DARK
RIVER
RISING

DARK
RIVER
RISING

ROGER JOHNS

Minotaur Books
New York

DARK RIVER RISING. Copyright © 2017 by Roger Johns. All rights reserved. Printed in the United States of America. For information, address St. Martin's Press, 175 Fifth Avenue, New York, N.Y. 10010.

www.minotaurbooks.com

The Library of Congress Cataloging-in-Publication Data is available upon request.

ISBN 978-1-250-11009-1 (hardcover)
ISBN 978-1-250-11011-4 (ebook)

Our books may be purchased in bulk for promotional, educational, or business use. Please contact your local bookseller or the Macmillan Corporate and Premium Sales Department at 1-800-221-7945, extension 5442, or by email at MacmillanSpecialMarkets@macmillan.com.

First Edition: August 2017

10 9 8 7 6 5 4 3 2 1

For Julie, my wife

Acknowledgments

One of the most gratifying things about the publication of this book is that I can now, very publicly, thank those who helped make it a reality: Julie Johns, my wife and counsellor and my endless inspiration—thank you for reading and for being there every step of the journey. April Osborn, at St. Martin's Press, who acquired and so expertly edited this book and, in so doing, changed the course of my life in the most amazing way—April, thank you for believing, I feel like I've won the lottery. Paula Munier, of Talcott Notch Literary Agency, who has been a wonderful agent—both a savvy guide as well as a patient and cheerful advisor. George Weinstein, who shepherded me into the Atlanta Writers Club and showed me how to make the most of everything the club has to offer. Terra Weiss, who read early drafts and made sure I did a thorough rewrite at the most critical moment. Grace Wynter, for bringing her deep understanding of story and character to bear on one of the later drafts. Jill Cobb, for reading it twice and offering so much thoughtful guidance on the protagonist. Geoff Chalmers, for being so generous with his many gifts—spiritual, mental, technical, and fraternal. Gordon

Prend, who read two early drafts and offered valuable insights and a ton of good advice. Maria de Boyrie, for reading and critiquing an early draft. The Roswell critique group, for their feedback during the beginning stages of the book. To everyone at St. Martin's Press who had a hand in this project—many, many thanks. David Fulmer, in whose Fiction Shop, all those years ago, I learned so many important lessons about writing. Dr. Baback Larian and Dr. Babak Azizzadeh, the most gifted surgeons I can possibly imagine. Their physical restoration, which was nothing short of astonishing, brought about an emotional restoration that enabled me to refocus my energies into my writing.

DARK
RIVER
RISING

ONE

Wallace Hartman had never seen a dead man move, but the guy in front of her was definitely dead, and definitely moving. He just wasn't going anywhere. There was a crudely sutured incision just below his rib cage and his abdomen heaved with a sinuous reptilian rhythm. Wallace's mind recoiled from what her eyes insisted was true—that a snake was slithering among his innards searching for a way out. The corpse looked like it was belly dancing its way into the hereafter.

All of the shootings and stabbings and beatings Wallace had worked on over the years had eventually run together into a slurry of lifeless recollections. As a Baton Rouge homicide detective and a nearly twelve-year veteran of the war on crime, she had grown almost numb to the endless parade of inventive atrocities the soldiers on both sides routinely inflicted on the enemy, but this snake business was in a class all by itself. It had been nearly a decade since she had thrown up at a crime scene, but now her streak was in jeopardy. She forced herself to focus on the details.

Strapping tape secured the body to a large wooden pallet. The hands were swollen and livid from the bindings. The end with the ankles was elevated with cinder blocks, so gravity would have kept blood flowing to his brain. He would have remained conscious even when shock dropped his blood pressure toward the lethal range.

"Take a look at this."

She turned toward the voice. It was David Bosso, a plainclothes narcotics officer who had arrived just before her. He was at the other end of the room—the office in a long unused warehouse. He was down on one knee looking at something under a broken ladder-back chair. One of the evidence techs had raised the blinds, improving a bit on the jaundiced light filtering in through the dirty skylights. The air was still and the stink in the room was so strong she could taste it.

"What is it?" She backed away from the body and walked over to Bosso, her boots rasping against the floor. The smell was taking a toll on Bosso too. His pained grin made him look like he'd been hit in the face with a skunk. "And how come you showed up here?" she asked, wondering why a narcotics officer would be an early responder on a homicide.

"I been trying to nail this guy for years," Bosso said. "In the last few weeks, his routine started changing. Made me think something was about to happen. We upped the surveillance, but he slipped through anyway. When I heard Dispatch sending cars to a homicide in this area, I had a bad feeling he might be involved."

Wallace leaned in, her hands on her knees. Several bags of white powder were nested in a knapsack. Maybe they would get lucky and find some usable prints on the bags. "Who is he?"

"Ronnie Overman. A big player. The main coke distributor for a Mexican cartel for the whole southern half of Louisiana."

"Is this a turf war?"

"Could be. Could be revenge. Could be a lot of things." He stood and hugged his arms around his chest. "Whatever it is, leaving the merchandise behind tells me it wasn't just a deal gone bad." He stared at the floor.

Wallace looked back toward the body. "Other than that incision, which doesn't look like it bled much, I can't see an obvious cause of death. I'm curious what actually killed him and what broke up the party."

"Whatever happened, you can bet this is just the beginning. There's bound to be a power struggle for Overman's organization—chaos for a while and probably more killing before it's over."

She closed her eyes to gather her thoughts. Instead, she found herself trying to imagine which specific day had condemned a laughing, wide-eyed little boy to the life that ended in this crummy warehouse in north Baton Rouge. Would anyone in this world see Overman's death as anything more than a coldly calculated opportunity? What were his last rational thoughts before the horror consumed him?

Her emotional armor was slipping. This was happening a lot, lately.

"Any idea who could've done this?"

"Not off the top of my head," David said. "Overman was way too big to do the grunt work hisself. He had people who handled all the lower echelon stuff. It would take something pretty important to bump him out of his regular orbit and get him in a position where they could take him down."

When Wallace looked again, Overman was no longer moving. She noted the time at 3:47. "What are these?" She knelt next to the knapsack and used a pen to point out a pair of clear plastic tubules embedded in the edge of one of the bags of powder.

"I don't know. I never seen anything like that," he said, looking closely. "But who knows what these shitheads do anymore? I mean, look at this poor bastard. Can you believe this?" he asked, nodding in Overman's direction.

Wallace shook her head. "We should get together on this later, but right now I need to talk to the guy who called this in." She stood and brushed off the knees of her cargo pants. She took a long slow look around, then left the office.

With practiced efficiency, she one-fingered her disposable gloves off and snapped them into an orange trash bag sitting just outside the exit door. She huffed in a few breaths of fresh air, then approached the officer stringing a perimeter of plastic tape in front of the building. "After the evidence techs are done, you and those two officers right over there start canvassing the area for anyone who saw or heard anything. Start around the building, then move into the surrounding neighborhoods."

"Will do, Detective." He backed away, snatching a quick glance at her as he continued to reel out the tape.

Wallace surveyed the parking lot, looking for Arthur Staples, the man who had found Overman. "Mr. Staples?" Wallace called out as she approached him. He had the rangy, rawboned look of a committed hiker. Flecks of gray showed in his mustache and at his temples. He was leaning back against the front fender of his motor pool sedan, idly drumming his fists on the metal. The logo for the City of Baton Rouge was painted on the door. He turned at the sound of his name.

"Thank you for waiting. How is it that you came to be in such a dismal place?" She stabbed her right thumb back over her shoulder. "Especially on a Sunday."

"I'm an engineer for the city. We recently acquired this property and we intend to demolish the present structure and then repurpose the land. I came to make an estimate of demolition expenses, site rehabilitation requirements, and potential environmental impacts. My plate is rather full these days so I end up working some weekends."

The engineer spoke in an almost perfect monotone, she noticed, but he punctuated his delivery with pauses and gestures, like an actor. She studied him for a moment. "The scene in there is making even the professionals a bit green around the gills, but you look pretty composed."

"I served in the Middle East and North Africa. I've seen these creative interrogations before."

"You think that's what this was? An interrogation?" Wallace asked.

"In my experience, torture is rarely just for sport. This was too well hidden to be a message to others, like dumping headless bodies in the public square might be. I saw the bags of white powder left behind, ruling out robbery. That suggests interrogation."

Wallace wondered how much snooping Staples had done, and whether he had touched—or taken—anything. "You seem well-versed in the lore of excruciating methods. What exactly did you do in the military?"

"I never said I served in the military." He gave her a slab-faced stare.

She matched his stare, noting the faint arrogance in his response, his disinclination to elaborate. It was a ballsy demeanor for someone surely sensible enough to know he'd be among the first to fall under suspicion for the carnage in the warehouse.

"When did you find this?" she asked. "As precisely as you can remember."

He pulled his phone from his pants pocket and consulted the call log. "I dialed nine-one-one during the minute of three thirty-two—as soon as I heard moaning. My cell service provider can get the time for you, down to the second, if you need it."

"Moaning?" Wallace arched one eyebrow, feeling a tiny spark of hope. "He was alive when you got here?"

"Briefly."

"Did he say anything? Or was he just moaning?"

"*Ingrate.* Just the one word. Just one time. Then, his eyes glazed over."

"Like he was accusing someone of being ungrateful?" Wallace asked.

"I am certain of the sound I heard. Assigning a meaning would be purely conjecture. His volume was too low and his enunciation was too indistinct."

Had she been in the right frame of mind, she might have found the relentless precision of the engineer's speech funny. Seeing his wedding band, she wondered about his playtime palaver with his spouse. Was it afflicted with similar exactitude? Did they calibrate their bedroom performance on a simple one-to-ten scale, or was it something more scientific? Maybe they used one-to-ten for every day, but some secret Richter scale for special occasions—with extra points for high volume and distinct enunciation.

A cacophony of slamming vehicle doors drew their attention toward the street. TV reporters.

"You wouldn't mind showing me your ID, would you, Mr. Staples?" Wallace returned her attention to the engineer. She read his momentary hesitation as a sign that he did mind, but he slowly withdrew his wallet from his jacket pocket, nevertheless.

"Your papers, please," he muttered like a Cold War border guard as he handed over his driver's license.

Wallace narrowed her eyes. "I beg your pardon?"

"Do you really think I had anything to do with this, Detective?"

"Should I?"

"No. But my daughter died of a drug overdose. If you are any kind of an investigator, you will soon find that out. Then you will have to consider the possibility this was a revenge killing."

"Do you believe the man in there was responsible for your daughter's death?" Wallace asked.

"I know he was." Staples repeatedly flexed and splayed the fingers of both hands. "He may not have personally sold Cynthia her last bag of dope, but he was obviously part of the machine that kills so many people like her."

"I'm inclined to think that if you had done this, you would not have called the police."

"Unless my intent was to make you think that if I had done this I would not have called the police."

"Don't toy with me, Mr. Staples. I can be unpleasant." Even

though she hadn't returned his license, he was reaching for his car door—*a little too eager to leave*, she thought.

"Step away from the vehicle, Mr. Staples. Do it now," she ordered, when she saw him dither. Confusion flickered across his face.

"Officer," Wallace called to a uniformed policewoman standing nearby.

"You're calling in backup?" Staples sneered.

"I'm searching your car."

"Not without a search warrant," he objected.

"I don't need a warrant. This car is city property. You have no reasonable expectation of privacy in it." She turned to the approaching officer. "Watch Mr. Staples, while I search his car."

"This is unbelievable." He plunged his hand into his front left pants pocket.

"No you don't," Wallace said, reacting to the sudden movement. She immobilized his hand and pinned him against the car.

"My phone," Staples ground out. "I was getting—"

"You're getting on my nerves," Wallace said. A quick pat down yielded nothing. "Now watch him," she said.

Other than a small briefcase, which contained only legal pads and writing implements, she found nothing in the vehicle that looked as if it even belonged to the engineer, much less anything that might connect him to the body in the warehouse.

Wallace stalked off toward her unmarked cruiser. She ran Staples's license through her onboard computer, but he came up clean.

"Are you done with me, yet?" he asked, when Wallace returned, giving her the same slab-faced look he had offered earlier.

"No. Not yet." She moved forward until she was well within the two feet of personal space she was sure he held dear—an intimidation tactic she had learned early on that had served her well. "As I'm sure you know, the success of an investigation can often turn on what information is made public and what's held back. Right now, you're the only civilian who's observed the crime scene. My people know how to keep quiet, so if details from this show up in the news, I'll assume it came from you and that could put a strain on our happy-go-lucky relationship." Wallace waited a few seconds. "Now I'm done." She turned toward her fellow officer. "See that he's escorted from the premises."

As she made her way back to her car, she tried to put everything into some kind of perspective. She was no expert on the managerial niceties of the cocaine business, but a major player getting his hands dirty on a routine wholesale transaction didn't strike her as commonplace.

If it was a declaration of war, as David Bosso thought it could be, then reprisals would be swift and bloody. When street sellers and foot soldiers got killed, it rarely provoked more than a tit-for-tat backlash because getting gunned down was part of their job description. The dramatic elimination of an alpha dog like Overman, though, might incite a more systematic retaliation. Other players might take advantage of the ensuing turbulence to advance their unwholesome agendas.

On the other hand, if it was just an intelligence gathering operation, as Arthur Staples suggested, then who was doing the gathering and what were they after? And had they gotten it?

The abandoned knapsack full of kilos undercut both of those theories or it at least made them seem incomplete. However, it did suggest another explanation. Maybe this really was nothing more than Arthur Staples avenging himself on the forces that killed his daughter, and trying to cover his tracks by making it look like more than it was. And maybe the man's irritating, confrontational attitude was intended to make her suspicious—to provoke her into searching him and his car. That way, when she found nothing incriminating, she would decide he was just an irksome but uninvolved citizen who had done his duty by calling in a crime. Crazier things had happened.

Just as Wallace's mind began to buzz, a profound wave of fatigue settled over her body. Normally, the surge of questions and possibilities that sprang up at the beginning of an investigation left her feeling energized. But sometime during the past several months it had begun to make her weary instead.

She had gotten into law enforcement to get career criminals off the street. She wanted to make sure the habitually harmful, the kind of repeat offenders who had destroyed her family, got locked up for as long as possible. The horror show in the warehouse made her question whether anything she did would make a difference.

6:30 P.M.

After what felt like an eternity, the last of the police and crime-scene techs packed up and left. For nearly three hours he had been standing dead still, roasting inside the air shaft just outside the office while the police and the techs did their endless bag and tag. Once he heard the last of them leave the building, he waited several more minutes. When he was sure he was alone, he quietly lifted away the grill covering the air shaft and left the warehouse.

Earlier today, he had watched from a discreet location as Ronnie Overman stepped out of the back of an SUV, then turned to help a smoking-hot young lady out after him. She had working girl written all over her, and Overman seemed to be enjoying her company.

Two Saturdays ago, he had watched them go through almost the same routine but he had lost the trail. He followed them into the lobby of a down-at-the-heels office building, and watched as Overman said something to the girl, pointed toward a sign for the restrooms, and then pointed at the elevator, as if to say *I gotta take a leak, I'll be right back, then we'll go up*. But Overman never came back. The girl made a quick call, and after a few minutes another girl showed up and the two of them left the lobby and disappeared into the sidewalk traffic. By then, it was obvious the drug peddler had probably slipped out the back of the building.

Today, though, he ignored the girl. Assuming things would go as they had two Saturdays before, he drove into the alley behind the building in time to see Overman walk out and slide into the driver's seat of a car. In an attempt at cleverness, Overman had altered his appearance a bit, but the walk was the same and that gave him away.

From there, he tailed Overman to the edge of a light industrial warehouse district, where Overman parked and then started walking. Once the destination became obvious he too parked, and watched his quarry disappear inside the warehouse. As he moved cautiously around the building, trying to assess the situation, he heard the prissy whine of a two-stroke engine fade rapidly into the distance.

It would have been nice to know how many others were already inside the building, but as he arrived at the door he had seen Overman enter through, the slippery devil was already coming back out. So he made his move.

All in all, things had worked out well, which he attributed entirely to the fact that he was a compulsive planner, yet willing to alter his plans to meet changing circumstances. Today's operation had been a particular challenge, though, because he had never killed before. Dispensing misery was nothing new. In fact, it was a particular interest of his, as any number of luckless young men and women had discovered when they slipped between his sheets expecting bliss only to find agony instead. But killing was different from hurting and he had forced himself to respect that difference.

Dealing with the snake had proved a bit tricky, but he quickly figured out how to handle the uncooperative reptile without getting bitten or losing his grip. He also spent time poring over anatomical diagrams of the human abdomen, so he could slice into Overman's body cavity without opening a major artery. Coaxing the balky creature inside had tried his patience, but its effect on Overman's reluctance to give up valuable trade secrets had been more than worth the trouble.

To his surprise, the only resistance his conscience offered to the whole business sprang from having to weigh the likelihood of getting what he needed against the prospect of being caught and killed. The twinge he expected when he pictured the actual bloodletting simply wasn't there. Maybe the possibility of great wealth blunted his feelings. Or perhaps he had stumbled into a hitherto undiscovered room in his emotional mansion—one which just happened to be a rather congenial place.

Forcing his thoughts back into the present, he threaded his way through the thicket of rotting crates and pallets behind the warehouse. The officers canvassing the area for leads were loud and easy to avoid, and he briefly entertained the idea of approaching them, posing as a stumblebum who had *seen something*, so he could send them off on a wild goose chase. But those games were best reserved for situations where the police approached him. Little would be gained by engaging them and risking later recognition, just for a few seconds of fun, especially since it was unlikely that anyone was aware of his presence in the area. No one had reason to be—yet.

He paused to use his reflection in a van window to straighten his clothes and fluff out his curly red hair, which had become matted with sweat while he waited in the sweltering air shaft.

As he made his way to his rental car, he contemplated the future. His visit with the now-deceased drug dealer practically confirmed that a serious development, something he had anticipated for a long time, had finally arrived. He still had to take possession of it. But that would be easier, thanks to the terrified yet very talkative Ronnie Overman.

Just having it, though, wouldn't be enough. It would also have to be put to work. Whether he could do that and live to tell the tale was not a given. One thing was certain, though. The bag of cocaine he had taken from Overman carried a kind of weight that went beyond its actual mass.

TWO

Instead of going directly home after meeting Overman at the warehouse, Matt Gable had come to his lookout point along the trail that ran through the wooded area between his house and the lab where he worked. He came here after every meeting because he knew there was always the chance someone—a confederate or even a competitor of Overman—might try to follow him. But Matt couldn't afford to have anyone discover his identity or his base of operations. During his years at the lab, he had worked out a pathway that led from the back of his yard, through the woods, all the way to the lab's access road. On fair-weather days he would run to and from work along the challenging trail. And on meeting days, like today, he used it as a way to check for, and if need be, shake off any pursuers. So far, he had been lucky and no one had tried to follow him. But something was not right. From his lookout point at the crest of a rise, he could see his house burning in the distance. He lowered his binoculars and considered his next move.

It was always possible that the blaze had been started by a frayed wire or an airborne cinder from some redneck's burn barrel, but it might also have something to do with the red-haired man he had seen entering the warehouse as he had sneaked away. The burn triggers he had installed inside his house were designed to go on active alert if his regular security system was disabled. Once that happened, the triggers would ignite in the event of an unauthorized entry.

The resulting fire would eliminate all evidence of the things that needed to remain secret. But it would also be a sign that his luck had finally run out and that he should probably do the same. Shit. He had the sinking feeling that a lot of difficult and dangerous work—not to mention an amazing piece of good fortune—was teetering on the edge of the abyss.

On the other hand, perhaps the fact that he was standing here *watching* the blaze instead of being caught up in whatever had started it was, itself, a piece of good fortune. It had taken nearly four hours to deposit all the cash he had driven away from the warehouse with. In order to avoid the federal scrutiny that always came from triggering the currency transaction reporting regulations, he had to break up the cash into numerous small amounts. For this, he had had to open several accounts, at banks scattered around Baton Rouge, all in the names of different businesses. Dividing the money into random, under-the-limit amounts and then going to ATMs and night deposit drops all over town to make the deposits was something he normally considered a huge pain in the ass. But today it might have actually *saved* his ass. *Maybe there was value in the growth of the bureaucracy after all*, he thought.

As he watched the fire, he tried to use his phone to check on his regular security and his other safeguards, but the security company website wouldn't load. The high droning wail of a fire engine drifted in on the evening air. He would assume the worst and find out the facts later.

There would be no time to cover his tracks at the lab, but his precautions would make it nearly impossible for anyone to figure out what he had been up to. Kevin Bell, the director of the lab, and his army of small-minded dorks would know something was going on, but Matt doubted they would ever figure out what. They were people who lived to think *inside* the box—not true scientists, just overtrained technicians who assumed the empire of truth was confined by the limits of their puny imaginations. Theirs would be careers of record-setting insignificance, with contributions too trivial to see except under the extreme magnification of an academic résumé.

There was no time to cover his tracks with Carla either. As if the thought had summoned her into the moment, his phone vibrated. He let it go to voicemail, like the other calls she had been pestering him with. She'd been a decent ride for a while, but her extra-eager-to-please attitude had moved at a fevered pace from entertaining to annoying, skipping completely over the boring phase. He had managed to get her out of his hair for a few days, by sending her to a conference on protein folding and she was no doubt calling to effervesce about how awesome it was. She might still prove useful, but his immediate plans didn't include her.

He hated to abandon his vehicle, but he had to make a clean break. That meant he had to get to the shack before nightfall. The trail marks he had scraped into the bark of some of the trees, a couple of feet above eye level, were getting difficult to see in the fading light.

Inside the shack he kept the untitled car he got from the kind of backwoods character one expected to traffic in bootleg versions of things that were once in legitimate commerce. It looked bad, inside and out, but Matt had restored the engine to top mechanical condition. He tossed his duffel in the trunk, then slid behind the wheel and pulled out of the shed, cruising along a pathway he had cleared to an unfenced field. From there, he drove along the edge of the field to a dirt road that eventually led him to the highway that would take him to Baton Rouge.

The most difficult part of moving on would be replacing the lab equipment he had free access to as a scientist at the lab. None of it would be terribly expensive, but some of it was specialized enough that it would be difficult to buy as a private citizen without attracting at least some unwanted governmental scrutiny. What he couldn't steal from the relatively unguarded research labs of small-town universities, he would worry about when the time came.

THREE

Wallace adjusted her car seat to a comfortable position as she watched the Staples residence. Yesterday, after her encounter with the engineer, she had tailed him from the warehouse back to his house and when he left the house after dark, she followed him into the night. He spent hours trolling through areas where street dealers and shooting galleries were common. But he never stopped and he never got out of his car. He just drove and drove, watching the street scene, always on the move. Clearly, he had been looking for something or someone. But shortly after ten o'clock he abandoned his quest and drove home. An hour after that, when the last of the lights inside the Staples's house went out, Wallace had also headed for home. Now she was back.

If Arthur's nocturnal ramble was in some way connected to Overman's death, Wallace doubted he would fess up just because she asked him politely. His attitude during their skirmish at the warehouse told her that if she hauled him in for questioning, he would probably just clam up and demand a lawyer.

Before doing something like that, she was going to try a less direct approach. Family members were often more sensitive to police pressure than the suspects themselves, especially if they thought they could protect a loved one from unnecessary public embarrassment.

The Staples's home was an older, well-kept tract house, situated in one of the borderland areas. At one time, Baton Rouge had been one of those places where genteel areas sometimes butted up against less fortunate territory, where poverty and prosperity sometimes eyed each other nervously across the width of a single street. Over the last thirty years or so, she had seen many of those border*lines* soften into border*lands* where old patterns of skin color, net worth, and national origin were re-forming into new, more hopeful social and economic arrangements.

Beyond some of the borderlands, though, there were still dangerous areas where street level power structures held sway and what the media reported as gang violence served as the equivalent of political campaigns and general elections.

When Wallace was a girl, her family had lived on the white side of one of the borderline streets. For much of her childhood, she had played with Craig and Berna Stephens, the black children who lived on the other side of the street—a practice that didn't sit well with some of the white folk in the neighborhood. The fact that Craig insisted on calling her "little white girl" hadn't helped matters.

She could still hear Craig's mother yelling across the yard. "Craig, her name is Wallace. You call her by her name. Are you listening to me?" His response was always the same. "Okay, Momma." Then five seconds later he'd be saying, "Hey, little white girl, you wanna play some Ping-Pong or something?" Even now, whenever their paths crossed, Craig sometimes called her little white girl.

At precisely 7:45, Arthur stepped into the carport from the side door of his house. He climbed into his car and drove in the direction of the freeway. One vehicle remained in the carport. Wallace started her car and pulled to the curb in front of the house. She got out and walked up the steps to the front porch. She rang the doorbell and waited.

"Who is it?" a female voice asked through the windowless front door.

"Detective Wallace Hartman, with the Baton Rouge City Police."

"If you're here to speak to Mr. Staples, he can't be disturbed," the voice lied. "Leave your card in the door, and I'll see that he gets it."

Wallace admired the woman's caution in making it sound like she wasn't alone in the house. "I know Mr. Staples isn't here. I just saw him drive off."

"Please face the window on your right so I can see you."

Wallace complied. She was waiting to be asked to show her badge and her ID, but she was startled when the door opened instead.

"How may I help you, Detective?" the woman asked.

She was about to deliver the standard lecture about not opening the door to someone just because they claimed to be with the police, when the woman spoke.

"I know who you are. You're Carol Hartman's daughter. You look too much like her not to be," the woman said, obviously reading Wallace's expression.

Even though this happened to Wallace from time to time, she still found it unnerving—but flattering, as well. "My daughter was one of Carol's students, so I met your mother on a number of occasions. Please," she said, standing aside, "won't you come in? I'm Wanda Staples—Arthur's wife."

Wallace took in the room with a quick scan. Wanda's spiky hair style had been daring a few years back and her outfit looked like it stood a decent chance of coming back in fashion. There were a few bargain barn prints on the walls and groupings of mass-market figurines were staged along the mantel. Where most homes would have had a television, an elliptical trainer stood instead. The furniture was old and ugly and the muted light filtering through the thin curtains gave the place a solemn feel.

"Why don't we sit?" Wanda asked, closing the door and motioning Wallace toward an armchair. She took a seat on the couch and faced Wallace. "Arthur told me he found a body," Wanda said, sounding as if they were discussing the weather. "I assume that's why you're here."

"May I ask what else he told you?"

"That it was a murder. I know he knew more than he was telling, but he's not exactly a chatterbox."

Wallace studied Wanda for any sign the woman knew more or might be hiding something—unnaturally steady eye contact, feet pointed away from the line of conversation—but there was nothing. Maybe Arthur had heeded the warning to stay quiet about the particulars of what he had seen in the warehouse. That didn't make Wallace like him, but her respect for him did go up a notch.

"In any event, what was it you wanted to speak with me about?" Wanda asked. She folded her hands in her lap and leaned toward Wallace, with an expectant look on her face. "Is Arthur under suspicion? Am I? Should I retain counsel?"

Wallace waited for several seconds. If she seemed too ready to answer Wanda's questions she would lose control of the conversation. Besides, "retain counsel" gave her away.

"You're a lawyer, yourself."

"I am. But you know what they say. A lawyer who represents herself has a fool for a client. And, in any event, I don't handle criminal matters. I'm part-time with a firm that practices public interest law. You know . . . the kind that doesn't pay very well."

"I followed Arthur last night. He spent a good bit of time cruising some very questionable neighborhoods. He wasn't doing anything illegal, but it was peculiar behavior, especially in light of the circumstances under which we met. I'm tempted to have him picked up so I can question him in a more formal setting. But I was hoping maybe you could shed some light on what he was doing. You know—less hassle, less of a spectacle."

Wanda shrugged, her gaze drifting slowly toward the floor. "I don't know where he goes when he takes off like that. He won't say, and I've given up asking."

Wallace could tell the woman was lying. "Well, he was moving through some pretty perilous precincts."

Wanda's nostrils flared as she tried to suppress a smirk. "You are your mother's child in more than just looks. Who but an English teacher's daughter would say 'perilous precincts' when 'shitty part of town' would do?" She paused. "But I wouldn't worry too much about it. Arthur can handle himself."

"What exactly did he do, before he became an engineer?" Wallace asked. She would come back to the subject of Arthur's drive around later, from a different angle.

"If you're asking whether he could have done whatever it is that was done in this crime you're investigating, the answer is yes, of course. But, under the right circumstances, aren't we are all capable of terrible things? What you really want to know is whether he *would* have done it." Wanda shook her head. "No. I don't believe so. He's seen enough killing and dying to last a lifetime."

Sensing there was more to come, Wallace watched as Wanda's demeanor softened, changing from self-assured to distracted. "A few years ago, we lost our daughter, our only child."

"He told me that. An overdose."

"Cynthia was smart and charming, and as a young girl she had Arthur wrapped tight around her little finger—a place he considered more exalted than the right hand of God. There's something so magical and so beautiful about some fathers and daughters." A wistful smile lit up Wanda's face. "Were you close to your father when you were a girl?"

"I'd like to think I still am."

"Then you know how that can be." Wanda stopped to collect herself. "But adolescence was difficult for Cynthia. It triggered things in her that neither Arthur nor I were prepared to deal with. She was changing faster than we could keep up with and she became hard to handle and impossible to understand."

Wanda's eyes glistened and she stared off to one side, fighting for control.

"Mrs. Staples, are you sure you want to do this?"

"I am. This is what you came for. Just give me a moment."

After several seconds of silence, Wanda began to speak again.

"This sort of thing . . . losing a child . . . it's a shattering experience. It ruined our marriage. When Cynthia started to run wild Arthur blamed himself. . . ."

"And you?" Wallace asked, filling in the blank Wanda left hanging.

"And me. But mostly himself. He adored her and she adored him. When she seemed to lose her devotion to their relationship, Arthur assumed it was because her idol had fallen. He was devastated. He was sure he'd failed her."

As the story unspooled Wanda grew smaller, tucked deeper and deeper into a corner of the couch. The breaks in her narrative grew longer and she stopped looking at Wallace altogether.

"At some point, after Cynthia was gone, he started his disappearing act at night."

"And you really have no idea what he's doing?" Wallace asked.

"He's rescuing people. Or so he thinks. He drives around searching for kids who look out of place. Sometimes he even goes in where the kids get high, where they're screwing the meth man for their next hit, places like the one Cynthia died in. And he physically hauls them out and takes them to shelters, hospitals, churches, any place that'll have them."

"This is a very dangerous thing he's doing. Surely he realizes it's suicidal."

"And surely you realize he's just trying to get someone else to pull the trigger," Wanda said plainly, finally looking Wallace in the eye again.

Wallace hadn't seen that coming, but the man's odd behavior at the warehouse suddenly made some kind of sense—the needless cultivation of suspicion, his hand darting into his pocket raising the fear he was going for a weapon. Wallace had seen her share of self-destructive people and she knew they sometimes tried to enlist others in their grim enterprise. Enough of them had managed to put themselves in the path of enough official gunfire to make *police-assisted suicide* a depressingly common term. She didn't know if that was Arthur's goal at the warehouse, but she knew from her own experience that grief and self-blame caused people to do irrational, unpredictable things.

She was also personally familiar with the strange logic of the penitent's mind and it didn't make sense that Arthur would jeopardize his kamikaze rescue missions—his chance at redemption—by putting himself behind bars on a murder rap, or getting himself killed. Arthur Staples was starting to look less like a suspect and more like a sadly mixed-up man.

"Don't judge him," Wanda whispered.

"I don't," Wallace murmured, rising to go. "Here's my card, if he thinks of anything."

As she drove away from the Staples house, Wallace wondered whether Arthur might not be doing more good with his crazy crusade than she was as a cop. He certainly seemed to be going about his business with the zeal of a true believer—something she had not felt in a long time.

MONDAY AFTERNOON

Mason Cunningham was the Deputy Assistant Administrator for Intelligence at the DEA. He had begun his DEA career as a special agent at the El Paso Intelligence Center, working the front lines of the war on drugs, so he had a badge and a gun. But the only time he drew his weapon, anymore, was on the occasional trip to the firing range. These days he rarely left his office.

Some years earlier, his regular interactions with the intelligence analysts at the Center had exposed him to the power of using mathematical tools to uncover the hidden engines of cause and effect that powered the drug underworld. To his surprise, he had become fascinated with how things like unemployment rates, wage levels, and climate change could be used to predict the magnitude and pathways of illicit drug flows. He became so enchanted with numbers that he had gone on to earn a doctorate in statistics, then made the jump to full-time analyst. After that, he had climbed the ladder in the Intelligence Division and now he occupied a nice office at the national headquarters in Washington, where he specialized in strategic intelligence.

Most of his time was spent overseeing the construction and operation of gigantic databases from the rivers of data generated by information gathering and drug enforcement activities across the country. He and his analysts devised algorithms that sifted the data, hunting for the sinister currents that flowed through the drug trafficking economy, with an eye toward policy planning and resource deployment. The patterns in the data were the important things. Individual events were just threads in the tapestry and rarely of any particular significance—until yesterday.

Yesterday, a very powerful system the agency operated—the National Drug Pointer Index—had kicked out a cross-match on a case in Baton Rouge, Louisiana. A cross-match meant that a person of high interest to the DEA also appeared to be the subject of a local investigation.

Cross-matches were hardly rare, but this one was unusual because it implicated a cartel-level player—the kind of person who would almost never fall under the scrutiny of local law enforcement. It was also unusual because the cross-match hadn't been generated by the person's name. It was based on his distinctive modus operandi. Mason hoped it was just a grisly coincidence, a copycat. If not, then Fernando Echeverría, a Mexican physician who had retired from the practice of medicine to pursue a new career as a cocaine kingpin, had left his calling card—a two-foot emerald tree boa—in the belly of one of his big-time distributors.

If Echeverría or one of his associates had entered the United States and done this thing, then an irritating little riddle that had been rattling around in Mason's head now had an answer.

The riddle had surfaced months earlier, when the data from south Louisiana started to look odd. It was nothing huge, but it was a change in the pattern, and the economics of it were all wrong. The number of cocaine dealers getting arrested had suddenly gone up. With more dealers off the street, the supply should have gone down and prices should have risen. But prices had fallen, instead. Mason took the problem to Don Brindl, his most talented analyst. Ten weeks later, Don walked into the analyst meeting and dropped a bomb.

"I might have found something," Don droned, paging through his notes.

Regardless of what he was about to say, every one of Don's presentations started the same way, with the same low-key delivery and the same unreadable face. In terms of mannerisms, Mason credited Don with the makings of an excellent poker player, which, in fact, he was. The occasional Friday night games among the analysts were usually object lessons on the futility of gambling—for everyone except Don. Tales of the man's casino exploits were legendary.

"Only might have?" Mason asked.

"I hesitate to be too emphatic," Don said. "But here's the bottom line. More dealer arrests should have reduced supplies and increased prices. And that would have happened if all these arrests had actually driven down the number of dealers. But it didn't. More dealers are getting popped because there are more dealers on the street—a lot more, even after all these arrests. And it's happening in new parts of town where the dealers haven't learned how to handle the cops."

"That would mean the street supply is going up, not down like we thought," Mason said. "Where is it coming from?"

"Practically speaking, there are only two places it *could* be coming from. Either the cartel that supplies the area is sending more or . . ."

"Or a rival cartel is moving into south Louisiana," someone finished.

The room went dead quiet.

"No way," a voice boomed from the back of the room. "A cartel war, in the States? Never gonna happen. The cartel in control is just moving more of its inventory into Louisiana."

"Exactly," another analyst agreed. "The energy business is big down there, and drilling is up. More people will have more money to spend on everything, including recreational drugs, so the incumbent cartel is just catering to rising demand."

Don faced the analysts with the same place-your-bets expression he had used to bluff so many of them into losing their money on so many occasions.

"Do you have any evidence that a new cartel is moving in?" Mason asked.

"The surrounding states are all controlled by rival cartels and street prices in those states have gone up. That means the supply in those states went down—went somewhere else. And the most efficient somewhere else would be someplace nearby—like Louisiana."

The room erupted into a buzz of geek-speak as Don's conclusions were debated.

"If a new cartel is moving in, then why aren't we seeing a spike in drug-related violence?" Mason asked over the rising din.

"I assume they're going in low and slow," Don said. "Until their position is strong enough to withstand any pushback from the entrenched players."

Mason knew a sneaky approach wouldn't last. Cocaine was a street-corner by street-corner business. Eventually, things would speed up and south Louisiana would become a flashpoint.

At one time, the Mexican cartels had more or less respected each other's territories but over time, as competition increased, turf wars had become just another cost of doing business. Until now, though, the fighting had stayed south of the Rio Grande where the traffickers still had law enforcement outmanned and outgunned. If the cartels were now willing to fight each other on United States soil, south Louisiana would not be the only theater of war.

"If you're right, this will mean serious changes in our tactics," Mason said. "It'll affect agencies outside of DEA and if we don't move fast enough, it'll get bloody before we can react. But we can't go around shouting that the sky is falling until your work's been independently verified."

On Friday, four days after Don's presentation, a second analyst had verified his work. Two days after that, Ronald Overman stumbled onto the front lines of what looked like the start of a cartel turf war and got caught lying down on the job. Then, late last night, the cross-match between the Overman case and Echeverría's snake trick had popped up. At that point, Mason decided there was a better than even chance the sky actually *was* falling. Now, he had to do something he hadn't done in a long time—saddle up and ride into town for an up-close, personal look at the situation.

The stakes were too high to rely just on data analysis. Statistics and cross-matches could tell you a lot, but some things had to be slogged out the old-fashioned way. Like who had actually put the snake inside Ronald Overman? Were the dealers who were getting busted by the boatload selling Echeverría's wares or were they the advance team for a new crew? Had anyone actually seen Echeverría or any of his top lieutenants in Louisiana?

If Mason just went with the numbers and said war was coming when it wasn't, he would end up wasting a ton of money and looking like a fool, with egg on his face. But if he read the numbers to mean the status quo was safe and sound, and the DEA got caught flat-footed while wholesale cartel violence ignited on United States' territory, he would look like a bigger fool, with blood on his hands.

FOUR

TUESDAY MORNING

H artman."

Wallace looked up from her desk. It was her boss, Chief of Detectives Jason Burley, cruising through the bullpen.

"My place," he said over his shoulder, as he strode into the hallway.

Wallace followed him into his office—a glass-walled affair that was utterly free of the usual sediment that builds up after a lifetime with the same employer. Despite being born decades before the dawn of the personal computer age, Burley had embraced the paperless office like it was a long-lost child. What little space he had was given over to old comfortable furniture and mementos from his and his husband's travels. Burley had been handsome once, but the stress of the job had stolen his looks.

"Close the door." He stood in the far corner of his office and used his right index finger to spin the smudged, school-room globe that sat on the scuffed credenza behind his desk.

"Sit." He pointed to a side chair as Wallace pushed the door shut.

"It makes me nervous whenever you spin that thing," she said, staying on her feet.

"Why's that?"

"Because you only do it when you're about to fling something into the fan."

"Nothing could be further from the truth," he said.

"That just means you've already flung it. This is about my new partner, isn't it?"

"Think of this as a promotion—to senior partner," he said in the unctuous tone that always marked the boundary between the calm and the storm.

"Oh, Jesus. Just tell me who it is."

"Michael Harrison."

"Medicated Mike?" She slouched against the wall and lifted her eyes toward the ceiling.

"Don't you call him that," Burley said, heatedly, motioning for her to keep her voice down.

"What *should* I call him? He never met a prescription pill he didn't like—a lot."

"He's been through rehab. He's been in front of the disciplinary board. He's done everything he's supposed to do, before he goes back on duty. And he's passed the test for detective," Burley said, ticking off each item on his fingers.

"That doesn't mean he has to be my cross to bear."

"You're an open pair."

"I happen to know there are two other open pairs—one longer than me. And, unlike me, neither has a chance of the gone partner coming back."

Burley gave her a steady five seconds of the don't-kid-yourself look that parents gave children who, six months after the dog disappeared, still believed it was coming home. "Those two open pairs are about to be joined in holy acrimony," he said. "That leaves you and Mike

Harrison. Unless you'd rather go with one of those open pairs. In which case I'll put Mike with the other one."

It wasn't a serious offer and Wallace dismissed it, instantly. Both of the unpartnered opens were trouble. LeAnne Hawkins was a serial temporary because her personality was so exasperating she could make the Buddha lose his cool. The other was a grievance artist who had been retired on active duty longer than Wallace had been an officer. Putting them together was obviously Burley's clever way of attempting to drive at least one of them off the force, and make Medicated Mike look attractive by comparison.

"There's no reason I can't go solo for a while longer," Wallace insisted. "I'm doing fine on my own."

"Not an option."

"Why not?"

"If you repeat what I'm about to tell you, I'll find a way to ruin you. Understood?"

She stiffened, sensing she was about to be handed an opportunity, wrapped in a turd, inside of a bomb. Her mentor, when she had become a detective, had taught her to be alert to the good fortune that being asked to do a favor represented. He had also counseled her not to mistake good fortune for a free lunch.

"Mike Harrison has a . . . sponsor . . . if you will."

"It just hit the fan," she said, slumping into Burley's side chair.

"Wallace, think for a minute. If I put Mike Harrison with either of the two fuck-ups I'm about to force on each other, there will be trouble in paradise before sundown. And Mike's guardian angel is in a position to make our upcoming budget review feel more like a cavity search."

"So I'm babysitting the third fuck-up?" She threw her hands in the air.

Burley flashed her a smile that came nowhere close to involving his eyes.

"Mike's obviously got the goods on somebody in City-Parish government and that somebody is squeezing you to keep Mike employed when he should probably be indicted, instead," she said.

"Everybody's entitled to a second chance," Burley said. "Mike Harrison included."

Typically, Wallace had enormous respect and affection for anyone who overcame difficulties that had been thrust upon them, but it was common knowledge that Mike's drug problem sprang from troubles he had manufactured for himself. Saddled with a family and colleagues that didn't share his undying devotion to himself, he had turned to amphetamines and painkillers—friends that reliably made him feel good and asked nothing in return.

"This is just temporary, right?" She tucked her dark brown hair behind her ears and stared at the floor, shaking her head.

"Provisionally temporary."

"Where do you learn to talk like that?" Wallace asked, half groaning, half laughing. She rubbed her eyes with the heels of her hands. She admired Burley's gamesmanship. He hadn't been chief of detectives for as long as he had, and successfully avoided every attempt to promote him, by being a dimwit. But she was getting tired of being moved around on somebody else's chessboard. Especially when there were landmines under the surrounding squares.

"Look at me," Burley said, suddenly serious. "This is a delicate thing. It's got to be handled by somebody who's got their head screwed on straight and tight."

Wallace stared at him, waiting for the punch line.

"And, you're the closest I've got."

Sensing that Burley might feel a bit of gratitude for helping him square away a problem, Wallace decided to see if she could wring something for herself out of the situation.

"The budget review you mentioned? I suppose this means my little project will get sidelined, again."

For three years Wallace had been pushing for funding for a big-data project that would help the department identify individuals most at risk for becoming repeat-offender drunk drivers, so that prevention efforts could be more efficiently targeted. Police departments around the country had awakened to the idea of predictive enforcement and the technique had been used successfully to target other types of criminality. But it had never been tried for the purpose Wallace had in mind, so getting the money was proving to be a hard sell. Burley's half-hearted smile let her know he had expected her to bring it up.

"Look, I know how important this is to you, and I know it's personal. But even with the cuts that are probably coming, there could be room for your project—at least on a trial basis. Help me get Mike Harrison back on his feet and I'll push as hard as I can for you. The Overman homicide you picked up Sunday would be just the kind of case to turn him around. A nasty crime, a victim nobody's gonna miss, but enough weight to make Mike feel like he's being useful again."

Wallace and Mike Harrison spent the rest of the morning going through her open cases, updating reports, and parceling out investigational duties. She was going to keep him on a short leash until she could get a handle on what he could do. In the meantime, she intended to limit him to chasing forensic details, interviewing witnesses, and doing computer-based research on suspects and persons of interest.

"This is just busywork," Mike said, waving his hand dismissively at the computer.

"It's detective work."

"It's bullshit busywork," he said, raising his voice. "I want to work on the stuff that counts."

"What are you talking about? This *is* work that counts."

"You don't get it. My reputation got messed up, so I gotta get back in the game, make a big play," he said, pushing back from the desk, standing directly in front of Wallace.

"Mike, please, just listen—"

"I want to work on something hot," he said, smirking, his crotch inches from her face.

Wallace stood and shoved him hard into his chair. "Promise yourself you won't make that mistake again."

"Come on," he said, laughing and squirming in his seat. "I was just—"

Wallace leaned over, her hands resting on the arms of his chair.

"Hey, hey, Detective. Why don't you two love birds get a room?" It was Tonya Eklin, head of the Sex Crimes Unit. She was standing in the doorway of a cubicle across the room, chatting with another of Wallace's colleagues.

Wallace backed away and sat down. "You'll want to mind your manners around me." She stared at him until he looked away. "Now, let's go back over the list of names I gave you," she said, subduing her frustration. "See this guy right here?"

"Arthur Staples? Yeah. What about him?" Mike asked, sporting a sullen look.

"He's a person of interest in the Overman homicide. Certain parts of his past are probably going to be forever closed off to us, but I want you to see what's on record for him, his wife Wanda, and their deceased daughter Cynthia, since the family moved to Baton Rouge. The circumstances of Cynthia's death may be important, so any names or places or events she was connected to, we need to know about them."

"Look, I was out of line, before. My apologies," Mike said, his eyes and nose reddening, his fingers drumming nervously on the desktop.

"Apology accepted," she said, softening her expression. She returned her attention to the computer screen. "At the end of every day, you'll have a progress report for each item on the list. Everything gets worked. Nothing gets neglected."

"I got it, I got it," he said forlornly. "Look, I'm just trying to get back in the groove, figure things out. Plus, I never had a female partner before."

"One more thing," Wallace said, standing up and putting things in her shoulder bag. "About a dozen kilos were taken into evidence on this case. I want you to go to the evidence room, and look at the bags themselves. Not the powder inside, the actual plastic bags. I want to know what they are and where they come from."

"Seriously? I'm chasing down sandwich bags? I said I was sorry."

When she looked down at Mike, he had a strange expression on his face. Wallace couldn't tell if he was going to laugh or cry.

"I need to talk to someone about an old, inactive case. I'll be back in a few minutes." She left the bullpen wondering which unremembered transgression had wheeled Medicated Mike into the debit column of her karmic ledger. The only thing more dangerous than an eager-beaver rookie was an out-of-practice veteran with something to prove and, in a sense, Mike was a bit of both.

5:30 P.M.

When Wallace got back, Mike Harrison was gone, so she pulled up the preliminary autopsy results on Overman, for another read-through. The coroner, normally a stickler for rules and schedules, had been so intrigued by the possibility that someone had put a snake inside the victim, she not only agreed to put him at the head of the line, she did the autopsy on a Sunday—a day they were not normally done.

The results had been released late Sunday night so Wallace immediately took the time to study them and transfer information from there into her official police report. In addition to confirming the presence and species of the snake—a juvenile emerald tree boa, native to South America—the coroner reported that all of Overman's fingertips had been crushed. Tightly spaced parallel groove patterns across his fingernails and the pads of his fingers indicated that pliers had been used. Wallace recalled the bloated, purplish condition of Overman's hands at the crime scene. The swelling had obviously obscured the plier marks. The crushed fingertips supported Arthur Staples's theory that Overman was being interrogated at the time of his death. Bits of cotton lint recovered from his oral cavity meant a rag of some sort had been stuffed into his mouth—no doubt to keep the noise down during the painful parts. And, interestingly, the coroner had determined that none of Overman's physical injuries, separately or in combination, had been fatal. A determination of the cause of death would have to await the results of the toxicology screen. Those would not start trickling in for at least another day.

After she finished reading the report, Wallace spent the rest of the day tidying up the details of other cases and compiling a list of online snake dealers who claimed to deal in emerald tree boas. She even called several, but none had made any recent sales. By the time she was ready to leave, Mike had still not returned.

As she gathered her things, her desk phone rang. She almost let it go to voicemail, but the DC area code intrigued her. *How pathetic,* she thought as she reached for the phone, that an out-of-town call from some unknown party could be a more fascinating proposition than heading home after a long, hard day.

"This is Detective Hartman." She sat on the edge of her desk, one foot resting on an open drawer.

"Detective, this is Mason Cunningham. I run part of the Intelligence Division at the DEA."

"How can I help you, Mr. Cunningham?"

"I'm not sure who would end up helping whom, but, at the moment, I'm trying to verify something. You're the officer of record on a homicide committed in your jurisdiction on Sunday. The killer left a rather unusual calling card."

"A calling card implies an identity. Are you saying you know who goes around doing this sort of thing?" She wasn't going to reveal any details, in case the caller was a reporter scamming for information.

"I do know of such a person. I don't know if it's the same person in your case, but I would very much like to find that out," Mason said.

"How many forms will I have to file, with how many agencies, before I can get the name of this sainted individual?"

"Fernando Echeverría."

"That was suspiciously easy," she said, as she scribbled the name onto her desk blotter. Surely this was just the bait on the usual federal hook—the old give a little, take a lot routine.

"Detective Hartman . . . we're on the same side."

"But not on the same team."

"Nicely put," he said. "How many forms will I have to file, with how many agencies, before I can get you to agree to throw a little information my way?"

Nicely put, yourself, she thought, but she would not be charmed so easily. "You seem a little too practiced at this type of repartee, Mr. Cunningham. How could you help me any more than you just did? I already have access to all the major state and federal crime information databases. As we speak, one of my officers is checking out the name you just gave me," she lied.

"Well, that last part is not true. I can see, in real-time, who's searching those databases, and there are no searches for Fernando Echeverría originating from Baton Rouge, or anywhere else for that matter."

Wallace remained quiet to see if he would react further to her little deception.

"It'll probably turn out that neither of us will end up helping the other very much," Mason continued. "But, I can tell you this— Echeverría is a very disagreeable person. If he or his heavies are in your neck of the woods, you can be sure big trouble isn't far behind."

"How did you even become aware of this?" Wallace asked.

"We operate a program that continuously compares information from DEA investigations to the information in local police reports to let us know when local investigations are targeting the same people we are. It searches by name and any other identifying feature that's common to both sets of information. Monday morning it kicked out a cross-match between one of your cases and one of ours. It matched on the snake."

Wallace knew the information from Overman's autopsy report hadn't gone into her official police report until she inputted it herself Sunday night. Whatever system her caller had, it was very thorough and very fast.

"With all that information, why do you need me at all? Why can't you just go on the assumption it's Echeverría, subpoena any of our records and reports you don't already have access to, and move forward with your own operation?"

"We may do exactly that. But, I can't afford to leave any stone unturned. I need more than just reports. I need street-level detail that's not in the written record, your and your colleagues' local knowledge of the players in south Louisiana. You know, personal cooperation."

"I hope you're not planning to use me to help you find this killer, then you whisk him off someplace where we can't prosecute. This was a really ugly crime. I'll want some really ugly justice."

"I'll do my best to make sure we don't stymie you," he said. "I can't promise more than that. I'm coming to Baton Rouge tomorrow morning, and I'd like to meet with you . . . unless that's not convenient."

"Tomorrow morning is fine," she said, wondering if his presence would, in fact, be fine, or if it would be a pain in the ass. The fact that a federal agent appeared to be taking her schedule into consideration instead of just announcing when and where her and her department's cooperation would be forthcoming, seemed odd—but odd in a good way. She tended to get along better with people who were burdened with quirky habits like good old-fashioned common courtesy. Maybe it meant he wouldn't try to take over her case. She knew of the occasional jurisdictional standoff between locals and the feds. Perhaps his diplomacy and his decision to come to Baton Rouge signaled nothing more than the importance of the matter.

"When will you arrive? I'll have someone pick you up at the airport," she said, bidding for control of the opportunity her caller represented.

"That's a nice offer, but I was planning to just rent a car. I'm also setting up meetings with the state police, sheriff's investigators, and the other federal agencies involved in drug suppression, so I'll need to be pretty mobile."

"Where will you be staying?"

"At the . . . let's see . . . the Istrouma Hotel."

"They have a rental car desk, there. Let us pick you up, take you to the crime scene—which is about halfway between the airport and your hotel—then drop you off. You can get your car at the hotel."

"Well . . . alright then. Your way sounds fine. I'll want to meet with you and with any of your officers on the drug beat who know the Overman organization."

"I can set that up, but we may not get all of them in one go," she said. "They tend to have erratic schedules."

"I understand," he said. "Thanks for whatever you can do."

"You're welcome. And listen, before we hang up, there's something you might be able to help us both with. The man who discovered this homicide—Arthur Staples—is a city employee whose history, beyond a certain point, gets murky. He had an obvious opportunity to kill Overman, and he's admitted to some sort of a motive for wanting him dead. You might be in a position to uncover information about him that is, so far, proving to be out of my reach."

"The illicit drug economy is really all my outfit deals with. Do you think he's involved with that?"

"He hinted he was once employed by Uncle Sam in some unusual but unspecified capacity."

"And you want to know if Uncle Sam gave him the skills to do what was done to Overman."

"Means, motive, and opportunity—the big three in my line of work. If you could throw a little light on the means part . . ."

She gave him what she had on Staples, but she wasn't sure how much effort she should expect him to put forth. Then again, he hadn't tried to force her cooperation or tried to impose any jurisdictional mandates on her. Maybe he was a fed who knew how to play nice. What would they think of next?

After they hung up, she called the head of the Narcotics Division to arrange the meeting Mason requested, then she called Mike Harrison to let him know when and where the meeting would take place. Mike didn't answer so she left a message.

FIVE

Your card says you're a Ph.D. Do you prefer Dr. Cunningham or Mr. Cunningham?" Wallace asked. They were in her unmarked cruiser, moving south through a blighted area, headed away from the Baton Rouge Metropolitan Airport.

"Mason is fine. And you?"

"Just Wallace. Ever been to Baton Rouge?"

"Never been in Louisiana."

When she looked over at him, Mason was staring straight ahead, not looking at the buildings or the people on the street. Whenever she traveled to a new place, she gawked at everything with a goofy country-come-to-town look plastered across her face. She couldn't be sure, but he seemed almost shy or ill at ease.

After a short silence, he continued. "When we spoke yesterday you said you would have someone pick me up at the airport. I wasn't expecting it to be you."

"The governor was busy."

Out of the corner of her eye, Wallace could see an eye roll and a strained smile disrupt the stony federal façade Mason had maintained since his arrival. Somehow she had gotten it in her head that a statistician would look about as exciting as the occupation sounded, but this guy definitely beat the odds by a fair margin.

"Anything new since we spoke yesterday?" he asked.

"We've got a time frame for when the killer left the scene," Wallace said. "The snake died around three forty-seven. A reptile expert the coroner consulted said it probably could have survived for around twenty minutes."

"Assuming twenty minutes is reasonably close and working backward from three forty-seven, that means the snake was inserted at around three twenty-seven. What time did your engineer find him?"

"At three thirty-two. So it was sometime during that five minute stretch when the killer took off."

"Which means he, or she, wouldn't have been too far away when Overman was discovered."

"We also found a baby monitor wedging open the door to the warehouse—the transmitter part that goes near the crib, which probably means—"

"—the killer was working alone or at least without a lookout," Mason said, finishing her sentence. "Clever. He kept the receiver with him, so he'd hear anyone approaching. They're cheap and they can send a signal over several hundred feet."

"You know a lot about baby monitors. You have little ones?" she asked.

"My sister just had a baby. I gave them a monitor. So, I did my homework first."

Under the basic rules of polite chitchat, Wallace knew this would be the place for him to ask if she had children, but he didn't. The silence felt like a missed opportunity.

"I've tried contacting snake dealers," Wallace said. "Maybe we can link a purchase to some personal information about the buyer like a credit card or an address. No luck, so far, though."

"It's low probability," Mason said. "There are a ton of breeders.

They all ship everywhere and it's easy to buy anonymously. Same with the baby monitor. It's doubtful you'll ever put a name to either one."

During the remainder of the drive, she filled Mason in on the particulars of her conversations with Arthur and Wanda Staples.

The warehouse was back from the road, in a light industrial district, in the southeastern part of Baton Rouge. A deep lawn overtaken by scrub trees and underbrush made it difficult to see from the street. Wallace pulled all the way up to the crime-scene tape.

"After we leave here, do you mind if we stop at that little taco restaurant we just passed?" Mason asked, as they got out of the car. "Breakfast on the plane was useless," he said, as they walked the rest of the way to the building.

"Too dangerous," Wallace said, pulling a key from her pocket.

"But you're carrying a gun."

"And I'm a really good shot, but salmonella is tough to shoot."

"Then maybe you know a place where the odds of survival are more in our favor."

Wallace opened the padlock the evidence techs had installed on the door and they went in.

"Has the pallet been moved?" he asked, pointing at the apparatus that had been Ronald Overman's last carnival ride.

"No. They were scheduled to take it away this morning, but after you and I spoke last night I told them to leave it until you had a chance to see it."

Wallace walked him through the scene, showing him where they had found the monitor, the knapsack full of powder, and the likely means of entry and exit the killer might have used. Mason wandered around the rest of the warehouse, looking into the other rooms and the main storage area that took up most of the building. Broken furniture and tattered, oil-stained cardboard boxes filled with bundles of paper were scattered around the floor. Sunlight poured in through large wire-glass windows high up near the ceiling. After a few minutes they made their way back into the office where the body had been found.

"Hold my feet," he said, as he lay down on his back on the pallet, assuming the position Overman would have been in.

Wallace moved to the raised end and took hold of his ankles. It felt like a strangely intimate act with a man she had spent less than half an hour with—a man with excellent taste in shoes.

Mason craned his head around. "Overman's field of vision would have been approximately the upper half of the wall my feet are pointing toward, the ceiling, everything to his left and right, and, to the extent he could tilt his head backward, the wall behind me."

"So?" Wallace asked.

Mason's head was tilted so far back his shoulders were elevated and the top of his Head was pressing against the pallet. His gaze was locked on the wall-mounted grill covering the air duct in the hallway across from the door to the office. "So . . . his last word—*ingrate*— might have been two words—*in grate*."

"You bastard," she laughed, letting go of Mason's ankles. He slid off the pallet and watched as she used a car key to carefully lift the grate from its mount. Behind it was the up leg of an air shaft just wide and deep enough for someone to stand in. A set of blurred shoe impressions was visible in the puddle of dust at the bottom of the shaft. She pulled her phone from her pocket. "This is Detective Wallace Hartman. Have one of the crime-scene units call me ASAP."

11:00 A.M.

"Are you always so clever?" Wallace asked, around a mouthful of breakfast burrito.

"Couldn't be a federal agent, otherwise," Mason deadpanned.

Wallace smirked. "So, what exactly makes this case so important that you needed to come all the way to Baton Rouge to look around and talk to me and my people?"

"About a week ago, one of my analysts developed something that puts a really dark spin on things."

"Like what?"

"It may be nothing, but it *could* be meaningful," he said, biting into his sandwich.

"Like what?" she asked again.

"Statistical stuff, which means it could be just an aberration in the numbers or an artifact of the methods we used, but . . . on the other hand—"

"Like what, for Christ's sake?"

"Sorry—like a turf war, a full-scale turf war, here in south Louisiana—just like the ones that're ruining northern Mexico."

Wallace's eyes got big as Mason walked her through the worrisome data and its implications.

"I thought the basic territories were settled," Wallace said. "Skirmishes every now and then, sure, it's a violent business, but a war? Here? That seems so . . . excessive."

"Agreed. But the territories are only as valuable as the money the cartels can squeeze out of them. Every location has a maximum profit potential, which always declines over time, so they look for new markets to improve their take."

"Would that be enough to draw a big shot like Echeverría up here?" Wallace asked.

"This part of Louisiana has been profitable for him. He paid for it with a lot of other people's blood and he'll fight for it again if he has to."

"So you see Overman as the first high-profile casualty?"

"Could be. Could be we're completely wrong about everything I just told you, and we just don't have enough information, enough data, to suggest the right way to think about it." He shrugged and turned his palms up in a who-knows gesture.

Was this guy for real? she wondered. Never in her many encounters with federal law enforcement had she ever come across one who didn't act as if he knew everything, much less one who was willing to admit he might be wrong. "Would you like another sandwich? Your first two didn't last very long."

"No, thank you. But this is really good. I think I'll stop here again on my way back to DC."

"How long do you plan to be here?"

"Until we can figure out who slipped Overman the snake. And I need to get a read on which cartel this new supply is coming from. Any luck putting together something with your narcotics officers?"

"All set for today . . . at one," she said, furrowing her brow.

"You seem unsure," Mason said.

"Not about the meeting. It's this whole business. I obviously don't have your expertise on these kinds of things, but it seems so unlikely that the actual head of a cartel would take such a huge risk and come here himself," Wallace said.

"You're right, of course. And I don't mean to imply that I'm looking just for him. It's the snake—his signature method—that bothers me. If it's a genuine signal that he or someone important in his organization was here, that says there's worry at the top. That tends to validate the war theory."

"Does your office maintain a list of those people—his inner circle?"

"We do. Other agencies do, as well. I checked them all. None of his known lieutenants entered the U.S. using commercial transport. But we shouldn't rule out Echeverría, himself, just based on some low probability."

"For a professional statistician, you seem awfully skeptical of statistics," she said.

"People with blind faith in the numbers are called *politi*cians, not *statis*ticians."

Humble, agreeable, and a quick wit. How had this guy slipped past Uncle Sam's guardians of the infinite grimness? And why was she keeping score?

"Besides, if the information Echeverría needed was something he wanted to keep close to his vest, something he was afraid spies inside his organization might reveal to his rivals, he might have done the deed himself," Mason said. "Just to limit who was in the know."

"Were you able to dig up anything on Arthur Staples?"

"Yes and no. No, because I ran into the same brick wall you did. But, yes, in the sense that I've seen this wall before, when the government is trying to shield its lethal operatives."

"Is it possible to get past this wall?" she asked.

"Not unless you know someone really important in the intelligence community."

"You're my most important someone," she said, utterly dismayed at her choice of words.

"Then you're out of luck, unless this case becomes a matter of national security."

"I'll interpret this veil around his past to mean that whatever he did for Uncle Sam, somewhere along the line he picked up the skills necessary to do what was done to Overman."

"Him and several thousand other former spooks out there with the same skill set."

"That's scary," Wallace said.

"Or comforting, depending on where you presume their loyalties lie."

"I'm not presuming anything. But if Arthur Staples is capable of doing what was done to Overman, then it's possible that he did it . . . either for his own motives—"

"—or on behalf of Echeverría. I thought of that after we hung up."

"Then surely you looked at his passport records, to see if he's been out of the country. Maybe you talked to your friendly neighborhood NSA agent, to get a look at phone, email, credit cards?"

"I'm trying, but it's not just push a button and there it is. Applications have to be filed. Passport records come from the State

Department, and they're slow and suspicious of every request. And you can forget about help from the NSA," he said, solemnly. "What?" he asked, when he saw her smirking. "Yeah, okay. I get it, I get it. The NSA bit was a joke."

SIX

After dropping Mason at his hotel, Wallace returned to the Homicide Division. Mike Harrison was nowhere to be seen. And maybe that wasn't so bad. While she needed him to be around, she didn't like being around him. But in spite of his absence, he had done what she asked and tracked down the source of the bags. He had left a write-up on the desk. They were osmosis bags, used in laboratories to equalize ion concentrations in adjacent fluid compartments—whatever that was. The name and web address of the manufacturer was at the end of his notes.

Wallace got the telephone number from the company website and called the sales department. After a bit of wrangling she convinced the person on the other end to tell her whether they had shipped any of the bags to customers in Louisiana. They had. To two customers—a researcher at the Tulane medical school in New Orleans and a scientist at the Tunica Research Laboratory, a federal facility in Bayou Sara, a small community northwest of Baton Rouge. She was about to call the Tulane med school when Mason came strolling into the bullpen.

"Detective Hartman," he said. "Long time no see."

"You're early. Did you have trouble finding a place to park?" She had known he would be showing up, but it wasn't until he walked in that she realized she had been feeling a sense of anticipation.

"It's such a nice day and the hotel is so close, I decided to walk over. We still on for one?"

"We are. But since you're here so early, you can earn your keep. Feel like throwing your weight around?"

"What have you got?"

Wallace showed him the information Mike had left and what she had learned so far.

"This seems almost too easy," Mason said. "I suppose you want me to wrestle with the federal lab."

"If you insist." She handed him the information she had on the lab.

"You ever heard of this place?" He set his shoulder bag on the floor next to her desk and pulled out a tablet.

"Nope. It's in the Felicianas, a fairly remote part of the state. A bit . . . feral, but historically interesting. Briefly British, then Spanish, and for about five minutes in the early 1800s it was part of the Republic of West Florida. Some people there still fly the old flag, the Bonnie Blue."

"You seem to know the area pretty well."

"Just the grammar school history," she said. "Nothing about the day-to-day."

"Well, let me see what I can dig up on this lab," he said, heading for an empty cubicle across the room.

Wallace called the med school and, after getting bounced around a few times, finally spoke to someone in the research group that had ordered the bags. The person on the other end assured Wallace that all of the bags had been used for their intended purpose, and that they would not be ordering more.

While she waited for Mason to finish his part, she scrolled through her phone calendar. A "Call Lex Today" reminder stared up at her.

Her thumb was poised above Lex's number, but at the last second she moved the reminder out one more day—again.

"I just got my office to send me a description of this Tunica place," Mason said, as he returned to Wallace's desk. He showed her his tablet. "They're trying to genetically engineer groundcover plants that will pull chemical pollutants out of contaminated soil and turn them into harmless organic molecules."

"Are any of the bags missing from their inventory?" Wallace asked.

"To find that out, they'll have to go lab to lab and do an inventory, which will take time. Which means somebody will call me back . . . someday. I say we just go out there and look for ourselves."

Something about his offhand way of suggesting the trip as a joint effort was appealing to Wallace. He seemed untroubled by the territorial jealousies that plagued so many in this business. He was definitely not cut from the same stiff cardboard as the typical Washington lawman. "Can we get in?"

"Of course we can." He flashed her a smug smile. "This afternoon, as a matter of fact. I had meetings set up with investigators from the state police, but I'm pushing those until this evening."

As one o'clock approached, Wallace did a quick tour of the floor, looking for Mike Harrison. No one had seen him and he wasn't answering Wallace's calls or texts.

After that, she and Mason looked through the evidence reports that had come back on the Overman scene. Presumably Overman had been armed, but no weapon was found. All of the blood at the scene belonged to Overman. And, except for the bags of powder, which were confirmed to be cocaine, the only other testable material had come from the air shaft a few hours ago.

The report from the canvassing officers was also uninformative. No vehicle registered in the name of Ronald Overman was found near the scene, nor were there any abandoned vehicles in the area that could be connected to him. The officers had done a door-to-door in the residential neighborhood near the warehouse but, in many cases, no one had been at home. And none of the residents who had been home had anything useful to offer. Addresses for the people they spoke to were included with the report.

"Looks like there's still a lot of ground to go over," Mason said, reacting to the skimpy results of the canvass.

"I've got a new partner," Wallace said. "You'll meet him in a few minutes. I'll put him on it." *If he ever shows up*, she thought. She called Mike's cell again, but it went straight to voicemail. She left yet another message reminding him about the one o'clock meeting, then she and Mason walked to the conference room.

The officers lounging around the room looked more like bikers and gang members than police officers and they presented a strange contrast to the clean, sleek, board-room–style furniture. Some sat at the table, others milled about. Wallace half expected Mike to be in the room already, schmoozing with some of his buddies from the earlier part of his career, but he wasn't there.

David Bosso, the narcotics officer Wallace encountered at the warehouse, opened things with a rundown on Ronald Overman and their unsuccessful attempts to dismantle his operation.

Overman had been under surveillance for years, but he was a clever operator who brought a true entrepreneurial spirit to his work. Starting as a street dealer, he had become a minor distributor and from there he had methodically taken over the territories of less gifted and less far-sighted players.

After that Overman had launched a business development campaign that would have merited a write-up in the *Harvard Business Review* had he applied it to a legitimate trade. He had aimed his efforts directly at the beating heart of the communities around him—youth softball and soccer coaches, scout masters, and even lay leaders in the churches—and he had been incredibly careful. No prosecutor had come close to getting a drug-related indictment against him, much less a conviction. It had been easier to jail some of the state's highest-ranking politicians.

Bosso was of the opinion that just before Overman was killed, his organization had been in the midst of an evolution—a change that exposed a brief vulnerability—and that someone unafraid to use harsh methods had seen it as a chance to strike.

"What made you think a change was coming?" Wallace asked, taking a swig from a bottle of water.

"Couple a things," Bosso said. He leaned back in his chair and put his booted feet up on the table. "First, he'd go off the radar for longer and more frequent periods. It's like we'd be watching him while he's tooling around with his people, then suddenly he ain't with 'em. His guys and his vehicles are there but he's gone. Plus, his organization occasionally leaks a little information. There was a fear on the inside that he was taking some . . . unnecessary risks."

"What do you think it all means?" Mason asked. He pulled the cap off his pen, ready to take notes.

"Sometimes when guys like this start doing stuff like that, it means they're trying to hide something from their own people. They don't want anybody to be able to see what their move is gonna be before they make it."

"Was this his first time to go to that warehouse?" Mason asked.

Bosso shrugged. "We don't know."

Beverly Drysdale, another of the officers, spoke up. Beverly was a master of disguise. At the moment, she looked homeless. Tomorrow she might look like a prostitute or a banker. "Look, Overman was a *very* cautious man. For him to go any real time or distance without his most trusted muscle around, it would have to be worth a lot of money—money he wouldn't necessarily want the people upstream in his supply channel to know he was pulling in."

"He was two-timing his suppliers?" Mason asked.

"He *mighta* been," Bosso said, gnawing the cuticles of his left hand. "He mighta been getting tutored for his GED exam or playing doctor with the mayor's wife. We just don't know." He eyed his cuticles with disapproval, then resumed chewing.

"Do you currently have anyone who was close enough to him who might have information they'd be willing to pass our way?" Wallace leaned forward in her chair, resting her elbows on her knees, looking at the floor. Bosso's hands were filthy and his toothy manicure was grossing her out.

"Not at the moment," Beverly said. "Our last useful source seems to be no longer employed with the Overman organization."

"Is he still among the living?" Mason asked.

"It's a she, and we don't know that either," Bosso said. "What about your side of the fence?" he asked, commencing operation cuticle-chew on the fingers of his other hand. "You got any federally funded tattletales inside Overman's crew?"

"If there were, I wouldn't need to be here, punching a hole in your day."

"Mr. Cunningham, Wallace told us you have some specific questions you wanted to ask," Beverly said. "This would be the time."

"First I need to share some information with you. Information that needs to stay . . . unpublicized," Mason said, cautiously. "If we can agree on that—"

"Most of the folks in this room are undercover, Mr. Cunningham. They're trusting you with their lives, just by letting you see their faces," Bosso retorted. "We know how to keep secrets," he continued, not bothering to look up from a careful study of both hands.

"I'm not calling your discretion into question," Mason fired back. "I'm flagging the information as something that hasn't been released. Its value would be lost if it got loose."

"We understand," Beverly said. "Let's just get on with this."

Mason began by laying out the data showing the sudden fall in street prices for cocaine and the rise in dealer arrests, then finished with Don's theory that cocaine originally earmarked for the surrounding states was being diverted into south Louisiana.

"Interesting idea," Beverly admitted. "If it's true, the potential for cartel-level violence would seem to be very high."

"What I'm seeing bears that out," Bosso said. "There does seem to be more and cheaper shit on the street. But how widespread that is, I couldn't say."

"As to whether the extra product is coming in from places like Mississippi and Arkansas, that would be anybody's guess," one of the other officers said.

"Based on your knowledge of the area, how feasible would that even be?" Mason asked.

"It could happen," Bosso said. "But geographic factors would limit where. There's only so many bridges across the rivers between Louisiana and Mississippi. Those are low probability because they're so heavily watched."

"That leaves the northern border of the parishes, between the Pearl River and the Mississippi," Mason said. "Detective Hartman tells me that's some pretty rough country. So if the cocaine is coming in from Mississippi, wouldn't that be a likely place?"

"That would actually be the very best place since it's so difficult to patrol and, obviously, sitting right on top of south Louisiana," Bosso said, pulling his feet off the table.

"I know most street-level dealers don't know which cartel produces their goods," Mason said. "But the ones getting arrested, are they giving up anything on the source of their stuff?"

"No. But like you said, they don't know and they don't give a shit," Beverly said. "For information like that, we'd need a really talkative individual who was high up in Overman's bunch. Which, at the moment, we don't have."

"What about who might have killed him?" Mason asked.

"Like I told Detective Hartman, the day Overman got wasted, other than the usual suspects—people trying to take his sandbox away from him—we're in the dark," Bosso said, returning his attention to his left hand.

SEVEN

It had rained heavily for about fifteen minutes, but now the sun was out full force, raising tendrils of steam off the hot streets. People on the sidewalks squinted against the glare reflecting off the rain-slick windshields and glass buildings. The dirt smell of the river, a few blocks west, was heavy in the soggy air.

"The area where Overman was killed is sort of on the way to Tunica," Wallace said. "Since we finished our meeting early, we have some extra time. I'd like to follow up the half-assed neighborhood canvass. Will that work for you?" she asked, as they drove away from the police station. Wallace felt her low opinion of Mike Harrison was vindicated by his failure to show up at the meeting, but she was also irritated at having to do the work she wanted him to do.

"I'm perfectly fine with stopping to do a little poking around in the neighborhood by the warehouse." He studied her closely. "Are *you*?"

Either she was losing her poker face or Mason was more observant than she'd given him credit for. "Am I so easy to read?"

"Your no-show partner getting under your skin?" He pulled his tablet from his shoulder bag and opened Google maps.

"Something like that."

Traffic was light as they headed northeast away from downtown. They rode in silence for several minutes. When she glanced over at him, he was focused on the tablet in his lap.

"I'm looking at the satellite view of the area around the warehouse." He swiped his finger across the screen and spread the image. "It fronts on a street called Choctaw Ridge and backs up to a large wooded area. What looks like a wide, well-groomed power line easement cuts through the trees and opens at a residential neighborhood about a mile away."

"So someone approaching from the rear would have had a sheltered pathway there and back."

"Any idea what this is?" he asked, pointing at what looked like a series of parallel brown bands in the otherwise uniformly green easement.

Wallace pulled onto the shoulder and took Mason's tablet, zooming in as close as she could. "It's close to the back of the neighborhood, so it's probably a community vegetable garden."

"People farm under high-tension power lines?"

"It's illegal, but they do it anyway. In fact, let's start there. Maybe someone was tending the pea patch and saw something."

Their approach to the warehouse took them through an old part of Baton Rouge. Residential areas built during the fifties and sixties transitioned into stretches of metal buildings and homes converted to commercial use.

As they neared their destination, Wallace turned off Choctaw Ridge and worked her way toward the neighborhood that lay behind and to the north of the crime scene. She stopped at the southernmost part of the neighborhood, nearest the mouth of the power line easement.

They parked and took off on foot, looking for the rows they had seen on the satellite image. The easement was about two hundred feet wide. Thick electrical cables drooped heavily between the huge skeletal towers that marched into the distance. About a hundred yards in, the cleared area turned sharply to the left. As they made the turn, the plowed rows came into view. It was indeed a garden—quite a large one. A group of men and women, all appearing to be in their sixties and seventies, were getting down to business with rakes and hoes.

"May I he'p you?" one of the women asked, as Wallace and Mason approached.

The crowd visibly tensed when Wallace introduced herself and Mason. As if a secret signal had passed among them, everyone dropped their tools and began to walk back toward the houses.

"Just take what you want," one of the departing women said over her shoulder. "There ain't gone be enough left for us to make it worth doing anymore, so don't expect nothin' after this. Take the tools too. We ain't gonna have no use for 'em."

"We're not here because of your garden," Wallace said. "We're investigating a crime that took place near here, a few days ago."

"You talking 'bout dat drug dealer what was kilt over on Choctaw?" one of the men asked in a wheezy voice.

"Yes sir. But we'll get to that in a minute. Is someone shaking you down, here? Cops?" Wallace asked.

The ones walking away stopped, but no one spoke. Wallace walked over to the woman who had spoken first. She had the dead-eyed, jut-jawed expression of someone who had been forced to submit too often.

"If you're being victimized by a police officer, tell me. I'll make it stop."

"You gone run on up to headquarters and complain for us?" the woman asked. "And then what? You make trouble for 'im, instead of stealin' from us the son of a bitch'll just get mad and come out here and start hurtin' people. You gone fix that too?"

"We're old, not stupid," one of the men said.

"In case you change your mind," Wallace said, handing the woman her card.

The woman stuck the card in a pocket of her work shirt, without looking at it. "I know you're tryin' to do right, but let's just leave that to the side, for the time bein'. You prob'ly wanna know if anybody here knows anything 'bout that fella in the warehouse?"

"Yes ma'am," Wallace said. "And I'm sorry if you've already been over this, but the officers who went asking around in your neighborhood the day it happened didn't have much luck finding folks at home. And please, tell me your name."

"I'm Louise Mautner. Most of us are retired and lots of us spend our time out here. Helps us make ends meet and it's good exercise. Them officers prob'ly didn't find too many folks at home 'cause a lot of us woulda been out here."

"Well then, thank you for taking the time now," Wallace said.

"How much do you know about the individual who was killed?" Mason asked.

"Just what was in the papers," Louise said.

"It happened Sunday afternoon," Mason added. "Was everyone that's here today, out here then?"

"My sister and I were here," Louise said, as she pointed to another woman in the group. "And those three men over there."

"We're most interested in the time between three and four," Mason said.

"Anything you can remember," Wallace prompted. "Even if it doesn't strike you as terribly important."

"Only thing we saw was some fool shootin' through here on a motorcycle," Louise said. "But there's lots a that goin' on, right along in here. Lots of folks on four-wheelers and dirt bikes and thangs like that."

"Then what made you notice that particular motorcycle?" Mason probed.

"Well, we pretty much know the people that ride around in here, 'cause they're from the neighborhood. This fella whadn't anybody I'd seen before."

"Fella? The rider was male? You're certain of that?" Wallace asked.

"Well, not absolutely certain, no. He was wearin' a helmet with a tinted visor, but he looked like he was built like a guy," Louise said.

"And he was going fast," one of the men said. "Most of the regulars is just cruising, out having a little fun. But this guy whadn't wasting time. He was loud and he was moving."

"Do you remember what the bike looked like?" Wallace asked.

"Not the make, or nothin'," the first woman said. "It was shiny black all over. What the kids call a crotch rocket."

"Did he exit the easement at your neighborhood, or did he continue in the easement past the subdivision?"

"He drove right out into the street at the corner and disappeared. You could hear him for a while, but once he hit the street I couldn't see him anymore," Louise said.

"Could you tell from the sound, which way he went?" Mason asked.

"East," Louise said.

"And, can you pinpoint the time?" Mason asked.

"Not exactly, no," Louise said. "I do remember we were on our way back to the house when the motorcycle went past. And when we walked in the back door, the clock in the kitchen said three-oh-five. I remember that 'cause I needed to put somethin' in the oven at three forty-five, and I remember thinkin' to myself that I had forty minutes to get cleaned up before I needed to start cookin'."

"How long between the time the bike went past and when you saw your kitchen clock?" Wallace asked.

"Prob'ly no more than five minutes, at the most," Louise's sister said. "A couple of minutes to go to the house, and another two or three to get the tools and the boots put away."

"Can you think of anything else?" Mason asked.

"No. Can y'all think of anything?" Louise asked, looking out at the rest of the group. The question was met with a muted chorus of no's and negative head shakes.

"This is going to sound like a strange thing to ask," Wallace began, "but do you mind if we walk back to your house with you?"

"What for?" Louise asked, suddenly suspicious.

"Just trying to get the time frame as close as possible. Do either of you carry a cell phone?"

"Of course. We both do," Louise replied.

"Would you mind comparing the time on your kitchen clock to the time on your cell phone? We'll wait out by the street."

"Sure. We can do that," Louise said, the suspicion draining out of her voice.

Mason and Wallace followed several steps behind the sisters as they walked from the garden toward the neighborhood. A few minutes later, Louise met them on the sidewalk in front of her house.

"The kitchen clock is two minutes ahead of my cell phone," she said. "So I guess we actually walked into the kitchen at three-oh-three, not three-oh-five. Is that what you wanted?"

"It is. Thank you," Wallace said.

"One last question," Mason said. "Is this easement a shortcut that people might use to get from the main road up there to somewhere north of here?"

"No. Just vacant land on out past the subdivision. Unless you're drivin' some kinda off-road vehicle, it'd be quicker just to take the regular streets back on into the neighborhood."

"Thanks, again," Wallace said. "It's possible we might think of a few more questions. Is there a way I could get in touch with you?"

"Sure," Louise said. She pulled Wallace's card from her pocket and called Wallace's cell.

Wallace's phone began to ring. "Is this you?" Wallace asked, showing her phone to Louise.

"Yes ma'am," Louise said, turning toward her house.

"Thank you," Mason called after her.

"It's probably time that we headed up to the Tunica Laboratory," Wallace said, as they watched Louise move slowly up the walkway to her front door.

"You look ready to play the what-if game," Mason said, in response to her thoughtful look.

"Stop getting in my head like that," she said, smiling. "You don't know me well enough." She paused. "So . . . what if we assume Mr. Crotch Rocket was a member of the cast in that little drama at the warehouse?"

"Then, based on your earlier calculation that Overman and the snake got cozy at about three twenty-seven, it looks like Mr. Crotch Rocket had already exited the stage about thirty minutes before that."

"Which means that there had to be at least two people with Overman. The guy on the motorcycle and the guy who stayed behind in the air shaft," Wallace said. "And it seems reasonable to assume the guy in the air shaft was the snake handler."

"So if the snake guy was there the whole time after Crotch Rocket left, then he and Overman were alone together for the thirty minutes between then and the time Arthur Staples arrived."

"We can't assume it was just the two of them in the warehouse at that point," Wallace added.

"True," Mason said. "But we know the motorcycle rider was gone—"

"Which raises the question of whether he and the snake handler were together or whether Overman encountered them separately."

"And we still don't know how Overman got to the warehouse, or how the snake handler in the air shaft got away."

"We don't actually know if the motorcycle rider is even part of this," Wallace cautioned. "It's just an assumption, at this point."

EIGHT

K evin Bell was the Director of the Tunica Research Laboratory, although, if he had many more weeks like he was having now, he wasn't sure how much longer his directorship would last. Late Monday morning, Carla Chapman had notified him that Matt Gable, one of the lab's most important scientists, appeared to be missing. Carla was Matt's principal research assistant and a talented scientist in her own right. She had returned from a conference late Sunday night and been unable to get Gable on the phone. She said she assumed he was working late.

On Monday morning, though, when Matt was not at the lab and still not answering his phone, Carla had driven by his house. When she discovered that the house had burned down during the night, she became alarmed and went straight to the police. They told her no one had been in the house at the time of the fire, so she had filed a missing person report and then returned to work. That was when she had called him to say Matt was probably missing.

After checking with security, Kevin discovered that Matt had exited the lab the previous Friday and hadn't been back since.

Monday afternoon Kevin had gotten Carla to walk him through Matt's lab areas, looking for some clue as to the researcher's whereabouts. What they found instead was a locked storage room that concealed what appeared to be functioning but unauthorized apparatuses. Kevin's best guess was that Matt had been diverting lab resources to some personal, probably illegal, purpose. There was no way he could tolerate any off-the-books shenanigans, especially when inspectors from his funding agencies would be descending on the lab in less than two weeks. Slow progress toward its goal and an increasing need for resources kept the lab under intense scrutiny and its continued existence seemed to hang forever in the balance. Kevin had to think of the greater good, so he had ordered Carla to disassemble the whole business and send it to the crusher.

Then, late Tuesday afternoon, the local police chief had called to see if Matt had returned or been located. Kevin assumed that if the police had taken an interest in Matt for reasons related to the apparatus in the closet, they would have shown up at the gate with a search warrant by now. Since they hadn't, he was relieved he had gotten rid of it. Going on the assumption that the less he appeared to know, the better off he and the lab would be, he had told the police chief the absolute minimum—that Matt's whereabouts were still unknown.

Today, he was finally starting to feel like some semblance of order was returning to his world. Even though Matt had still not surfaced, Kevin was content to let the local police handle the search for the rogue chemist. He was also feeling pretty clever about having Carla destroy the stuff from the closet, instead of doing it himself. If push came to shove, he could very plausibly claim ignorance of the matter and Carla would certainly be in no hurry to admit to anyone that she had been a participant in the destruction of evidence.

Kevin's intercom chirped. It was his administrative assistant.

"Dr. Bell, two individuals showed up at the front gate, demanding to be admitted to the lab."

"Why are you telling me this?" he asked. "Surely you remember we're not a tourist attraction. And last time I checked, gate security was capable of informing uninvited guests that they're on federal property and subject to arrest and detention if they fail to vacate the premises immediately."

"Well, one's from the DEA and the other one's a detective from Baton Rouge. The DEA guy was waving around an order from somebody important, saying it's okay for them to be here."

"Have their credentials and this so-called order been authenticated?"

"Yes sir."

"Really?" Kevin said. "Have they been allowed inside the gate?"

"They have."

"And where are they now?"

"Right out here with me."

"Why didn't you tell me about this as soon as you knew about it?" he fumed.

"I'm doing that right now, Dr. Bell."

"Have them wait," he said icily, struggling to maintain his composure.

3:30 P.M.

"Detective Hartman, Mr. Cunningham, please come in," Bell said, after forcing Wallace and Mason to wait nearly fifteen minutes.

Wallace took an instant dislike to Bell. His tone reeked of the artificial charm people used when hospitality was the furthest thing from their minds.

"Detective Hartman and I are pursuing different but possibly related cases," Mason began, after everyone was introduced. "Our investigation has led us to your doorstep."

"Given what you do for a living, Mr. Cunningham, would I be

off base if I inferred that there's a drug angle to your being here?" Kevin leaned against the front edge of his desk but didn't offer Wallace or Mason a seat.

"You're not off base," Mason replied.

Wallace explained how the osmosis bags had focused their attention on Tunica.

"So, your theory of the case is that our agricultural research mission is just a thinly veiled cover for a federally funded cocaine plantation," Kevin said, looking skeptical and annoyed.

"No," Mason replied calmly. "Our theory is that a little friendly cooperation from you will keep an army of DEA agents from crawling over every square inch of this place while you sit on your hands and watch." He sat in one of Bell's side chairs, then set his bag on the front of the desk.

"Mr. Cunningham, I assure you I was joking."

"Dr. Bell, there's nothing funny about this case," Wallace said, wandering behind his desk to peer out of the window. "This is a large facility. It's possible that some out-of-the-way corner is being misused."

"You're absolutely correct, Detective." He turned, giving her a nervous look. "Let's begin again, shall we? How is it that the two of you believe I can be of help?"

"We'd like to know if any of the osmosis bags from your inventory have been used, and if so, who has access to them or has been using them," she said.

"It will take some time to determine that. If the bags were part of the general inventory, we will have a record of which section requisitioned them, and from there, we would move on to who used them. If, on the other hand, they were acquired specifically for a certain section, we'll have to query the section-level inventory custodians."

"We'll wait while you make the calls," Mason said.

Kevin spent the next several minutes calling the supply custodians.

"I see. Thank you." He had a stricken look on his face as he hung up. "The bags were purchased specifically by Section Seven."

"Can you make the relevant persons in Section Seven available to us?" Wallace asked.

"Dr. Sarah Bleeker is the head of the section. Unfortunately, it seems the entire allotment of bags has disappeared, and the custodian has no record or recollection of anyone getting them from inventory."

"How is that possible?" Wallace asked. "Don't you have internal controls?"

"No system is perfect, Detective," Kevin said, drumming the fingers of both hands on his desk.

"Perhaps we should speak with Dr. Bleeker, and decide from there what our next move will be," Mason said.

"Of course," Bell said. "I'll arrange it immediately."

Forty-five minutes and several conversations later, Wallace and Mason realized they had hit a wall, when they finally discovered that the bags had been purchased for a scientist who no longer worked at Tunica. It was possible that the departed scientist had used them before he left. Or maybe he had inadvertently packed them and taken them when he went to his new position and the requisition had been lost. Such things happened from time to time, they were told. They got the scientist's contact information from Bleeker, then headed toward the parking lot.

4:45 P.M.

As she and Mason walked toward her car in the Tunica lot, Wallace called Mike Harrison, but he still wasn't answering his phone. She and Mason stopped in the shade of a huge oak while she wrote Mike a detailed email about how to contact the former Tunica scientist who might have used or taken the bags and what she wanted Mike to ask him. Her flare of frustration over Mike's persistent absence subsided after she reminded herself she could give him work without them having to be in each other's presence. Since the partnership was only temporary, perhaps a long-distance relationship was the best posture for things.

"We've been focused on who the bags were sold to in Louisiana, but it's possible they came from out of state," Mason said, as they strolled through the lot toward Wallace's car. "Part of my analyst's theory is that the new cocaine showing up around here came from out of state. If the scientist you've got your partner calling doesn't pan out, we'll need to broaden our inquiry."

"While we're waiting on that, what's your next move?" she asked.

"A few things. I still have meetings with the other law enforcement agencies in Baton Rouge. And my folks in DC are trying to pin down Echeverría's movements over the last few weeks. If anything puts him inside the U.S., I'll go to wherever he was to see if he can be traced from there to here."

"Detective? Could I have a word with you?"

Wallace and Mason turned at the sound of the voice. A thin woman who looked to be in her midthirties, with a lab coat slung through the strap of her shoulder bag, was hurrying toward them. Her long brown hair was in a loose braid at the back of her neck. A pair of expensive-looking glasses compensated for her slightly owlish eyes.

"You're not getting the whole story," the woman said.

"Am I looking for a story?" Wallace asked.

"I know you're investigating something at Tunica. I was just coming into the research building when you were walking out with Dr. Bell. I heard him call you 'Detective'."

"Who are you?" Wallace demanded.

"Carla Chapman. I work at Tunica for Matt Gable. I'm one of the scientists in his section."

"And . . ." Wallace said.

"And I happen to know that whatever Dr. Bell told you, it's not the whole story."

"If you have something to say, Ms. Chapman, you have our full attention," Mason said.

"Not here. It's too risky. There's a park a mile or so down the road, if you take a left out of the front gate. It has covered tables and benches, where we can sit and talk. I'll meet you there," she said, pulling her keys from her purse and striking off toward the other end of the lot.

NINE

5:05 P.M.

The park was deserted. Concrete tables and benches situated on gum-speckled slabs were scattered around a treeless expanse of unruly grass punctuated with patches of red clay hardpan. Poles set into the corners of the slabs supported corrugated aluminum canopies that provided the only shade. The tables had seen a lot of meals but not a lot of cleaning. A few of the canopies were tilted at odd angles because someone had backed a vehicle too close and bent the support poles. Garbage was foaming out of trash barrels that looked like they hadn't been emptied since Reconstruction. The sun was baking the stink of stale beer and rotting food out of the garbage.

"Since you don't know what Dr. Bell told us, you must believe you know something you're sure he doesn't," Wallace said, after they settled at one of the tables.

"Most three-year-olds know stuff he doesn't," Carla replied, "but that's not what I meant. Do you mind if I know who you two are? I'm taking a big risk talking to you, so I'd like to know who I'm dealing with."

"I'm Wallace Hartman, a detective with the Baton Rouge Police Department. And this is Mason Cunningham, with the DEA." They both offered their credentials, but Carla seemed satisfied with the introductions and didn't bother to look at the proffered identification.

"I know that whatever Bell told you isn't everything, because he ordered me to help him cover something up."

"That's very interesting," Mason said. "Exactly what would that be?"

"Matt Gable, one of the main researchers at Tunica, the one I work for, is missing. Since at least Sunday night." Carla paused, shifting her gaze from Wallace to Mason.

"Please go on," Wallace urged.

Carla told them about how her inability to contact Matt had eventually led her to his burned house on Monday morning, her dealings with the police in Bayou Sara, the little town near the lab, and about her and Kevin Bell finding the hidden apparatus in the storeroom.

"What was the hidden lab stuff for?" Wallace asked.

"We don't know."

"Bell never mentioned anything like that to us and he didn't show us anything inside any storerooms," Mason said.

"That's because he ordered me to take everything down and destroy it."

"You're kidding me," Mason snapped.

"I'm not. But I didn't destroy anything either. I took it all apart and packed it in storage crates and hid it behind some other things in the storage room."

"Could you reassemble it?" Wallace asked, waving away a squadron of flies.

"I think so. I made sketches and notes as I took everything apart."

"You obviously think it's connected to Matt's disappearance?" Wallace said.

"It's the only clue I have. That's why I saved it." Her gaze drifted and her demeanor shifted into a lower gear. "That's why I followed you just now."

"The two of you were involved," Wallace probed, keying on Carla's sudden change in mood.

"We were, but we never registered the relationship with HR," Carla admitted. "We didn't think it was anybody's business. It didn't interfere with our jobs, and we kept it out of the workplace, so we felt like we were entitled to our privacy." Her shoulders sagged and she stared at the ground.

"Tell us what's known about the circumstances of the fire," Mason said.

"So far, nothing," Carla replied. "The local police say an investigation is underway, but I don't get the impression there's any urgency to it. They did say that no one was in the house when it burned."

"Is it possible that Matt set the fire himself?" Wallace asked.

"I can't think of a reason he would, and I can't imagine why anyone else would either. He was renting, so it's not like he would get insurance money for it."

Mason stood and paced in front of the table, his shoulders hunched and his hands stuffed in his pockets. "Could the fire be connected to the stuff you found hidden in the storeroom?"

"I don't know. This wasn't some kitchen-counter lab fire, if that's what you're getting at. He wasn't cooking meth or anything."

"Is it possible he's seeing someone else?" Wallace asked.

"I don't think he would trash his career for something like that. Besides, I know he loved me. We had only been seeing each other a few months, but things got serious really fast. Don't ask me to explain it, but I don't think this has anything to do with another woman. Matt's in some kind of trouble."

"What about family somewhere?" Mason asked.

"He's an only child and his parents are both dead. He has distant relatives somewhere in South Dakota, but they're not close. They haven't spoken in years. And anyway, if that were the case, he would have gotten in touch. He hasn't, so my assumption is that he can't." Carla's face crumpled and her eyes brimmed.

"Mason and I may meet with the local police to see if they have any leads on Matt's whereabouts."

"The local police aren't taking this seriously."

"What makes you say that?" Wallace asked.

"Because they're moving too slow," Carla blurted, her emotions escalating. "When I went to file a missing person report, I explained about how devoted Matt is to his work—that he would never just disappear without telling anyone. And all I got was a bunch of slow-walking *we have to follow procedure* bullshit."

Wallace was about to speak when Carla cut her off.

"And I could see in their eyes, what they're thinking. That I'm just some starry-eyed girl who won't face the fact that he's off with someone else. I mean, for Pete's sake, his damn house burned down, he won't answer his phone, his lab was full of a bunch of shit nobody even knows what it is. Does that sound like somebody tomcatting around to you? Police can be such bastards. Present company excluded, I'm sure," she added.

"Do the police know everything you just told us?" Mason asked, mopping his brow with a handkerchief. "Do they know about the funny business you found in Matt's lab?"

"I didn't find out about that until after I talked to them on Monday so, no, they don't know about the lab."

"Why haven't you told them?"

"We all had to sign nondisclosure agreements at the lab. If I talk about internal matters to outsiders and Bell found out, he'd fire me and maybe Matt too."

"But you're telling us," Mason pointed out.

"If I tell the local police and they blab it to Bell, but they don't do any kind of real investigation, then I get fired for nothing. Somehow the fact that you came all the way out to the lab to look made me think you were serious about looking into this. That makes it a risk worth taking because you might actually help me find Matt."

"Surely the locals are doing the standard things—a motor vehicle alert, phone and bank activity. What are you holding back?" Wallace asked, in case Carla was being cagey.

"I'm not holding back. Look, they haven't even bothered to do a decent search in the woods around his house. If somebody who lived near the forest disappeared, wouldn't you make that some kind of a priority?"

"What would make the woods near his home more likely than any other place to look?" Mason asked. He sat back down and began rolling his sleeves up to his elbows.

"Sometimes Matt ran to and from work along a trail through the woods between his house and the Tunica access road. I don't know the actual route, because I never went with him. I'm not a runner and I don't like being in rough country."

"Can you show me where Matt started his runs?" Wallace asked.

"Sure. When?"

"Now, if you like," Wallace said. "One more question, though, before we leave. Do you know what an osmosis bag is?"

"I'm a professional chemist. Of course I do."

"Did the secret apparatus from Matt's storeroom lab involve any osmosis bags?" Mason asked.

"No. There was nothing like that in the stuff I took down," Carla said.

"Could the apparatus be modified so that the bags would need to be part of it?"

"Sure. Any lab setup can be modified any way the chemist needs it to be. But you would have to know what the setup is intended to do, before you could guess about someone else's work."

5:30 P.M.

Wallace and Mason followed Carla to the burned ruins of Matt's house. It had been an older frame house built in the pier and beam style. The firefighters had arrived too late to save anything. The tops of the brick piers and a bathroom sink still attached to its drainpipe like a huge white flower were the only things visible above the drift of ashes.

Pine woods surrounded the lot on three sides. Every house in the neighborhood was on a large wooded tract. Carla led them through the backyard, then through a break in the foliage. Shade from the trees gave them a little relief from the heat. The air was sharp with the turpentine scent of pine sap and the forest floor was slippery with leaf litter and pine needles. A few yards in, they came to an area where the bare earth was exposed.

"This is where he would start," Carla said. "It's maybe two miles, I think, from here to the access road that takes you to the guard gate at the lab. In that direction," she said, pointing off into the trees. "Matt said the terrain was pretty difficult, but he's very athletic."

No one spoke for nearly a full minute as Wallace did a slow turn, studying the forest in the direction Carla indicated. Because of the deep layer of pine needles there was very little scrub vegetation and the ground had a springy feel. Shafts of sunlight stabbed through the canopy of the treetops.

"I have to get back to the lab," Carla said, breaking the silence. "I've got some time-sensitive tests running and I'll need to look in on them, pretty soon."

"That's fine," Mason said. "Just make sure to leave those crates you hid exactly where they are, for the moment. Don't do anything that might indicate they even exist."

"Here's my number," Wallace said, handing Carla one of her cards. "Call me if anything turns up. And let me have your number in case we have more questions."

"Sure," Carla said, pulling out her phone and calling Wallace's number. "Is that good enough?"

"Perfect, thanks."

"Will you let me know if you find anything out there?"

"I will," Wallace assured her.

"I wonder where the trail is?" Mason asked, as they watched Carla walk away.

"See those streaks of paler brown going off in that direction?" Wallace said. "Where the color of the pine needles is vaguely lighter than the rest and it looks less cushiony?"

"Sort of. Maybe. Now that you point it out."

Wallace looked deeper into the trees, her eyes scanning along the floor of the forest, then darting back and forth among the trees. She walked a few steps deeper into the woods.

"Are you thinking of trying to follow this?" he asked.

"It has to be followed." She looked back at him. "A halo of peculiar circumstances is forming around this place."

"I meant you personally. Shouldn't we leave the cross-country tracking to the pros?"

"Why would you assume I'm not a pro at this?" Wallace demanded. "Because I'm a girl?"

"Exactly," he laughed.

Wallace looked at him, trying to keep her face from betraying the curiosity his whimsical attitude was stirring. "You're not like any fed I've worked with before."

"Is that good or bad?" he asked, staring off into the trees.

"I'll let you know," she said, not entirely sure what the answer was. "In any event, once upon a time, my brothers and I did a lot of hunting in woods just like these. I still know how to find my way around pretty well."

"Once upon a time?"

"My older brother died a few years back. After that, my younger brother and I sort of lost our enthusiasm for it."

"I'm sorry. I wasn't trying to pry."

"And you weren't. I'm the one who brought it up." She waited a moment to see if Mason would pick up the thread of the conversation. When he didn't, she looked back toward the burned house. "Obviously, Matt Gable is of prime interest now, but I'm thinking that even though Kevin Bell is a deceptive little prick, he's not involved."

"Agreed," Mason said. "If he were, he would never have let Carla see the apparatus in Gable's storeroom. He would have destroyed it himself. But Matt and the Tunica lab itself . . ."

"They no longer pass the smell test." Wallace squatted down near one of the pale areas, then turned to look back into the woods.

"Do you want to run this trail right now?" Mason asked, following behind her.

"I'm out of my jurisdiction. We'd have to clear it with the locals first. I can't afford to get accused of claim jumping and trampling on evidence," Wallace replied. "It should be easy to follow, though. It's pretty clear what he was doing."

"Really?" Mason asked, looking at his phone. "Those pale streaks you pointed out don't seem like much to go on, and Google Satellite shows nothing but tree cover and a few creeks, from here to Tunica. If there's a trail in there, it's well hidden."

"Okay, city boy, does Google show this?" she asked, using a stick to point out a scrape mark about seven feet above the ground on a nearby tree trunk.

"Not that I can see, on this tiny screen," he conceded, smiling at her gentle dig.

"And just to keep our vocabulary straight, wherever it is you come from I'm sure those things would be creeks," she said, pointing to the image on his phone. "Around here . . . they're bayous."

"Got it. Bayous."

"How much do you know about birds?" she asked, turning her attention back toward the remains of the house.

"Beyond the basic wings and feathers bit, not much. Why?"

"I'm just wondering what kind of a bird lives in a birdhouse that's wired for electricity."

Mason followed her gaze to a tree a few yards from where the left rear corner of the house had once been. Attached to the trunk, about fifteen feet above the ground, was what looked like a well-crafted birdhouse. A wire, almost the color of the bark, ran from the back of the birdhouse, down the trunk and disappeared into the ground. Scorch marks on the bark of the tree, and several others nearby, showed where the blaze had apparently burned away branches that would ordinarily have obscured the birdhouse from casual inspection. Sunlight glinted off a reflective surface just inside the round entry hole in the front. As they looked at it, Mason's phone signaled an incoming message.

"Maybe we can borrow a ladder from a neighbor," Wallace said, heading toward the street.

"He's dead," Mason said, studying his phone.

"Who?" she asked, alarmed he might be referring to Matt Gable.

"Echeverría—a plane crash, in northern Mexico." He held the phone in her direction.

"When?" She moved up next to him to look at the screen.

"Yesterday."

"So he could have been here, and was on his way home," Wallace said, stepping back and looking at Mason.

"Could have been. It looks like his plane was shot down."

"That should be easy to confirm. Do we participate in aerial interdiction down there?"

"No. Not in northern Mexico. And apparently it wasn't a Mexican government takedown, either."

"A rival cartel?" she asked.

"That would certainly support our turf war hypothesis. And it could easily be the case. Some of these newer cartels are operating like military units, with the training programs and heavy weapons to show for it. Shooting down aircraft is nothing new and hardly beyond their capabilities," Mason said.

A gun-metal gray, late-model Dodge Charger, with BAYOU SARA POLICE stenciled in orange on the door, cruised to a stop at the curb alongside Wallace and Mason. The driver's window descended in perfect synch with the car's deceleration. The painfully thin driver was hunched up in the seat, as if he were far too tall for the size of the passenger compartment.

"I'm Jamie Whitlock, the Chief of Police here in Bayou Sara. Are you all friends or family of the individual who's been reported missing from this address?" Whitlock asked, giving Wallace and Mason a slow, obvious threat assessment.

"Neither," Wallace responded, then introduced herself and Mason.

"Then would I be wrong in assuming that your next stop, today, Detective Hartman, was gonna be at my office, to apprise me of your presence and your activities in my jurisdiction?"

"It would have been our first stop, but we got sidetracked by an opportunity that presented itself before we could get there. An opportunity we didn't think would be wise to pass up."

"So, if I'm hearing you correctly, you and Mr. Cunningham were driving directly from Baton Rouge to my office," Whitlock said, giving his statement only a hint of a question mark at the end. "Because, if that's the case, I guess I missed the call where you phoned ahead to see if I would be in and available to meet with you."

"We'd love to have the meeting with you right now, Chief Whitlock. Our situation is a bit more complicated than a run-of-the-mill courtesy call to request permission to poke our noses into your department's business."

"I love complicated. Why don't we walk and talk, since it looks like you and Mr. Cunningham were about to have yourselves a stroll through the neighborhood, anyway," Whitlock said, extricating his six foot eight inch frame from the car.

"Your department wouldn't happen to have a twenty-foot extension ladder, would it, Chief?" Wallace asked.

"Will we be carrying this ladder around just for the exercise, or did you have a more conventional use in mind?"

"It'll be easier to show you," Wallace replied.

As they led Whitlock back toward the burned house, Mason and Wallace took turns telling him the basics of what was going on, including their visit to the Tunica facility. Wallace noticed that she and Mason quickly fell into a rhythm, each knowing what to tell and what to hold back, without having worked it out ahead of time. By the time they finished talking, they were standing beneath the birdhouse in Matt's backyard.

"Estelle," Whitlock barked into his phone, without preamble. "Send Jake and a twenty-foot extension ladder to that house that burned three nights ago on Juniper Drive. Tell him I got a suspicious-looking box I want him to take a look at and tell 'im I'm tapping my foot waiting on 'im."

Whitlock looked at Wallace and Mason with a disbelieving grin. "I got it now. You two were about to go looking for a ladder when I rolled up."

"Just for a quick peek," Wallace said.

"Nobody will be doing any peeking into that little box up there until Jake has had a chance to go over it first. Just look at what's left of this house. You'd expect to see part of the frame—at least some of the boards and the contents visible in the ash. There's nothing left here *but* ash," he said, his voice rising as his hands flew about his head. "The Fire Chief estimates it burned in about half the time it would normally take for a house of this type to burn."

"Well, that certainly raises an inference of arson," Wallace said.

"I don't think there's even a shadow of a doubt about that," Whitlock fired back. "Anyone who would use such a powerful accelerant to burn the main structure might have also rigged the little contraption in the tree with some sort of explosive device." Whitlock looked from Wallace to Mason. "Jake's had some training on this kind of thing, so we're gonna let him have first go at it."

"Boy, do I feel like a damn rookie," Wallace whispered.

"Better than feeling like a dead rookie," Whitlock responded.

As soon as Jake arrived, Whitlock walked over to explain what he wanted.

Jake set up his ladder against the back side of the tree so he could keep the trunk between himself and the birdhouse. Using a series of flat and magnifying mirrors on extensible rods, he examined the exterior of the birdhouse. Finally, he used a small camera on a long goose-neck to peer inside.

"What do you see?" Whitlock called out.

"Three things, Chief. One, there does not *appear* to be an explosive device inside the box. Two, the glint the detective and the investigator saw through the door hole was the reflection off a camera lens. And, third, there's what looks like a mobile hotspot stuck up under the peak of the roof inside. You know—the gadget you keep near a laptop when there's no Wi-Fi around."

"Is there any way to tell what the camera is seeing?" Wallace asked.

"Not with the equipment I have with me," Jake said.

"Could you take the camera out and download the pictures it's taken?" Mason asked.

"It doesn't look like the kind of camera that stores anything. With that hotspot in there, it's probably just sending whatever it sees to some place off-site, and maybe it's getting recorded there."

"Can you tell where it's sending to?" Wallace asked.

"Should be possible, but that's not anything I have the equipment or the know-how to do."

"Chief Whitlock," Mason said, "I have access to folks at DEA who do this sort of thing for a living. With your permission, I can have someone here by morning."

"I'll want name, rank, and serial number on anybody you bring in, and I'll want it *before* they commence operating in my jurisdiction. And, because there's an open arson investigation and a missing person report connected to this place, I'll want whatever you find out."

Wallace could tell from Whitlock's tone that he was still ticked off about her and Mason's failure to get his blessing before making themselves at home in Bayou Sara.

"You get everything we find," Mason said, pulling out his phone.

"One more thing, Chief," Jake said, as he began climbing down the ladder.

"What's that?"

"See that tree at the front right corner of the lot, about four or five feet this side of the utility pole?" Jake said, pointing. "It's got a little box on it that looks a whole lot like this one."

They all walked toward the tree Jake was pointing at. "These are surveillance cameras," Mason said. "Not home safety devices."

"Right you are," Whitlock drawled. "To provide safety they'd have to be a deterrent and to be a deterrent they'd have to be visible."

"And these would have been fairly well hidden until the fire burned away those limbs," Wallace said, pointing at the scorch marks on the tree. "The bad guys won't be scared off by what they can't see."

"The question is what were these cameras watching for?" Whitlock said. "What was Matt Gable so afraid of?"

"What if he didn't put the cameras there?" Mason asked. "Maybe his employers were concerned about the kind of company he kept? Maybe they thought he was selling their secrets."

"Would the kind of off-the-wall plant research you said they do at Tunica call for secret surveillance like this?" Whitlock asked.

"Possibly. Plant patents can be enormously valuable," Mason said. "And industrial espionage is very profitable."

"Well, regardless of who put the cameras here and why, the fact that they were hidden says somebody was worried about something," Wallace said.

The clang of metal on metal drew their attention toward the street. Jake was strapping the ladder to the rack on the top of his truck.

"Jake," Whitlock hollered, just as Jake was about to climb into the cab, "I want you and Sophie out here standing guard on these cameras until Mr. Cunningham's people can get here to take a look at 'em tomorrow. Sophie stays 'til midnight, then you come out and relieve her until whenever the feds get here."

"Done, Chief," Jake replied, as he finished packing his gear.

"At a minimum," Whitlock began, returning his attention to Wallace and Mason, "we find out where these cameras are sending their feeds and I'll bet we get a good look at our firebug."

"Is there anything yet on the whereabouts of the missing Matt Gable?" Wallace asked.

"Not a damn thing. We've asked the judge for permission to look into his phone and banking records, and we've put out an all-points on vehicles registered in his name—all the usual first steps—but we haven't heard anything yet. The records request has been in for less than twenty-four hours and Judge Castro gets a bit testy if he thinks I'm trying to hustle him along."

"What about a check on Gable's current location using his cell phone? You don't need a warrant if you've got a valid missing person report," Wallace asked.

"Nothing on that either," Whitlock said. "We called the law enforcement desk at all the cell service providers, and gave them the number for Gable that the Chapman woman listed on the missing person report. We've got a standing notification request in case he ever turns his phone on."

"I need to make some calls to get the technicians lined up for tomorrow," Mason announced, as he started toward Wallace's car. "This may take a few minutes."

"Chief, I'm really sorry we didn't come to see you first, but we had no idea we would end up right here," Wallace began, sensing this might be a good time to mend fences. "We came from Baton Rouge straight to Tunica and we intended to go to your office after we left there. But Carla Chapman followed us away from the lab. She and Matt Gable were . . . are a couple, and she's worried. She spotted us when we were at Tunica and thought we might know something."

"I'm glad you bring that up, Detective. That confirms something for me—namely, her interest in this Gable fellow. When she filed the missing person report, she started out as if she were doing so as a colleague, all formal and businesslike. But I think the general consensus around the station was that her concern went a little deeper than that because, after she got it in her head that we weren't moving fast enough, she got downright surly."

Mason leaned back on the car and waited for his call to be answered. The barest beginnings of a new theory about Matt Gable had begun to materialize. In order to test his new idea, he would need to reexamine some of the information Don Brindl had used to calculate the size of the cocaine supply in Overman's territory. His call to Don's office went straight to an out-of-office message. He left a voicemail asking Don to call, as soon as he could, then he called Neil MacKenzie, the section secretary.

"Neil, this is Mason. I just tried to call Don, but got an out-of-office message. Am I missing something, because I don't remember that he was going on vacation or traveling for work?"

"He's home, sick as a dog, but he checks in periodically. Do you need me to try and get him to come in?"

"No thanks. I left him a voicemail, and I have his cell number."

As soon as Mason ended the call with Neil, he called the head of the technical section to arrange for someone to come to Bayou Sara to figure out where the birdhouse cameras were streaming their feeds.

As he walked back to where Wallace and Whitlock were still conversing, he could see that Wallace was having a rough go of it with the chief, who was probably still lecturing her on the fine points of interdepartmental etiquette. The tension was evident in their postures. Whitlock had positioned his tall thin frame a shade too close, forcing her to tilt her head back at an awkward angle just to maintain eye contact.

"Here's the information on the techs who will be here in the morning to check out these contraptions on the trees," Mason said, offering Whitlock a slip of paper.

"Thank you much. I'll be waiting to hear from you." Whitlock grinned and ambled off toward his car.

"I don't think my career will survive any more fooling around in his jurisdiction unless we notify him first," Wallace said, pointing at the departing police chief.

"Does that mean we forget about Matt Gable's running trail?" Mason asked her, as the chief pulled away.

Wallace shook her head. "As long as we promise not to move or remove anything, or obscure any footprints, he said we can take a look."

"Seriously?"

"Unofficially, but yes. He says his police force and his budget are both too small to do a major grid search on his own and it'll be another day and a half before the sheriff can free up enough deputies to help. But Whitlock, himself, actually did a careful look through the woods behind the house—a couple of hundred yards in an arc around the back of the lot. But he didn't find anything suspicious."

"What if Gable's lying out there, injured or something?" Mason asked, shrugging into a palms-up gesture.

"If he had gone for a run through the woods, then his cell phone would probably be on. Even if he was too hurt to make a call, it could still be located. But Whitlock says it's not showing up."

"He's convinced Matt's off with another woman somewhere," Mason stated flatly.

"Yep—and that the husband or boyfriend of the woman he's off with burned the house as revenge, and now Matt's too scared to show his face in these parts."

"Then why do you want to waste time traipsing around out in the trees?"

"Matt may not be the only thing out there worth finding. He's a hider. He hid a secret lab inside his regular lab. There were hidden cameras around his house and I'm willing to bet he put them there himself. And—"

"And, since it looks like arson was involved, maybe the house was burned to keep something else hidden," Mason finished.

"Very good. And, if Matt had other secrets, where better to hide them than out there somewhere? He wouldn't have taken the time to mark his trails if they weren't important."

"Did you tell Whitlock about your Matt-the-Hider theory?"

"Nope."

"Naughty, naughty."

"Just pragmatic," she said, with an unashamed, yeah-so? expression. "His permission was conditioned on *how* we'll be searching, not *why*."

"You would think that finding these cameras would get him a little more fired up about looking into things."

"Oh, he's fired up. While you were off communing with your people in DC, he and I had quite a chat. It seems he's a rather compartmentalized thinker. Until he knows where the camera feeds are going, he says he can only speculate about who put them there and why, and that none of that speculation suggests a direction for the investigation."

"But you could have suggested a direction by telling him your theory of Matt hiding things."

"Which is still just speculation. Besides if he gets too fired up, he might want to start calling the shots. That might not slow you down, because you're federal, but it could put me under his thumb."

"Your approach to things is very . . . uhm . . ."

"Pragmatic. Surely that's the word you're looking for." She smiled, then looked down her nose at him with a tread-carefully expression.

"That is precisely the word," he conceded.

"And by the way . . ."

"Yes?"

"When we were leaving the lab you said you had a few more things you wanted to do. You never finished the list."

"Well, finding out where the increased cocaine supply in and around Baton Rouge is coming from is critical," Mason said.

"Anything else?"

"Why must I show all my cards first? Your turn."

"The most important thing is the secret stuff Carla found in Matt's lab. It needs to come out of Tunica as soon as possible," Wallace said.

"It does, indeed," Mason agreed. "And it needs to be examined by some serious federal experts, so I'll want to accompany whoever the federal marshal sends to assert custody of it."

"Not so fast," Wallace said, raising a cautionary finger. "That equipment could very well be evidence that's related to an already-committed crime under state law—a homicide—and for all we know kidnapping and arson might come into the picture as well. The state crime lab gets first dibs."

"In fact, we don't know that it's evidence of anything, other than possibly some shenanigans by Matt Gable—federal shenanigans at that," Mason said, his voice taking on a subtle peremptory edge. "Carla Chapman said the apparatus didn't include any osmosis bags, so there's no definitive link, at this point, between your homicide and the stuff in the storeroom. So, why would you want it or think you need it?"

"I just told you why," she said, planting her feet wide and leaning toward him, her hands on her hips. "Those bags are rather unusual items. Until we can exclude a connection between the ones we found with Overman and ones that were at Tunica, I have to assume that somehow it's a link between the lab and my case. What I can't understand is why you're so interested in it."

"Look," he said, elbows at his side, his palms up, "it's federal property, it stays in federal custody, and it gets examined by federal scientists."

"That's not a reason. That's just you being a big shot. Bravo," she said, pressing her palms together in a kowtow.

"Okay. I can see I'm getting under your skin—"

"Can you really?" she asked, with a phony smile and a wide-eyed glare. She turned toward her car and started walking.

"Of course I can," he said, calmly, as he followed along beside her.

"Well then, try this on for size," she said, brushing past his irritating composure. "Let's assume Matt was kidnapped. We know he wasn't kidnapped from a federal facility because Kevin Bell told us lab security showed him leaving the place Friday evening. So, unless he was kidnapped *and* taken across a state line, it's a state matter. And if the stuff in the lab holds some clue to Matt's situation, then we're looking at a state crime that just happens to involve federally owned evidence."

"Hard to argue with that," he said.

"Thank you—"

"But I'm going to."

"Look, buster, I'm as fun-loving as the next person, but don't start playing games with me." She stopped and leaned toward him, her face inches from his. "Some people you can do that with. I'm not one of those people."

"Have you ever tried to get a state court to issue a warrant authorizing a search and seizure at a federal facility?" When Wallace didn't answer, he was about to ask the question again but her expression told him she was about to yank up the welcome mat.

"Look, I'm just trying to figure out the best, fastest way to get at this stuff," he said, instead.

"Twice," Wallace said. "I've done it twice. Once it went off without a hitch. The other time I got nowhere, because my federal counterpart took such an obstructive attitude."

"How long did it take you to get the warrant?"

"Not very. Where are you going with this?" She stepped off the curb and walked around to her side of the car.

"I see this whole business breaking down into three pieces. Who gets the stuff from Gable's lab, how quickly it can be gotten, and how it's analyzed after it's out of Tunica."

"Is there some reason you can't just get the evidence out of Tunica and then turn it over to the state lab? You'll obviously get any and all information we develop." She pulled open the door to her cruiser and slid behind the wheel.

"How certain are you of the range of capabilities at your lab?" Mason asked, stowing his satchel in the footwell behind his seat and then climbing into the front.

"Is that what this is all about? You're worried we're just a bunch of local yokels who can't tell a Bunsen burner from a hat rack?" She slammed her door, rocking the car.

"I'm not worried about anything," he said, coolly. "I just don't know, so I have to ask." He slammed his door and stared straight ahead.

"As far as I know, we can do what any other lab can do. Anything that requires exotic equipment or really high-end chemistry that isn't cost effective to do in-house, we have consulting contracts with the relevant science departments and med schools at every major university in the state. If it can be done, I'm sure it can be done here."

"Good. Then we're settled."

Wallace reached for the ignition but pulled her hand back and then turned to face him. "You know, it occurs to me that besides your lame Uncle-Sam-owns-it-so-Uncle-Sam-gets-it gambit, you've never made a case for why you even care about this stuff."

"While you and Whitlock were having your little come-to-Jesus meeting, it occurred to me that Gable's connection to your case and mine—assuming he's connected at all—might be that he's developed a new, more efficient technique for extracting the cocaine powder from the coca plant itself. Faster, less costly, higher yield."

"Would it have killed you to say that earlier?" she asked, shooting him a sidelong glance as she started the engine.

"I was debating whether to bring it up at all. A major advance in that direction was made several years ago, so I don't know if further developments of any significance are even possible. I'm just grasping at straws. I don't really have any facts to support my thinking. So, technically, my enhanced-extraction idea might be as lame as my Uncle-Sam-owns-it idea."

"Just for the sake of discussion," she asked, forcing herself to speak calmly, "could a more efficient extraction technique account for the supply discrepancies your analysts found?"

"It would depend on how much of an improvement it was, and the scale of the operation. Even a dramatic improvement wouldn't have much impact unless it was used on a big enough fraction of the harvest," Mason pointed out.

"If every square foot of his lab space was devoted to such a process, would it be enough?"

"I don't know. But let's say the stuff in the storeroom was just a proof of concept and that, once he debugged it, he ramped it up on an industrial scale."

"Could something that big be hidden somewhere out there? In the woods behind Matt's house, maybe?"

"Possibly, but I'm not a chemist so I can't say for sure."

"If he actually figured out something like that, and word leaked out, it seems like a lot of nasty people would be trying to get their hands on it."

"And on him, which might account for his currently unknown whereabouts."

"Well, this opens a whole new window into the matter," Wallace said, staring off into the trees lining the road.

"Which is why I'm so concerned about what happens to the things Carla so thoughtfully set aside. It will have to be made operational again."

"Surely, with Carla's notes and sketches, that won't be a problem," she said.

"Assuming we can figure out what chemicals he fed into it, where in the process they went in, at what temperature, and so on. There could be a lot of variables."

"So, do you want to get a federal warrant, or am I going to be doing this?"

"I'll get it," Mason said. "It'll be easier."

As they traveled back to Baton Rouge, Mason spent the better part of the drive time arranging for one of the legal officers in the DEA's Resident Office in Baton Rouge to get a warrant with an order of seizure issued and delivered to the federal marshal. Mason and the marshal would pay a surprise visit to the Tunica Research Lab, bright and early, the next morning.

"We need to think of a way to lessen the blow this is going to have on Carla," Wallace said. "If it weren't for her, we wouldn't know about this stuff. And, once Kevin Bell finds out she kept it, he's going to rough her up."

"Bell tried to have her destroy evidence. Instead, she reported it to the proper authorities—you and me. So I don't think he'll be in a position to do much damage. Plus, we can't afford to ignore the possibility this lab stuff represents."

"I'm not suggesting we ignore anything. I'm just looking out for someone who took a risk to help us. You never know when you'll need to go back to that well."

"She went out of her way to help herself," Mason said, the peremptory tone creeping back into his voice. "That was pretty clear. She's interested in having us find her boyfriend. If she didn't have a very personal stake in this, you can be sure she'd have never chased us down and the things in that storeroom would have been destroyed."

Wallace didn't fancy herself the sensitive type, but she also wasn't the type to be callous without provocation. She had never gotten completely comfortable with the collateral damage suffered by decent people like Carla, who just happened to fall into possession of what turned out to be dangerous information. The casual arrogance of some in the law enforcement community always struck her as wrong, and coming from Mason it was disappointing and confusing.

"Will you call me, once you and the marshal are done?" Wallace asked, bringing her focus back into the moment. "I want to be at the crime lab when the stuff rolls in."

"Sure, but I thought you were going to show off your professional tracking skills tomorrow. Remember? Over the hills and through the woods."

"I'm not leaving Baton Rouge until late in the morning. New reports on what they found at the warehouse might come in, plus I need to visit someone. Colley Greenberg."

She waited a few seconds to see if Mason would ask who Colley was. But he didn't.

"Mike Harrison is just a temporary partner," she said. "An interim gig until Colley, my regular partner, comes back from medical leave."

"I hope his recovery is speedy. And, look . . ." He hesitated, staring down at his feet.

"Yes?" Wallace said, turning toward him.

"You know . . . I could have done a better job of negotiating this business with the stuff from Gable's lab." He looked up at her. "There was no need for me to inject all that friction into it. In Washington,

I'm so used to fighting tooth and nail for every little scrap. Sorry. Can we back that up and pretend I acted like a grown-up?" He extended his right hand toward her.

"We can," she said, taking her hand off the wheel to shake his, her chest tightening a bit.

"Thanks. It wouldn't have been good to leave that standing between us. You never know what kind of problems that can cause down the road."

Wallace turned to look out of her window. "So, just to make sure, you *do* want to go with me tomorrow on my little cross-country expedition?"

"Yes, I do. I assume that after the stuff from Matt's storeroom arrives at the lab you'll be heading back to Bayou Sara?"

Wallace continued to gaze out of her window.

"Wallace?"

"Sorry, what was that?" she asked. That was the first time he had called her by her first name.

"After Gable's stuff arrives . . . you'll be going back to . . ."

"Right. Bayou Sara. That's the plan. What?" she asked, when she noticed him studying her.

He continued to stare at her for a few seconds, his brow furrowing, the left corner of his mouth pulling to the side. "My electronics technicians—they're coming up from the New Orleans Division—should be rolling into Bayou Sara to look at those cameras at about the time we get things buttoned up at Tunica, so I'll have the marshal drop me off at Matt's house. I'll wait for you there."

"Perfect."

They rode in silence for several minutes. The next time she looked over at him he had fallen asleep with his head leaning against the window.

When they reached the hotel, Wallace squeezed his shoulder until he woke up.

"Oh, sorry," he said sheepishly.

"Don't mention it. You snore at the same pitch as the engine noise, so it was actually kind of soothing."

"Really?" he said groggily, then grimaced when it became obvious she was making fun of him.

As Wallace drove away from the hotel, she found herself puzzling over Mason's decision to partner up with her for the excursion to the lab. She hadn't expected it. No other federal agent she'd ever met would have included her in what was really *his* investigation simply because it was an efficient way of doing things. All the rest of Uncle Sam's tribe viewed such unforced generosity as treasonous, but for Mason it seemed second nature.

Their little skirmish over the things from Matt's secret lab proved he could play the role of the straight-ahead, federal buzz cut, but then he'd been so quick to make amends. And yes, he was nice looking. She hadn't expected that, either.

8:00 P.M.

Once she got back to the police station, Wallace spent half an hour at her desk checking progress on other cases. Nothing clamored for her immediate attention. Mike Harrison had yet to call her back, but he had left a report for her on the desk, with a note explaining that he had had to duck out to attend to some personal business that had come up at the last minute.

She pulled up the city-wide duty roster and noted the unit number and the names of the officers who had daylight patrol duty in the area that included Choctaw Ridge, where she and Mason had met Louise Mautner and the other gardeners under the power lines—Marcels and Romer, in Unit 107. With a quick call to a fellow officer who worked out of the North Baton Rouge substation, she learned that Marcels was the long-timer on the beat and that Romer had been riding with him for less than a week.

She left the building trying to focus on the case, but as she made her way to her car, her mind kept straying back to Mason and she had to keep reminding herself that she didn't need a man in her life—especially not one who lived and worked so far away. But she kept thinking about him anyway. She had been so confident that she had retired that part of her life. A part that, at one time, had been as perfect as such a thing could be on this side of heaven. But all of that had been snatched away.

On the few occasions when she had mustered the courage to try again, she found she could go only so far before the old fears took over. As soon as she found herself beginning to care she retreated. Caring meant responsibility and responsibility raised the possibility of failure. And failure had proved itself capable of deadly consequences.

TEN

WEDNESDAY 8:30 P.M.

The curtains in Matt's second-floor motel room were parted just enough for him to look out the window with a pair of binoculars. Directly across the highway, he could see the door to room 119 at the Heart of the South Motel, as well as the glass-fronted office two doors to the right. He was registered under his real name in room 119, and he had paid with one of his Matt Gable credit cards. He was registered under a phony name in the motel where he presently sat and he had paid with cash. The only people he had seen at room 119 were the housekeepers. When they saw the DO NOT DISTURB placard he had left in the key slot, they moved along to the next room.

He had been waiting nearly three days to see if anyone else would show up. His food stock was dwindling and his back was killing him from sitting in the crummy club chair in front of the window. A problem with his cloud storage account kept him from checking the feeds from the birdhouse cameras, so he still didn't know who had triggered the burn on his house in Bayou Sara. And he had spent so much time staring through the binoculars he felt as if his eyes might never again focus properly. When the lure of sleep grew too strong he used a video camera hooked to his laptop to do the watching for him. Upon resuming his post at the window he would review whatever the laptop had recorded while using the binoculars to keep tabs on current goings-on.

He was on the cusp of believing that his back trail was clear when a man wearing civilian clothes stepped out of a rental car and headed toward the motel office. The man's gait and his bushy hair reminded Matt of the red-haired man he had seen walking up to the warehouse the day he met Ronnie Overman. He was about to dismiss the recollection as paranoia, but when the man entered the motel office and the light shone back through his copper-colored hair, Matt froze.

His goal in using the two-motel head fake had been to find out if anyone dangerous had managed to get a fix on him. He had always known Overman would eventually take too great an interest in his operations, but the man across the street felt like a different sort of trouble.

The ability to track him to the Heart of the South Motel implied access to government capabilities. Although it seemed unlikely that government auditors drove rental cars at night to out-of-the-way motels just to make sure Uncle Sugar's scientists weren't making off with too many federal test tubes. The man might be a cop, although cops tended to travel in pairs.

Maybe he was a private investigator, or someone Overman had hired to eliminate Matt's position in the supply chain. Maybe Overman was in league with the red-haired man. Stranger things had happened.

The most critical question, now, was how to proceed. He could either try to shake the man off, or string him along and maybe learn more about him, or confront him. But, confrontation seemed fraught with all sorts of dangers—a desperation play.

Hopefully, this would be only a temporary complication. After all, as far as Matt knew, the man had been unable to locate him until he had used the credit cards with his real name. So, at least the man appeared to be no more capable than regular law enforcement.

Tracking Gable to this dung-heap motel had been a snap. Two credit card charges for someone named Matt Gable, both at businesses on the east side of Baton Rouge, had done the trick. One charge was for a boatload of nonperishable food items, indicating that Matt was either considering a sizable donation to a local food bank or he was planning a lengthy holiday off the grid. The other charge had been for a room at the Heart of the South Motel. Getting access to the credit card records was as simple as greasing the palms of unscrupulous card company employees. One simply had to know the right websites to troll through.

"What can I do for you?" asked the young fellow sitting behind the desk as he looked up from a massive textbook.

The desk sat just behind the registration counter and was mostly hidden under big, unstable-looking piles of what must have been months' worth of motel paperwork. Why, the man wondered, did so many mom-and-pop enterprises use piling systems instead of filing systems? How did they keep track of their business? He found it unsettling to have to look at other people's crapped-up spaces.

"I have business with one of your guests, but it seems he's forgotten our meeting. His name is Matt Gable. He said he would meet me here in the office, right around this time, but it must have slipped his mind. And he's not answering his cell phone. Maybe he left word with you, as to his whereabouts?"

"Not with me. Maybe he left something while I was off duty," the clerk said, rummaging through slips of paper piled next to the telephone. "Don't see anything, sorry."

What a fool-proof messaging system, the red-haired man thought.

Surely nothing of importance could escape the iron grip of a scheme based on scraps of paper strewn about a cluttered desk.

"Perhaps you could point me toward his room and I'll get out of your hair."

"Can't do that. Privacy rules and all. But I'd be happy to call his room for you, and let him know he has a visitor. Who shall I say is here?"

"Ronald Overman."

"No one's answering," the clerk said, after several rings. "Shall I leave a message?"

"No, thank you. Maybe you've seen him?" The man gave a brief description of Matt he had crafted from an old photograph, hoping it would be enough to trigger something.

"I don't think so," the clerk said, trying to appear as if he were giving the description thoughtful consideration while sneaking the occasional peek at his textbook.

"Perhaps the person who registered him would be able to help. Would there be any way to speak to that person?"

"Well, that would be either me or Mr. Pinion, the owner," the clerk said, consulting the computer. "I don't personally remember the gentleman myself, but that dudn't necessarily mean anything. We got a pretty steady stream a people through here, and after a while, they all start to look alike, if you know what I mean."

No, the red-haired man thought. He had no idea what the jabbering clerk meant. The notion of being so unobservant was repellant—little different from being dead.

"Well, looky here," the clerk chirped, putting on an idiotic aw-shucks drawl. "It was me what signed 'im in," he said, continuing his hayseed charade.

"Would you happen to remember anything that might be help-ful? Our business is somewhat time-sensitive, so I would hate to miss this opportunity because of a mix-up in communications."

"Seein' this sign-in screen kinda jogged my memory. I do recall the guy, but he dudn't look exactly like what you said. One thing I do remember is that right after he checked in here, he walked directly across the street to the motel you can see if you turn around and look."

"Could you pin down the time frame a bit for me?" the red-haired man asked, turning to look at the motel across the highway, thereby shielding the rise in his emotions from the clerk.

"Mmmm. I don't feel right giving out that level of detail without a guest's permission. You know what I'm sayin'? But it probably wouldn't mean much, anyway. They got a restaurant over there. We don't have one here. So, your guy probably tootled on over for a bite to eat."

The red-haired man continued to look toward the motel, trying to block out the clerk's mind-numbing drone.

"Mr. Pinion shut down the restaurant here a couple a years back."

The motel across the street was a two-story structure. All the rooms appeared to face the street.

"It's just dead space, now. Old man Pinion claims motel restaurants are more trouble than they're worth."

Perhaps old man Pinion would consider sealing his blabbering clerk in one of the abandoned restaurant's unused refrigerators.

"In any event, like I say, it probably dudn't mean much since I kinda doubt he's been over there chowing down for three solid days."

"Good Lord, I should hope not," the red-haired man said, perking up at the mention of three days. "Have you seen him since?"

"Naw. But I'm only on the desk about half the time."

"Well, you've been helpful," the man said, continuing to scan the doors and windows of the motel across the street.

"Seems to me that Mr. Pinion could find something profitable to do with that old restaurant, y'know. I mean, he's still paying the note on this place, so as long as he's gotta pay for it, you'd think he'd try and get something out of it, wouldn't ya. If it was me . . ."

How very clever. The red-haired man marveled as the ingenuity of Matt's two-motel ruse tumbled into place. He had almost mistaken the bait for the fish, but not quite.

Matt flinched as the red-haired man's magnified stare bored straight into his binoculars. He knew the man couldn't see him, but the thin, knowing smile on the man's face told Matt that the man was on to his ploy. Matt watched as the man's gaze scanned slowly from room to room. When he felt sure the man's attention was far enough away, Matt lowered his binoculars, eased out of his chair, and backed away from the window. Like most motel rooms, Matt's room had only one door—a front door. He moved quickly through the darkened room, into the bathroom, and closed the door before turning on the light. The window was small, but maybe he could snake through.

A tiny movement in the curtains of a room on the second floor caught the red-haired man's attention. The curtains were parted only a few inches, the room was dark, and the light on the walkway in front of the room was low—but the curtain had moved. Of that he was certain. Had someone been at the darkened window, trying to look out without being seen? Someone who might have been watching the Heart of the South Motel? Someone who might have improvidently brushed against the edge of the curtain as he pulled back from the window?

"So, you know, he could rent the damn thing out as a store or something," the clerk maundered on. "Any contribution to fixed costs drops straight to the bottom line. My accounting professor says that's just elementary business, and . . ."

The red-haired man exited the office, careful not to take his eyes off the window where he had seen the ripple in the curtains. The honk and hustle of the street drowned out the endless spew from the motormouth clerk. He picked up the pace, counting windows from his target to the stairs that rose from a breezeway up to the second floor. *Seven windows to the right.*

He dodged through the first two lanes of traffic to a grassy median, then paused to gauge the oncoming cars. He darted across, not even bothering to flip off the horn-blasting motorists. So far, the movement at the window had not repeated. Maybe it wasn't even the right room. Maybe Matt wasn't there after all. No, he was there. It made no sense for him to risk using his real name to rent a room, and then just disappear without waiting to see if it drew any attention. And because the ploy would depend on keeping a close watch on the room at the Heart of the South, the red-haired man assumed he had been seen scanning the rooms from the office window. Matt couldn't possibly know who was in pursuit, but the tricky chemist would now know someone was hard on his heels and he was probably in the midst of a hasty departure.

While the red-haired man felt certain the front door would be the only door to the room, he also knew there might be a balcony or a window at the back, through which his quarry might try to escape. The trio of teenaged skate punks cruising the lot could help him manage that little problem.

"Gentlemen," he said expansively, trying to get their attention over the grind of their wheels.

All three stopped in unison, turning to look at the red-haired man. As suddenly as they stopped, they all turned away and began pushing off again.

"Gentlemen," he began again. "There's money to be made for a few minutes of easy effort."

Again they stopped. This time they picked up their boards and swaggered over. Their baggy outfits looked like they were on a lengthy sabbatical from the world of soap and water. The added stink of stale weed smoke made them almost unbearable.

"We look like we need money or something?" one of them taunted, as they assumed a casually custodial formation around the man. The one doing the talking sported an ugly grin and a tattered porkpie hat. "We might be millionaires for all you know. Jackie . . . ain't you a millionaire, bro?"

"Fuck yeah," Jackie snorted. "Just like you."

"In that case, I withdraw my offer."

"In that case," Porkpie said, mimicking the man's tone of voice, "why don't we just withdraw some money from your wallet?"

As they moved in, the man spun smoothly on the balls of his feet and slammed a straight right squarely into Porkpie's relentless grin. The blow sent the punk skidding backward on his heels before landing him hard on his tailbone. The man grabbed Jackie by the waistband and drove a knee into his groin. As Jackie's eyes rolled back and his jaw sagged, the man slammed the butt of his hand upward into Jackie's chin, clacking the boy's teeth together.

"Here, catch." He shoved the groaning lad toward the retreating third boy, then darted toward the stairway.

The bathroom window was a mistake. Matt got his head and one shoulder through, but the window was too small and too high. He was off the floor with no place to put his feet. No way to push the rest of himself out. Fighting free of the window, he hurried back into his room.

He tossed his duffel on the floor near the door and then he pulled the mattress from the bed, leaving it covered in its dark spread. He balanced it on its long edge perpendicular to the front wall, about a foot from the door frame. Reaching from behind the mattress, he opened his door a few inches, then pulled his hand back. He heard footsteps approaching on the walkway outside. The footsteps slowed, then stopped outside his door.

Seeing the open door, the red-haired man paused to assess the situation. His encounter with the skate punks took less than thirty seconds and he hadn't taken his eyes off the door for more than a few seconds at a time—surely not long enough for Gable to slip away. Sensing a trap he reached into his jacket and drew his gun. Squatting with his back to the wall, just outside the edge of the door frame, he reached over and gently pushed on the door with the muzzle of the gun. Quietly, the door swung inward several inches. The interior of the room was cloaked in matte-finish darkness. The meager light filtering up from the street was unhelpful.

"I know you're in there, Gable, and I'm in no mood to fool around. You don't want to end up like your good buddy Ronald Overman. Let's do this the easy way, shall we?" Peeking around the bottom of the door frame he saw a thin stripe of light under the bathroom door. He slipped across the threshold. In the added light, as the door opened wider, he saw the mattress to his right. He hesitated.

Matt shoved the mattress, trapping the man against the wall and leaving his path momentarily clear. He snatched up his duffel and darted from the room. The duffel caught on the doorframe and yanked him to a stop. His feet slid from under him and his head banged onto the concrete walkway, bringing forth a sickening groan. He scrambled to his feet and lurched toward the stairs.

As he turned into the stairwell, footsteps accelerated behind him. He jumped the last few steps to the landing. His rubbery knees crumpled and he tumbled sideways into the wall. His pursuer, gun in hand, appeared on the top step. Panic took over and Matt pin-balled mindlessly off the wall and careened down the last few steps. The red-haired man strode onto the landing behind him.

"Stop. I'm sick of fucking with you, boy."

Matt froze.

"Turn around," the man said calmly. "Gently . . . put the bag on the ground." He slowly descended, his gun in a two-fisted grip pointing squarely at Matt's midsection. "Do it."

Slowly, Matt turned and gingerly lowered the bag to the pavement and began to back away.

"I didn't say back up. Stand still." The man continued his cautious descent. He had to take control of Matt and the duffel before others noticed the situation. At the bottom of the stairs, just before he left the cover of the stairwell, he thrust the gun into the pocket of his jacket, but kept it pointed in Matt's direction. He stepped quickly onto the sidewalk.

Then a skateboard slammed wheels-first into his face, sending him reeling back onto the stairs. He flailed with both hands, trying to break his fall.

"Catch *this*, motherfucker." The kid raised his board and slammed it down on top of the man's head, then he raced away, quickly merging with the shadows.

The moment the skate punk struck his first blow, Matt had grabbed the duffel and dashed toward the street. As he worked his way into proper running posture, his panic began to subside.

His car was parked near a building several doors down from the motel. In less than a minute he was there. He yanked open the driver's door, slung his bag onto the passenger seat, and slid behind the wheel. He fired the engine and sped smoothly into traffic.

ELEVEN

Wallace pulled to the curb in front of Colley's house, then waited—sorting through her feelings and putting on her game face.

Colley Greenberg had been Wallace's partner since she had joined the ranks of the Homicide Division two years before. As a rule, partner assignments were made by department brass. They paired newbies with experienced hands they considered compatible. But because Colley had mastered the department's inconvenient knowledge—the inventory of hush-hush favors and closeted skeletons that gave those lower down the ladder the occasional bit of influence over those clinging to the upper rungs—when his long-time partner took early retirement, Colley had been given free rein to select his new partner.

On top of that, because chronic illness made his continued presence on the force an iffy proposition, he had been ready to hand off his accumulated wisdom and experience. But he hadn't just wanted a new partner, he wanted a protégé—someone with a keen mind and the heart of a lion. He wanted Wallace.

Wallace, on the other hand, had been praying for someone else—almost anyone else, in fact. Colley was so skilled at getting cross-wise with his superiors that many times his career had hung by a thread. Wallace believed she had prospects, so she didn't want to be hitched to a train that so frequently thumbed its nose at the tracks. But praying, like golf, could produce the right result even when you did it wrong. So it hadn't taken her long to discover that her prayers had been answered. Colley *was* someone else. His reputation turned out to be a poor proxy for the man himself.

As Colley had told her, a few months after they started working together, it was as if the moment had been fashioned with exactly her in mind. As if just when the season had come for him to pass things along, she had materialized in the lane ahead, her hand stretched back, ready to take the baton. And Wallace could tell from the sum of their daily interactions that Colley felt as if he were racing toward her, eager to show her all the magic in his bag of tricks. But his darkening prognosis a year into their partnership made her feel as if, suddenly, she were running toward him. It had made her think of a childhood vacation her family had taken out West.

It was the last day on the outbound leg of their journey into northern New Mexico. They wanted to go all the way to the giant Shiprock—the colossal, jagged upthrust of rock that sits utterly alone on a vast expanse of the high plains. Its shape suggests a stately three-masted schooner cruising on an empty auburn sea and it is so enormous and the plain so otherwise unoccupied that it's visible from an impossibly great distance.

Even though they knew they would be racing against the sunset, they headed toward the mountain anyway. They continued, even when the roads turned from asphalt to gravel to nothing but tire tracks on the dirt. But it seemed as if no matter how far they went, the damn thing never got any closer. Then, just as the monolith began to claim a bigger share of the view ahead, the sun started plunging toward the western horizon. They found themselves speeding through the artificial twilight of the big rock's shadow, knowing they would never reach the thing itself before the sun set for good on their day and on their trip. Wallace's mother cried when they were forced to give up the chase—something Wallace hadn't understood at the time.

Wallace walked slowly from her car to the front door of Colley's house. She knocked and waited. Stella, Colley's wife, answered the door. Her look was enough. As Colley descended deeper into the world of some-days-are-better-than-others, Stella's front-door demeanor had been whittled down to a good-day look and a bad-day look. Today brought a bad-day look.

Colley and Stella had married at a time when mixed-race couples were an unwelcome rarity in the South. Stella was an archaeology professor at LSU. The police department had hired her to do the forensic excavation of three bodies buried beneath an old house in Zion City—a black enclave in the northern reaches of East Baton Rouge Parish. Colley swore it was love at first sight for both of them, but that Stella had repeatedly rejected him for what she termed *impossible irony*—as an archaeologist she would dig up the past, but as a white cop's black wife she would bury his future.

Stella told Wallace that at one point in the early days of the marriage she almost bailed out when it looked like her initial reservations were proving to be all too true. The straw that nearly broke the camel's back came when she and Colley walked into a restaurant up near the Capitol, where they ran into one of Colley's fellow officers and a couple of his civilian friends. The man started in their direction. His bully sneer and his hey-y'all-watch-this glances at his tittering confederates telegraphed the all-too-familiar scene about to unfold.

"Well, if it ain't Colley Greenberg. And you must be Mrs. Collard Greens."

Colley's fist flashed up. The big man hit the floor. And Stella almost bolted.

Fighting criminals was dangerous enough, she said. Fighting the rest of the world, as well, was likely to bring Colley's life and their marriage to an untimely end. "Find a less violent way to deal with the hecklers or find a new wife," she'd told him.

"Just go on back," Stella said. "He's in front of the TV."

"Colley, it's me," Wallace announced, from the doorway of the den at the back of the house.

He looked up and lit up at the sound of her voice. He was lying on the couch, watching the news, which he muted as she approached.

"Hey, kid," he responded. "Have a seat. You got time, or is this a drive-by?"

"I've got time," she said, sitting cross-legged on the floor by the couch.

"How's your new case going—the Overman thing?" he said, immediately cutting off any opportunity for Wallace to steer the conversation into maudlin territory.

"I'm not even going to ask how you know about it. It'll make me paranoid. But it's going . . . somewhere. To tell you the truth, I can't seem to bring it into focus."

"Why's that?"

"It's got a lot of big, shiny, interesting pieces, but how they fit together isn't so obvious. Plus, Burley stuck me with Medicated Mike for the time being, although I'm thinking Abdicated Mike might be more accurate because he's never around. On top of that I'm working with this guy from the DEA who thinks the key to this whole business is that Baton Rouge might become ground zero in a cartel-level territory dispute. Throw in a missing government scientist and his secret lab, who might or might not be connected, and that's how it's going."

"*How* they fit together comes after *whether* they fit together. Do they?"

"Well, before Overman was killed, he was tortured in a really gruesome way."

"Snake in the belly. I heard."

"Colley, if you already know everything about the case, why did you ask me how it's going?" she laughed.

"I just know the basic facts," he said, grinning. "I'm more interested in your thoughts on the matter."

Wallace could tell Colley missed the game. That he wanted to be back doing what he was so good at. Somehow the emotional elephant Colley had tried to keep at bay, by talking shop, was now sitting squarely in the middle of the room.

"Well, this snake business is apparently a trademark method used by a really charming man named Fernando Echeverría, the head of the Mexican cartel that's been supplying south Louisiana—and Overman—for years, so there's that connection."

"What about the missing scientist?" Colley asked.

"Matt Gable? It's weird, but the bags the cocaine was found in— the bags themselves—might be the connection. They're not plain old grocery store items. They're something called osmosis bags. The kind of thing that only comes with big-girl chemistry sets."

"So the merch with Overman was repacks, not the bricks that come up from the growers?"

"I won't know that for sure unless I can get the lab to tell me whether it's been cut down to street grade, but Burley is starting to pinch pennies. I can't see him giving me the okay to spend money on a purity test until we've got somebody to prosecute."

"Listen to you. Since when did you start worrying about big bad Burley?" Colley chuckled.

"Since I don't have blackmail on half the department, like you do."

"What do you know about these osmosis bags?"

"It's high-end stuff. The bag maker ships all over the place and its middleman distributors sell worldwide. A supply of the bags was shipped to a federal lab in Bayou Sara but they and Matt Gable are now missing under fairly odd circumstances." Wallace told him about

Kevin Bell and Carla Chapman, and about Matt Gable's secret lab and the hidden cameras.

"I'm just thinking," Colley said, chewing his lower lip, his gaze unfocused. "There might be a way to get that coke tested *and* clarify any connection between Matt Gable and the late Ronald Overman."

"Would you mind thinking out loud?" Wallace asked, bringing a smile to Colley's face. Asking the other to think out loud had become one of their rituals as they worked through cases together. She stood and started moving around the room.

"Did I ever tell you about that time I went to Colombia? Back in the eighties we got this grant to do an interdepartmental exchange with some of our counterparts down in the cocaine capitals of South America. You know, one of those things where we get a look at their methods and their madness, and they send a few of their guys up to the States to get a look at ours."

"Kind of," she said. "Just that you went. I got the impression you thought it was mainly a load. Just something the politicos could point to when they needed to make it look like they were doing something."

"Well, it was that, mainly. But I did, in fact, learn one interesting thing while I was there. Back then, before the worldwide market for cocaine got so well-developed, there were areas down there where there was so much cocaine around, it was as common as beach sand. And one of their guys was telling me that they had come up with this interesting way of figuring out just what part of what mountain or what valley a particular drift of this stuff had blown out of. Each area had its own version of the process they used to get the powder out of the coca leaves. I mean, they all used the same chemicals, but they used them in different proportions and concentrations and whatnot, and they were always tinkering with it, trying to find out how to get the best yield. Anyway, each cook's extraction and purification process left faint chemical traces that were a little bit different from the ones the others used."

"Molecular fingerprints?"

"Exactly. The government scientists down there learned to look for those chemical traces in the stuff they seized. That way the police could know which direction to point their guns."

"Surely Mason, our visitor from DEA, would know about stuff like that, don't you think?"

"One would think," Colley conceded.

"Do you know if these traces survive all the hands this stuff passes through to get up here?"

"No idea. The crap that distributors and dealers use to cut it down to street grade is different from the chemicals the cartel cooks use to extract the powder from the leaves, so it's possible. And since Echeverría is Mexican, he's a middleman, not a producer, and all the cocaine he's moving would come from just one cartel in South America. So batches cooked up around the same time could all have the same traces in it. And for sure, the people close to the retail end are not going to throw away time and money trying to purify it. So those extraction traces may still be there, just buried a little deeper at each step in the supply chain."

Wallace stopped pacing and perched on the arm of a chair, her eyes focused in the distance. Colley watched serenely as she computed the possibilities. Slowly, she surfaced from some deep pool of thought.

"We've got the stuff from Overman, and we're about to lay our hands on the gear from Matt Gable's hidden lab. If the chemical fingerprints in the coke we found with Overman point toward Echeverría, and we can link the bags to Matt Gable, then we have a link between Echeverría and Overman, and a link between Overman and Gable. Or if there's coke residue in Gable's secret labware . . ."

"And that's the linchpin. Burley won't stand in your way if testing the coke will help you line up a set of connections like that. Do you have any product you know for sure comes from Echeverría?" Colley asked. "For comparison purposes?"

"I'll have to find that out." She went quiet, again, her eyes closed in concentration.

"Would you mind thinking out loud?" Colley asked.

Wallace smiled at the question, but only half-heartedly. The old routines were comforting, but they were also making Colley's absence an even starker reality. "I'm arranging these three guys at the corners of a triangle and trying to see the connections between them. Isn't this what you would do?"

"It's exactly what I would do," Colley said. "Just remember—"

"I know . . . the case might be more complicated than a triangle."

"Right, and—"

"I know, even if we can show that Overman and Matt Gable are connected by those osmosis bags, that won't tell us which direction the goods were flowing."

"It won't tell you what that hidden lab was all about, either."

"Or whether the purification traces are inconclusive or point to some other cartel."

"Listen to me," Colley said. "All of a sudden, I don't like this case. It's making me nervous. Be careful, will you?"

Wallace gave him a startled look. In all their time together, regardless of the situations they faced, Colley had never once told her to be careful.

"Why are you saying that?" she asked.

"If you get that coke tested, and the chemical fingerprints belong to some other cartel, your new friend from DEA's gonna look like a genius with his cartel war idea, which means the two of you could find yourselves standing in the middle of some really hateful crossfire."

Wallace drove toward the state crime lab. Despite Colley's warning, she felt the thrill that came when a case started cracking open a bit. It was like a runner's high—the endorphin rush that persistent effort called forth. Maybe Colley's idea would clear the fog a bit. She was just starting to soar, when her phone rang. She lost altitude quickly when she saw it was Carla Chapman. She checked the time. Mason and the marshal would have finished their evidence grab by now and it was very likely that the waves it stirred up were swamping Carla's boat. Wallace almost chickened out and let it go to voicemail, but resolved at the last second to give up faintheartedness for the rest of the day.

"Detective Hartman," she said, bracing herself.

"You fucking bitch. You and that dog turd you hang around with just ruined my career."

"Whoa. Take it slow, there—"

"I am taking it slow," she blared. "I can't believe you did this. I tried to help you, and you have completely fucked me over."

"If you'll remember, you're the one who brought it to our attention in the first place, and you knew the risks involved. You spelled it out quite clearly for us. Surely you didn't expect us to just leave that stuff where it was." Wallace was amazed that her words and her attitude had the same insensitive tone she had faulted Mason for less than twenty-four hours before.

"But there was no need for a search warrant and a dawn raid. I would have gladly hauled it out and given it to you, and Bell would never have been the wiser."

"Even if that's true," Wallace continued, trying to soften her words, "how would you have done it without getting caught? Plus, even if you were successful, you would have further compromised any evidentiary value it might have. And on top of that, it wouldn't have kept you safe anyway. For it to do us any good you would eventually have to testify about where it came from. The light was going to shine on you at some point."

"What do you mean *further* compromised it? If I hadn't done what I did, all that shit would have been compromised into powdered glass by now."

"Sorry. Poor choice of words. What I'm getting at is that anytime something is moved from its original setting, its validity as evidence is diminished. Once it's changed from the state it's originally found in, the person who made the change will have to testify as to what it was like before they changed it. Testimony is always less reliable than physical circumstance. Always. If you had taken the further step of removing it from Tunica on your own, the only connection between it and Tunica would be your say-so. At that point, any evidentiary value it might have would be extremely low."

"So what are you saying? That I'm the one who screwed up my own career, by trying to do the right thing?"

"I'm saying it's a risk you knew you were taking," Wallace said, again alarmed at how much she sounded like the side of Mason she liked the least. "You came to us. We couldn't just ignore what you told us."

"This is all just so shitty," Carla whispered and began to cry.

"Listen, I'm not a lawyer, but I know that Bell can't fire you for refusing to commit an unlawful act. And destroying evidence is an unlawful act."

"Kevin Bell is a dickhead, not a dumbass. He didn't fire me for saving the glassware because—you're right—that would expose him to the charge that he ordered an illegal act. This isn't him retaliating against a whistle-blower."

"Then what?" Wallace asked.

"He's saying I violated the terms of my employment by not registering my relationship with Matt with the lab's HR office."

"That's a firing offense?" Wallace asked. "How did he even find that out?"

"You told the Bayou Sara chief of police, and when he called Bell to see if Matt had turned up yet, he just happened to mention it."

Wallace pulled her car to the side of the road and got out. She felt like she was going to be sick. She remembered telling Chief Whitlock about Matt and Carla's relationship, but she hadn't foreseen that he might spill the beans to Carla's boss. Now Carla had lost her job and Wallace felt responsible—and negligent.

"Plus, Bell is saying the stuff that was seized, he had never seen it before, that if it was ever part of anything at the lab, that *I* was the one who hid it from *him*. His story is that because Matt and I were involved, I was engaged in some kind of cover-up to protect Matt. And since we never registered our relationship, he says that's just further proof that I was trying to keep things from him. And since Bell and I were the only ones who saw the things in the closet, there's no one to contradict his version of the story."

"I'm sorry things worked out this way. Truly. I don't know what I can do, but I'm sorry."

"I know. Me too," she said, her voice cycling from angry back to despondent.

"You said, a minute ago, that you and Matt *were* involved. Past tense. Has something changed since we spoke to you in the park?"

"Isn't that sweet, that you're so concerned about my love life. But no, sorry, I can't help you. Matt hasn't called to give me the official heave-ho."

The line went quiet for several seconds, then Wallace could hear Carla crying.

"You know, I'd almost be willing to forgive him for dumping me if it meant knowing he was okay."

"Carla, I feel really bad for getting you in trouble, but this case is turning scarier by the minute. There's already one dead body—"

"What dead body?"

"A drug dealer was killed in Baton Rouge, four days ago."

"You can't possibly think Matt is connected to something like that," Carla moaned.

"We don't know what to think, at this point. What my instincts tell me, though, is that the possibility that Matt is connected to the homicide in Baton Rouge is growing, not diminishing."

"That's absurd." A faint echo of her earlier hostility had crept back into her voice. "He could never do anything even remotely like what you're saying."

"I hope you're right. But that will be determined by the evidence."

"I know you're just doing your job," Carla said after a long pause. "It's just that a few days ago everything seemed just about right. Now my whole world has been turned inside out. And not because I've done anything wrong. It's just not fair," she said, finally winding down.

"Listen, while we're on the phone, I need to ask you something. The stuff that was just seized from Matt's lab is on its way to the state crime lab in Baton Rouge."

"So?"

"We need your help to reassemble it."

"You're kidding, right?" Carla said. An ugly chill edged into her voice. "Let me see now—you get me fired from my job, you ruin my career, you all but accuse my boyfriend of being a murderer involved with drug dealers, yet you still have the nerve to ask me to help you?"

"You would be helping us find Matt, or at least find out about Matt," Wallace said, immediately regretting her ham-handed attempt at leverage.

"You're a real piece of work, Detective."

"Please," Wallace pleaded, brushing past Carla's whine. "I've got a dead body and a scientist missing under suspicious circumstances. I hate the way things have turned out for you, but I can't *not* follow the trail where it leads me because of your, or anyone else's, bruised feelings."

"You said, a minute ago, that a connection between Matt and this drug dealer was looking more likely. How much more likely?" she asked, her tone thawing a few degrees.

"I don't know. Cases evolve. Assumptions change. All I can say is that when I first started down this path, it looked like a real longshot. Now, my instincts are telling me otherwise."

"If something concrete has changed your thinking, I'd like to know what it is. That's only fair, after what this is costing me."

"I'm telling you what I can," Wallace said, trying not to sound evasive. "Look, we're letting precious time slip away. Will you help, or won't you?"

"I can try," Carla said, sounding defeated. "That's assuming my labels haven't been removed. But I'm getting the distinct impression you're not really telling me anything."

"At this point, there's no way for me to know what information might be dangerous for you to have. If Matt's disappearance is connected to something he knew, your knowing it could endanger you as well." Wallace waited to see if Carla would push for more, but she didn't. "Do you want me to pick you up? I can take you to the lab."

"Just give me the address of this place where you want me to go. I'll drive myself. I don't want to go with you and then be stuck there when you get called away on something else."

The moment she ended the call her phone rang. She almost didn't want to look at it, afraid it might be Carla, again. But it was Mason.

TWELVE

Detective Hartman," she answered, not wanting Mason to know she had programmed his name with his number.

"Hey. It's me. We're done at Tunica, and the evidence is on the way to the crime lab."

"I know."

"You've heard from Carla."

"Boy, have I. And you owe me big-time for taking all the shit for both of us. Her career is toast, and she's angry and confused."

"Typical informant's remorse," Mason said.

"That's nice. When you put a name on it, it makes it so neat and clean. I'm already feeling ever so much better about the wreckage," Wallace shot back.

"Great. Well, listen then, the marshal tells me he'll be there in about forty-five minutes, give or take, depending on traffic," Mason said.

"I'll be waiting for him," she said, irritated that he could remain so composed when she was so determined to provoke him.

"So, how is Colley?" Mason asked, catching her completely off guard.

"He's putting a brave face on a dismal situation, as usual."

"I'd like to hear the story, later."

"Alright," she said, unsure if he was really interested or just trying to make nice. "I need to make a call before I get to the lab. I'll see you in Bayou Sara in a bit."

As she pulled into the parking lot at the lab, Wallace called Carla to let her know when the material from Matt's lab would be arriving.

Connie Butterworth was a senior analyst in the Drug Analysis Section at the State Police Crime Lab. She and Wallace had been pretty good friends in high school. Because of her wild-child lifestyle she was regarded as the most likely to die young in pursuit of better living through chemistry. Some thought it odd when she chose a career analyzing drugs instead of consuming them. She might have drunk her weight in alcohol during the latter part of her high school days, and she might have been more than just a bit friendly with more than just a few of her classmates, but Wallace knew to a certainty that Connie had never been a drug user. Connie had not discouraged the rumors, but she hadn't invited any monkeys onto her back, either.

Wallace occasionally needed a favor from the crime lab and she had asked Connie a few times. But she kept her requests rare and never liked to ask by telephone. She felt like she needed to go the extra mile and ask in person if she wanted Connie to do something special.

Besides, Wallace liked driving around the area where the lab was located. It was part of the main campus of the State Police Headquarters, situated next to a park that sprawled on the site of the old Downtown Airport. The area formerly occupied by the runways and taxiways was mainly tennis courts and ball fields now. The control tower was long gone, but one of the original Quonset-style hangars was still standing. It had been turned into an office building, though, and a new façade made its original shape and function difficult to discern. Over the years, thousands of kids, Wallace included, had played thousands of innings on the softball fields, then snuck across the street to do the mall-rat thing. The place was soaked with memories.

"Hey, Wally Girl," Connie said, as she strode across the lobby. The sound of her teenage nickname in Connie's whiskey-throated drawl brought a girlish smile to Wallace's face.

"Hey, Connie. I need your help with something that's . . . a bit out of the ordinary."

"I get off at six. I know these two guys who are into—"

"Not that out of the ordinary."

"Oh, you mean forensically speaking."

"Bingo."

"And, let me guess—time is of the essence."

"As always. But I think you'll at least find this one interesting."

They left the lab building and headed for the walking paths in the park across the street. Wallace spent the next several minutes explaining Colley's idea about how small traces of the chemicals the cartels used to extract the powder from the leaves were like fingerprints that could identify the source of a particular batch of cocaine. She also filled Connie in on the story of the missing Matt Gable and his extracurricular science project and Mason's theory that Matt could have developed a new extraction method.

"If this guy Gable has developed some sort of superefficient extraction method," Connie said, "that would mean he had the actual leaves from the coca plants. In that case, there would be no way to link his product with any of the powder cocaine coming straight from South America. His method would be different from the cartels' and it would leave different traces. So, you could show that

Gable's and Echeverría's products were different—you could eliminate the possibility of that kind of a connection—but you couldn't
connect them."

"Then let's put Echeverría aside, for the moment, and focus on
Gable and Overman. Let's say there is cocaine in this glassware we
seized from Gable's lab. And let's say the extraction traces from that
match the traces in the coke we seized from Overman. That would
connect Overman and Gable, wouldn't it?"

"Well, it would establish the possibility of a connection, and you
could probably get a jury to believe that it's a pretty strong connection, but that's all."

"If they match, why wouldn't that be conclusive?"

"Well, two batches extracted by two different people, just by
sheer coincidence might have identical traces, within the sensitivi-
ties my tests are valid for. I mean, it's unlikely, but things like that
do happen."

"Is there a way to raise the probability that a match means two
samples are from the same batch?" Wallace asked.

"Sure. Test more than one sample from each source. It's very unlikely that several samples over any real length of time would match
exactly, unless they're from the same source. Three samples from
each source, taken at different times, should do it."

"We don't have that. We just have the one batch from the Overman case, and a lot of unknowns from Gable's lab."

"Well, these extraction traces would be just one marker we could
test for," Connie pointed out. "Instead of testing multiple samples
for one marker, we could test the Gable sample and the Overman
sample for multiple markers. If all the markers from both samples
turn out the same, then the probability they're from the same source
goes up."

"Besides extraction traces, what other markers could be tested?"

"Isotopes and alkaloids."

"I'm lost already."

"As the coca plants grow, they take up different amounts of isotopes from their environment and produce different amounts of alkaloids, depending on growing conditions, location, and the variety of coca plant involved."

"Are these things affected by different purification processes?"

"No. They're in the cocaine molecule itself. Changes in the cultivation practices made these markers pretty unworkable for a long time, but some new science has made them the gold standard again."

"So you could compare the amounts in two different samples, and if they match, they come from the same variety of plant and the same general area?"

"Yep. And since each cartel controls fairly specific growing areas, that would also give you a pretty good idea whether they're from the same source or not."

"So if you compare a sample from the Overman crime scene and the glassware from Gable's lab and they match for all these markers, we can say they came from the same source? We can connect Gable and Overman?"

"We can say there's only a teeny tiny chance they came from different sources. You're getting a whole lot closer to that legal certainty you're looking for."

"The items from Gable's lab are being set up in one of your vacant lab rooms later today. If I get you the piece from the output end of Gable's setup and a sample from the Overman scene, could you compare them for both markers?"

"Of course."

"How quickly?"

"Actually, pretty fast."

"I don't believe it. There's no one in the entire state ahead of me?"

"Quite a few, in fact."

"Won't you get in trouble for jumping the line with my stuff?"

"I've got a little bit of power," she said, with a huge grin. "You're not the only person around here who's been asking me to do something out of the ordinary."

Wallace walked back to the room where the glassware would be reassembled. Nothing had arrived yet, so she called Mike Harrison. He still didn't answer, so she called the Evidence Division. Joe Lumpkin, who had been on the force nearly as long as Colley, took the call.

"I'm stuck at the state crime lab for a while and can't get to a department computer," she told him. "Do you have time to check on something for me?"

"Sure," Joe said. "What do you need?"

"Has anything come back on the prints or DNA in the Ronald Overman case?"

"Gimme a sec." After a minute he said, "Not much here. Lots of hairs were recovered from the air shaft, but unless you got somebody's to compare 'em to, they won't help you much."

"What about fingerprints?"

"Only prints ID'd so far belonged to the victim."

The air shaft in the warehouse had been an intake, so over the years it would have sucked in a great deal of material. That meant there would be a lot of testable stuff, but getting through it would take time and a budget she didn't have.

"Anything? Anything at all?"

"Sorry, kid. Nothing."

"Thanks, Joe," she said, and hung up.

She was about to step out for a minute when the crates from Gable's lab arrived. Carla arrived a few minutes later and sat in the back of the room, refusing to even look at Wallace. After explaining to the evidence tech what she wanted done with the contents of the crates, Wallace left for Bayou Sara.

THIRTEEN

NOON

Wallace stopped in front of Matt Gable's ruined house. Mason and Chief Whitlock were standing next to one of the trees that held a hidden camera. A circular scaffold platform surrounded the tree and a waist-high rolling rack loaded with electronic gear was parked on the platform where a technician was hard at work.

"Find anything?" Wallace asked, as she walked up.

"Yes and no," Mason said. "We know how the cameras work, but we haven't been able to break into their cloud storage, yet."

"Are we certain they're storing what they see?" she asked.

"The cameras are sending to a website. The site is protected and it looks like the protection is pretty strong."

"Can your techs break in?"

"Probably, but they've done all they can for the moment. They're taking the cameras down and moving everything to a place where it's a little easier to work. We've got some really talented hackers back in Washington trying to get into the website. We'll know more when they know more."

"Ready for our little romp through the wilderness?" she asked, pulling her hair back into a ponytail.

"Chief Whitlock, would you care to join us?" Mason asked.

"No thanks. A walk in the woods without at least a chance of shooting at something edible seems like a waste of a good walk to me. Just remember our little deal."

"Any chance you could send someone to pick us up and bring us back to my car, when we get to the other end?" Wallace asked.

"Yes ma'am," Whitlock said, as he sauntered back toward the street.

Wallace and Mason entered the woods at the place Carla had shown them. The sun was baking a clean, sharp scent out of the vegetation. As they moved deeper into the trees, the frantic rustle of small animals and the kvetching of birds in the limbs overhead grew more frequent. They went slowly, at first, but as Wallace caught the rhythm of Matt's system of scrape marks on the trees, she picked up the pace.

The gentle terrain was punctuated by occasional rises. In some places the trail led around the rises and at others Matt had evidently climbed over. Twice the trail ended at a stream where Matt had apparently run along the streambed before returning to dry land. At these points, Wallace and Mason were forced to use trial and error, walking some distance upstream and downstream until they found where the tree marks resumed or they could tell from worn spots on the bank where Matt had exited the stream.

They moved without speaking, with Wallace in the lead. Their footfalls were their only contributions to the forest noises. Occasionally, instead of concentrating totally on the trail, looking for telltale signs of the missing scientist, Wallace found her thoughts straying toward Mason, just as they had the evening before. But today was different. She wasn't having the same allergic reaction to thinking about him. And the more she thought about his request for forgiveness, after their sparring match over the materials from Matt Gable's lab, the more it blew her away. It had been a long time since she had encountered a man with enough moxie to call a foul on himself like that.

And now, with him walking the path behind her, she was starting to wonder whether he was thinking about *her*. He hadn't given off any obvious signs in that department. And she hadn't caught him in any of those head-to-toe appraisals she knew men gave her when they thought she wasn't watching—something she had never gotten truly comfortable with, perhaps because she had been a late bloomer. It hadn't been until her late teens that she had completely forsaken gawky for gangly. And it had taken until her midtwenties to go from gangly to lanky. It was only now, as she navigated through her midthirties, that her corners and edges had begun to soften a bit.

She needed to stop and refocus but as she turned to announce a rest, her peripheral vision picked up something that didn't fit. It was about fifty yards off the trail. The space between the trees was a little darker than her eyes had come to expect. She stopped, signaling for quiet.

As they drew closer, she could see it was a crudely built shed. Cautiously she moved toward it, unholstering her weapon as she went. She motioned for Mason to stay behind, then she began to circle the shed, darting from tree to tree. Only after the gaping doors came into view and she could see that it was empty did she reholster her sidearm.

"Watch where you put your feet," she cautioned, pointing at the tire tracks leading from inside the shed into the field beyond. Using her phone, Wallace took several close-ups of the tracks.

"They go off in this direction," Mason pointed out.

They followed the tracks. Parallel tire-flattened furrows in the tall grass showed the path a vehicle had taken along the edge of the field.

"Let's go back to the shed," she said. Using a GPS app, she texted the shed's location to Whitlock. Her phone rang almost immediately.

"I hope those coordinates aren't the final resting place of Matt Gable, Ph.D.," Whitlock drawled.

"There's a shed here, some ways off the trail. What look like fresh tire tracks—car tire tracks to be specific—lead away from the shed, then go around the perimeter of a nearby pasture. We don't know where they end up."

"How big is that pasture?" Whitlock asked.

"Too small to be used as a landing strip, if that's what you're thinking."

"You're reading my mind, Detective."

"Too small and not enough level area. It's big enough to be a drop zone, but only a helicopter or a hot air balloon could take off and land here. I think the shed and whatever vehicle was in it are the main event. We're going to move along and try to pick out the rest of the trail. Can your guys take over on the shed?"

"As soon as we can. Any sign of Gable himself?"

"Not yet. No bodies, no dead smells, no buzzards circling overhead."

"Can you send me shots of those tire tracks?"

"Will do," she said.

"Ready?" she asked Mason, after she finished sending the pictures to Whitlock.

"Aye, Cap'n."

They continued in silence, for another twenty minutes. The terrain inclined gradually, but steadily, until they arrived at the foot of a rise. A foot-worn path rose from the forest floor for several yards, eventually curving back to the left. Wallace's phone told her they were close to the Tunica access road. As they ascended, the path widened and led beneath a tall, dense patch of scrub overhanging the trail. In the cavernous cleft beneath the overhang a black Ducati motorcycle rested on its kickstand. A Tunica Lab parking decal in the shape of a lazy triangle was affixed to the rear fender.

"Well, well," Mason crowed.

"I get a gold star for bringing us out to this miserable place," Wallace said. She photographed the motorcycle, its tire treads, and the license plate, then texted the images along with the coordinates to Whitlock. Then she sent the picture of the motorcycle to Louise Mautner—the woman she and Mason had spoken with in the garden under the power lines—asking if it was the crotch rocket she and her friends had seen the day Overman was killed.

Within sixty seconds, Whitlock texted back that the bike was registered to Gable.

"Look," Mason said, pointing back in the direction they had come from. They had gained enough elevation since leaving the pasture that they could see over the treetops back along the trail. The rooftops of some of the houses in Matt's neighborhood were visible in the distance. Between two of the houses there was the empty space where Matt's house had been.

"Matt could have seen his house burning from here, and decided to hit the road," Mason said.

"I'm starting to think the good Dr. Gable had a healthy streak of paranoia in him. He saw his house going up in flames, so he ditched his bike and fled in a car he had hidden in the shed."

"Which raises the question of why he felt the need for such preparations," Mason said.

"Just because you're paranoid, doesn't mean they're not out to get you," Wallace replied. "If this is the motorcycle our friends under the power lines saw, then almost certainly Matt was at the warehouse with Overman. That means Matt was dealing with some very dangerous people. Maybe he was afraid they would turn on him."

"Let's keep moving," Wallace said, leading them back onto the trail.

"What if my new theory is correct?" Mason began. "That Gable actually figured out a way to significantly increase the yield from a given quantity of coca leaves."

"Do you think bales of leaves were being dropped in the pasture back there?" Wallace asked.

"Maybe. Maybe Overman was getting the leaves and turning them over to Matt," Mason continued. "They could've had some arrangement, but then Overman got the idea Matt was skimming or overcharging."

"Or maybe Matt was using Overman to try to sell his method further upstream—"

"And the people he was trying to sell it to got their noses out of joint at having to pay for something they thought could be theirs for the taking, so—"

"So Echeverría or one of his people came up here to do the taking," Wallace finished, as they emerged from the forest onto the access road. "Let me call our ride." She texted Whitlock that they were ready to be picked up. She was about to reopen their discussion when her phone vibrated.

"Detective Hartman, this is David Bosso."

"Yes, David, and please just call me Wallace."

"Something's changed since we spoke with you and your boyfriend from DEA."

"I'm listening," she said, letting the dig pass. Turning away from Mason, she lifted the hem of her T-shirt and wiped the perspiration from her face.

"You wanted to know if we had anybody deep enough in Overman's organization who could maybe shed some light on his recent comings and goings. If you're willing to get your hands a little dirty, I may have something for you. You ever heard of a guy named Stacky Vincent?"

"Not that I can recall." She sat on a log near the edge of the roadway and watched Mason as he wandered back a few steps into the edge of the tree line.

"A real creepazoid. But . . . he's got a connection that might be useful."

"What's his story?" she asked.

Mason reemerged from the trees several steps from her, fiddling with his phone. He looked in her direction with an inquisitive expression. She patted the log next to her and motioned him over.

"Couple a years ago he happened to spend a few days in the same holding cell as our good buddy Ronald Overman, who, believe it or not, was waiting to bail out on a DUI. Stacky was back on the street before Overman was, and the theory is he musta done Overman a favor. Something Overman didn't want anybody from his regular band of douche nozzles to touch."

"Okay . . . ?" she said, as Mason sat down next to her.

"So Overman was grateful enough that, once he made bail, he gave Stacky a job. Just as a jerkoff member of his entourage, but he's somebody on the inside. You know, drive him places, pick up and deliver. Shit like that."

"Why would this guy be willing to turn?" She put her phone on speaker and held it between her and Mason. They both leaned in to listen. "Do we have any leverage?"

"We might have. It's kinda weird. See, Stacky had this old aggravated battery charge from about two years ago that was never prosecuted. And, well, fortunately or unfortunately, depending on your point of view, the victim of said battery died about an hour ago. Nothing's happening on it just yet, but if we're willing to push a little, we might be able to get the DA to at least threaten to bring it as a manslaughter charge. Then you could tell Stacky that, in exchange for whatever it is he's got that you need, you would try to talk the DA into reducing the charge."

Wallace was having trouble concentrating on the call. Mason's scent was invading her airspace. It was just him—no cologne or soap smell—just him, and it was making her head swim.

"It took the vic two years to die?" she asked, recovering her focus. "For something like that to turn into manslaughter, doesn't there have to be some kind of, you know, direct link between the original act and the eventual death of the victim?"

"That's just it. The agg battery, which was the reason Stacky happened to be in the same cell with Overman to begin with, was because of a fight between Stacky and the now-deceased victim. During the altercation, the vic took a knife to the abdomen. It was the vic's own knife, but Stacky was the aggressor in the fight. Exactly how the knife came into play, and exactly whose hand was on the knife at the critical moment, was never crystal clear. But, apparently, there was enough there to make it look like they could pin it on him."

"Why was it never prosecuted?" She looked over at Mason. He seemed to be listening intently to the call. Even though she was tired from the hike through the woods, his proximity was causing a surge of nervous energy.

"Stacky had information on some guys who were going into the bomb-making business. How he knew that, I don't know, but he did. In exchange for rolling over on the would-be bombers, the DA agreed not to prosecute the battery. Since it was never prosecuted to begin with, there's no double jeopardy bringing it as manslaughter now."

"I still don't see a connection between the original act and manslaughter."

"The knife was dirty. It caused an infection of the body cavity, uh . . ."

"Peritonitis," she blurted, trying to hurry him along. She needed to get up and walk off all this energy.

"Correct. Apparently, the docs could never get it under control. One a those drug-resistant bugs. And in two years' time it went from bad to worse."

"What's the victim's name?" Her knees started jumping.

"Farrell Macklin."

"Do you know if the DA will have any interest in this?"

"Macklin just died, so it's probably too soon to tell. Plus, this is an orphan crime—something nobody gives a shit about. Unless there's family out there, pushing on it, stuff like this usually just falls through the cracks and gets forgotten. There's no system for keeping track of people who might die someday from a crime committed against 'em way back who knows when."

"Then how did you happen to hear that Macklin died?"

"He was my little sister's first ex-husband. At least now I ain't gotta lean on him for rugrat payments."

"Is your sister going to file a complaint, so we can get an arrest warrant?" Wallace willed her legs to remain still.

"She will if I tell her to."

"Good, because I can't see this guy getting too worried if we pick him up without a warrant. He'll know the DA isn't interested, so he won't have any incentive to play ball."

"Like I said, she'll do it if I tell her to."

"So, if we can get this thing going, do you know where we can find Mr. Vincent?"

"That won't be a problem. Are you telling me you're interested?"

"I am. But since it's a homicide, I want in on the arrest."

"You got it."

"David . . . why are you doing this? This'll burn one of your bridges into Overman's organization." If the call didn't wrap up soon, she felt like she might explode.

"You're assuming you'll be the only one interrogating this fuckup. I got a lotta open investigations this guy's gonna help me out with."

"But you don't need me on this. You could bring him in without me being involved at all."

"Think of it this way. You're Colley's partner. I owe Colley a few favors. We all know the time for paying up is . . . growing short."

A wave of emotion crested over Wallace at the mention of Colley's situation, and all the energy drained out of her. She went silent for several seconds, then turned to look at Mason. He was giving her a worried look.

"You there, Detective?" Bosso asked.

"Yeah, I'm here. Listen, thanks for doing this. Call me when it's showtime."

"Stay by the phone 'cause it shouldn't be too long."

Their ride back to Bayou Sara arrived just as Wallace ended the call. It turned out to be Jake, the guy who had taken the first look into the birdhouses. Jake took a few pictures of the bike, then wrapped it in a plastic sheet and stuck an evidence sticker on the sheet. After that, they loaded the bike into the bed of Jake's pickup and headed back to Wallace's car.

During the drive, Whitlock called to give Wallace the results of the records search on Matt. Several hundred dollars had been taken out of a personal checking account on Sunday night and his credit cards had been used twice in the last few days. The latest charge came from a motel on the outskirts of Baton Rouge. The Baton Rouge PD sent a car over but there was no sign that Matt had actually stayed in the room. If he had ever been there, he was gone now.

"Do you have a photograph of Matt?" Wallace asked.

"I've got a head shot Carla Chapman gave us when she filed the missing person report."

"Can you scan it and send it to me? I just found out I'll have a chance to interrogate someone who could shed some light on how Gable fits into this business."

"Will do, Detective. But don't forget me now."

"No chance of that. You get what we get," she said, hanging up, then turned to Mason. "I'm inclined to push this thing with Stacky Vincent as fast as I can. Do you want in on the arrest or just the interrogation?"

"Just the interrogation. How long do you think the warrant will take?"

"A few hours, at least. David's got to type up the application and affidavit, then get it in front of the magistrate. My guess is it'll happen sometime tonight."

FOURTEEN

B y the time Jake had dropped them off, it was too late for lunch and too early for Mason's meeting with the state police investigators, so Wallace drove them to the police station.

Wallace sat at her desk and checked messages, then pulled up the file on Stacky Vincent's unprosecuted aggravated battery.

Mason took an empty chair a few cubicles away from Wallace's, and called Don Brindl's cell, but the analyst didn't answer, so Mason left a message. "Don, this is Mason. Sorry to bug you while you're home sick, but I need to clear up some details from the presentation you made at the analyst meeting two Mondays ago. Call me on my cell, as soon as you get this."

Before he could hang up, his phone showed an incoming call from Don.

"How are you feeling?" Mason asked.

"Sorry, I couldn't get to the phone quick enough, and I may not make it through this call in one go. Anyway, I don't feel so great. But I'll live. What's up?"

"Let's go back to your theory about the source of the new cocaine that's coming into south Louisiana. I've got a competing theory I want to bounce off of you, about where that extra supply might be coming from."

"I'm listening."

Mason rattled off the highlights of what he had learned about the Overman homicide, his trip to Tunica, the disappearance of Matt Gable, and the strange things Carla Chapman had found in Gable's lab. He finished by telling Don his theory that Gable might have developed an improved method for extracting the powder cocaine from the leaves.

"It would have to be a hell of an improvement to produce enough cocaine to account for the changes we're seeing. And it wouldn't account for the falling supply in the nearby states."

"Those may prove to be unrelated events," Mason said. He caught a sudden movement out of the corner of his eye and turned to look. Wallace was rocking gently in her chair, studying her computer screen. He watched as she drew one foot up onto the seat and draped an arm over her knee. With her other hand she absently wound her hair into a twist and piled it on top of her head. Loose strands trailed down her neck.

"Hello. Anybody home?" Don asked.

"Sorry, I got lost in my notes for a second," Mason said, realizing he had missed something. "What were you saying?"

"I was saying that for your theory to work, Overman would have to be getting hold of the coca leaves themselves. Have you found anything to support that?"

"There's an isolated patch of cleared land in the woods near Tunica, and there are signs Gable has recently spent time there. It could have been used as a drop site for the coca leaves, but I don't know if that actually happened."

"This is quite a story," Don said, his voice taking on an almost manic intensity. "When can we test this equipment from Gable's lab, to see if you're right?"

"As we speak, it's being examined at the state crime lab. They've promised to turn it around as fast as possible, so we should know something in pretty short order."

"The state lab?" Don asked, sounding incredulous. "That's crazy. We should be in control of this, not some backwater shop nobody's ever heard of. Have our people do it."

"I'm confident we're getting top-drawer work here, so I think we'll be okay."

"Who's going to reassemble this stuff from Gable's lab?"

"His lab assistant, Carla Chapman."

"Can she do it?"

"She's our best bet—our only bet, actually."

"Could she be involved in Gable's disappearance or Overman's death?"

"She pursued us. She told us about the stuff hidden in the storeroom and she filed the missing person report. If she was involved, why tip off anyone about anything? Why invite all that scrutiny?"

"Could be a manipulation calculated to make her look unlikely as a suspect?"

Mason had to admire Don's thinking—the same game-within-a-game strategies that undoubtedly fueled his success at the card tables.

Wallace stood and walked out of the detective area and down the hallway. Mason struggled to keep his thoughts from following her. "I've seen her up close," he said. "I think she's for real. If she's bluffing, she's damn good. Not someone you'd want to play poker against," Mason said, gently ribbing his colleague.

"I'll remember that," Don laughed.

"She and this guy Gable were involved on a personal level, so she may know more than she's saying, but we're not currently looking at her."

"Who's we?" Don asked.

"Me and Wallace Hartman—the local detective I'm working with."

"It he doing you any good?"

"Not he. She."

"She good-looking?"

"Indeed. She's a head-turner," Mason said in a low voice so none of Wallace's fellow detectives would overhear him. "But that's not why we're on the phone."

"Suddenly you're whispering. Hmmm. That probably means she's close by. You gonna go for it?"

"Are you gonna get your mind back on this case?" Mason responded, testily.

Don sighed. "Never mind. Another one slips away. Oh, well. Listen, have you got any leads on this Gable fellow?" Don asked. "Seems like he could be the key to everything."

"I think you're right, but so far, he's managed to remain invisible. Carla Chapman filed a missing person report, so the Bayou Sara police are looking, but they've had no luck. They got access to his phone and financial records and Gable, or somebody, we don't actually know who, registered at a motel in Baton Rouge under his name, using one of his credit cards. But he's not there. A sizable withdrawal was made from his checking account the day he went missing. So, it looks like he's on the move. In any event, when will you be back in the saddle?" Mason asked.

"I don't know. I think I've got some kind of stomach flu, and it's keeping me on a short leash. Do you need me to go back in?"

"No, thank you. No need to spread that around. Unless this flu business is just a con so you can have a long weekend in Vegas."

"Not this time," Don laughed. "Which is too bad because I'm feeling pretty lucky at the moment. So, how long will you be in Baton Rouge?"

"Until I can get some clarity on who killed Overman and why and where the extra cocaine is coming from. Whether it's a turf war or there's some new science in the picture."

"Are you staying near the capitol building?"

"I'm staying at the Istrouma Hotel, downtown, so it's not too far away," Mason said. "Why do you ask?"

"You know how some guys want to see a game in every major league baseball park? Well, my dad's bucket list was to tour every state capitol building. We never finished the list, but Baton Rouge was one of the ones we made it to. In the lobby, you can still see the bullet holes in the wall where some crazy guy gunned down Huey Long, the former governor. It's kind of creepy, but it's worth seeing. And, from the top of the building, you can get this view of the Mississippi River that's really just unbelievable."

"I'll keep that in mind, if I have time for any sightseeing. Listen, I have to go," he said.

A tall, barrel-chested man had entered the room and started pawing through the papers on Wallace's desk.

"Sorry I missed that meeting, yesterday," the man said to Wallace as she strode back into the room. "Did I miss anything important?" He followed her gaze to Mason, then he looked back at her.

"Mike, look, if you're not going to take this assignment seriously, then tell Burley you want something else," Wallace said.

"Why are you climbing up my ass? I miss one little meeting and you think the whole world's come to an end."

"You haven't returned my calls or my messages, either. Where were you?"

"I told you, in the note I left. I had some personal business that came up."

"What kind of personal business?" Wallace pushed.

"The none-of-your-business kind."

She motioned him close and spoke in a low voice. "It wouldn't be the kind that would keep you from passing a random piss test, would it? That might make it hard for us to get along."

"Fuck you," he spat, turning away.

"Answer my question," Wallace demanded, cocking her head to the side, studying him carefully. Others in the room had begun to pay attention to them.

Playing to the audience, Mike shifted into full bullshit mode, an open expression on his face, his palms outward in surrender. "Hey, that stuff's behind me," he insisted. "I'm cured, now. Praise Jesus, I'm all cured," he sang, feverishly clasping his hands and raising them heavenward like a revival-tent supplicant.

"You're skating on thin ice, mister." Wallace lifted her hand when she saw him gearing up for more theatrics. "Don't. I don't like being lied to. Especially not by a partner." She cut him off, again, when it looked like he was going to say something. "You just do the work I put in front of you, but don't expect anything more out of this."

"This ain't how partners work," Mike intoned, tick-tocking an index finger side to side.

"It is when one isn't being truthful with the other. When one isn't willing to put her life in the hands of the other." She thought back through her first encounter with Mike since his return, less than thirty-six hours ago. She didn't need a drug test to tell her what his pageant of moods and his secretive, erratic behaviors meant. He had fallen off the wagon. Her anger gave way to concern and her expression softened.

"Don't look at me that way," he said, a hurt expression taking over his face.

"Mike. Sit," Wallace commanded. "You have to be patient with this. Detective work is different from your other gig. Colley started me on research and—"

"Now you're patronizing me. I can see what you're thinking. Just write down what you want me to do, and leave it on the desk. I'll be back." He hurried from the room.

"Mike," Wallace hollered after him, then dropped into her chair.

"Your new partner?" Mason asked.

Wallace looked up to see him staring at her. Everyone else in the room had returned to their work, apparently unimpressed by the low-caliber drama. For some reason, Mason's gaze was making her feel embarrassed and tickled at the same time, like when the cat drags a dirty bra into the living room just when the new hot guy comes over for the first time. She bit her lower lip and squeezed her eyes shut, fighting hard not to laugh. When she opened her eyes, he was still looking at her, and she gave up the fight.

"Ever see one of these before?" she asked, once she stopped laughing. She pulled the final autopsy report from the envelope and placed it next to Mason's tablet. "It came in while we were gone."

"No, but gruesome doesn't bother me, if that's what you're worried about. But before we get into that, look at this," he said, holding up his tablet for her to see. "Just since I've been sitting here my office has forwarded more news on Echeverría's last movements. It's not much, but the Mexican authorities confirmed that his plane was headed south at the time it went down, and they back-traced its flight plans as far north as Monterrey, Mexico."

"So he could have been on his way home from points even further north."

"He could have, but there's no way to know from this."

"Will whoever is sending you this information be able to trace the flight plan further?"

"I don't think so. There are too many unregulated airfields in that part of Mexico, and no one in Echeverría's position is going to give the government any more information than they have to. His pilots could have filed a plan for one destination but taken him somewhere else, instead. So it's possible that what I'm showing you now is not entirely accurate."

"I suppose the chances of someone having seen him here, or along the way, are pretty slim."

"We should certainly ask this guy, Stacky Vincent, when we get our chance to question him."

"Any luck getting into the camera feeds from Matt Gable's house?" Wallace asked.

"Not yet, but promises continue to be forthcoming. Let's look at the autopsy report."

She flipped first to the section on cause of death. The killer had forced a hypodermic syringe with a large bore needle deep into Overman's left nostril, puncturing the cribriform plate—the paper-thin floor of the cranium just behind the bridge of the nose—and injected a massive dose of a highly concentrated cocaine solution directly into the cerebrospinal fluid surrounding Overman's brain. The coroner estimated that such an abrupt and massive chemical insult would bring death within five to seven minutes.

"Shit. Whoever did this is a real humanitarian," Wallace intoned.

"This is one of Echeverría's known methods for winding down the party."

"Does this make you more or less convinced that Echeverría is in the picture?"

Mason shrugged. "It could be a copycat, but it would have to be a copycat with some inside knowledge."

"Here's something interesting," Wallace said, pointing to the External Examination section. "Now we know how the killer got Overman to sit still long enough to be strapped to the board."

Two small, closely spaced puncture wounds were discovered just above Overman's Adam's apple, indicating that he had been Tasered.

"Overman would have frisked anybody he was meeting. The Taser had to come in with someone he didn't know was there. Our hypothetical third person?" Mason proposed.

"Unless someone went to the warehouse early and hid the Taser," Wallace said.

"We're getting nowhere. We need a physical link between the players at the warehouse."

"Well, we may be able to get a little clarity on that," Wallace said. She recounted her visit with Colley and her subsequent conversation with Connie Butterworth at the crime lab.

"How come it took all day for you to tell me this?" Mason asked, obviously irritated. "Everything I get, I'm shoveling in your direction, the minute I get it. I thought we had a deal."

"We do. I'm sorry," Wallace said, clearly contrite. "I wasn't holding out on you. We just got caught up in so many other things today, it slipped to the back of my mind."

"When will the results of these tests be available?" Mason asked, defrosting a bit.

"I don't know. Connie is running the cocaine we seized at the Overman scene right away. Then she'll test whatever we bring her from Matt's lab as soon as we can figure out which are the output pieces."

"Then let's make sure that apparatus gets reassembled as soon as possible," he said, then returned his attention to the report.

They paged through the remainder but found nothing of interest.

"I'm heading out," Wallace said. "Can I drop you at your hotel?"

"Sure. In an hour I'm meeting with two state police investigators at a restaurant a block from my hotel. Just don't forget to call me once you get Stacky Vincent on the hot seat."

6:00 P.M.

The meeting with the state police investigators was short and unhelpful. They had no concrete data or any anecdotal evidence that would support or undercut either of the theories Mason and Wallace were currently considering. Maybe his meetings tomorrow with the sheriff's investigators and two special agents from the FBI's Baton Rouge field office would prove more fruitful.

After he returned to his room, he showered and put on fresh

clothes. He fired up his tablet and found an email from the technician who was working on the birdhouse cameras. The email had a link to a website, along with a password. The homepage of the website had password-protected links for "Front Camera" and "Back Camera." The password was for the "Back Camera" link, which took him to a page with a list of dated video files.

FIFTEEN

Traffic was heavy, so the drive from the crime lab to her house in Bayou Sara took Carla over an hour and it gave her a headache. It had taken her and the evidence tech until nearly five o'clock to uncrate and lay out everything. Just being at the crime lab had put her in a prickly mood. Having to return the following morning felt like cruel and unusual punishment. All she could think about was a hot meal, an icy gin and tonic, and being left alone. Then the doorbell rang. She looked through the peephole and saw a man standing a few feet back from the door. "Who are you and what do you want?" she asked, trying to sound as inhospitable as she felt.

"Detective Capelle with the Bayou Sara Police Department," he drawled. "I'm following up on the missing person report you filed on a Mr. Matt Gable."

"Have you found him?" she asked, a note of hope creeping into her voice.

"Don't know. I got some photos—actually they're screen grabs from security cams—taken at two businesses, the last couple of days.

If you wouldn't mind lookin' at 'em and see if you can verify it's him in the pictures."

"Oh my God," she said. "Show them to me."

"This one's from a gas station outside Shreveport," he said, holding a grainy image up to the peephole. "The other one's from a restaurant in Tyler, Texas."

"I can't make out anything. I'll let you come in, but show me your ID first."

"I 'preciate your caution," he said, holding a leather placard with a badge mounted in the center. He quickly flipped the placard around and held it close to the peephole. A card behind a scuffed plastic film identified him as Detective Casey Capelle.

"Come in, Detective," she said, pulling the door open. "The place is a mess, sorry."

"Not a problem." He pushed the door closed as he followed her inside.

"The light's better over here," she said, heading for the cluttered table situated beneath the serve-through window that linked the dining area to the kitchen. "Things have been pretty crappy for me, lately. I'm almost afraid to be hopeful."

"Hope lifts us high, so the snap of the rope is more . . . effective."

"What an awful thing to say," Carla said, turning to face the business end of the man's gun.

"But true, wouldn't you agree?" His drawl had disappeared.

Carla stood dead still. She noticed makeup smeared inexpertly under the man's eyes and over the bridge of his swollen nose. The corner of a bandage was visible under the man's curly red hair.

"Who are you?" she asked, backing away, struggling to hold her panic in check.

"Don Brindl. Does the name mean anything to you?" He scrutinized her face. "Does it?" he demanded, when she failed to answer.

"No. No, I've never heard of you. Please . . . just let me—"

"I'm going to give you a series of instructions. You must follow them precisely. First . . . and this is very important . . . move slowly. Second, keep your hands where I can see them at all times. If you make a sudden movement or if I lose sight of either of your hands, even for the briefest moment, I'll put your brains on this lovely rug. Understood?"

Carla nodded slowly. The man's calm tone, so inappropriate to the situation, caused her fear to spike.

"Sit," he commanded. "Right here in this chair. I see you've noticed my amateurish attempts to cover some recently acquired battle scars. You're not the only one who's been having a crappy time of it lately."

Carla's lower lip trembled, and she was sweating profusely. A droplet of perspiration started to tickle and itch as it ran between her shoulder blades.

"Both hands flat on the table in front of you," the man instructed.

She very badly wanted to scratch but, mindful of the man's threats, she kept her hands where he could see them. Sweat began to bead on her scalp and forehead. A tiny rivulet prickled her skin as it slid alongside her nose, catching at the corner of her mouth.

Don studied her discomfort. "You're doing very well," he said, rubbing distractedly under his left eye, uncovering a deep bruise hidden by the makeup. "Excellent self-control. I know how tempted you must be to wipe away those little droplets. Maddening, isn't it? Makes you appreciate the power of the legendary Chinese water torture. Although I think it may have actually been invented by an Italian."

"What do you want from me?" she whined.

"I want you to tell me where every one of your communication devices is. Cell phones, tablets, laptops, hard line telephones, everything."

As Carla told him, Don made a list of the devices and their passwords. After that, he persuaded her to reveal the personal email address she used to communicate with Matt Gable. Using plastic wrist ties, he fastened her hands through the slats on the back of the chair and her ankles to the legs of the chair. Then, he went through the house gathering the devices.

"Now, let's get down to the reason I'm here," he said, rejoining her at the table. He placed a small digital recorder on the table in front of Carla, then pulled a small stack of index cards from the inside pocket of his jacket.

"I'm going to show you these cards, one at a time. Each card will have a different message printed on it. You will recite what you see. I will record what you say. Simple enough?"

Carla slowly nodded.

He slid a card across the table until it was right in front of her. "Now, read." He pushed the Record button.

"Matt, listen, I can only talk for a second. You have to call me. Please. I have to—"

"Wait," Don said, pressing the Stop button. "Do it again. And this time, try not to be so wooden."

"Why are you doing this?" Carla asked in a panicky whimper.

"Because Matt Gable is a fucking genius. He's found something that will change the world. And I intend to have it."

"I don't know about anything he's found, and I don't know where he is. I swear to God I—"

"But I'm pretty sure he knows where you are. So I need you to dangle the bait. I'll call him using your phone, then play your increasingly frantic messages into the phone. Once I've got him sufficiently wound up, he'll be dying to do the very thing he knows he shouldn't."

"Just call him. I'll say whatever you want me to."

"I don't think so. A live performance is too risky. You might blow your lines and spoil the show. You might go off-script and shout a warning. Or maybe the two of you have some sort of prearranged code word, something totally innocent-sounding that you could use to secretly tip him off. Sorry, but we just can't take those kinds of chances."

"What if he doesn't answer? I've been calling him for days, but he never answers and he never returns my calls."

"That doesn't matter. In fact, if he answers I intend to hang up. These messages will be for when he doesn't answer. Desperate voice-mails from you will have a more dramatic effect. So, let's get back to our little project, shall we? Ready?" Don pressed the Record button and pointed at her.

"Matt, listen, I can—"

"Cut," he shouted in mock exasperation. "I can see now that you are one of those people who just doesn't take direction very well. But I have an idea."

Stepping behind her, Don took hold of her right index finger and bent it backward until it made a gristly popping noise. Carla blanched and tried to recoil. A low, forlorn wail slithered from her lips as Don ground the muzzle of his gun hard into her right cheek.

"Now say it like you fucking mean it."

SIXTEEN

7:00 P.M.

It was dim and quiet inside the church, with that middle-of-the-week empty feeling. Fresco saints glared down from the vaulted ceiling and the vague scent of old incense laced the air. Faint sounds produced solemn echoes. As a young man emerged from the confessional with his head hung reverentially low, Wallace took his place in the penitent's stall.

"Bless me, Father, for I have sinned. It's been at least three popes since my last confession."

"Wallace, you have to stop doing this," the priest scolded without conviction.

"Maybe I've sinned and I need forgiveness," she teased.

"I'm certain you have and you do, but I'm your little brother. If this confession is as . . . impure as your last one, I'll have to go to confession myself, just for listening to it."

"Oh, come on, Lex. Aren't you supposed to give me absolution before you dish out the grief?"

"Aren't you supposed to actually confess your sins first?"

"Well, I don't want to scandalize you. What if I just go through them by commandment number? You know, I could say that I violated the Third Commandment three times, and I rang up one number Four and a couple of Sixes, and so on."

"I'm on a tight schedule. Just add them up and give me the total."

"Without some detail, how will you know if I'm being truthful and whether I'm truly sorry?"

"Good point. Are you really here for confession, or is this something else?"

"Something else," she confessed. "I just haven't seen you for a while. That's all."

Lex and Wallace and their older brother Martin had been those storybook siblings parents dreamt about. Adult life took them in different directions, but they had still seen each other often, and spoken almost daily. Martin's death ended that. What were once naturally and frequently intersecting orbits came to require effort after Martin was killed. The fact that it took effort made Wallace and Lex self-conscious. Somehow neither had noticed, until he was gone, that Martin was the linchpin in the trio. Now, they went long periods without contact. Eventually guilt would trump self-consciousness and one of them would call the other. They would make plans to get together. Sometimes they followed through.

"Father Rudanski from Texarkana, we went to seminary together, he's passing through tomorrow, on his way to visit his father in Pascagoula. He's stopping by for lunch. Why don't you join us?"

"That sounds like a class reunion. I don't want to get in the way," she said, a bit disappointed at being offered only third-wheel status. "On second thought," she backtracked, "that sounds fine." The presence of the other priest might keep things lively. "What time?"

"Come by around eleven." When Wallace didn't respond, Lex pushed. "I can tell there's something else on your mind."

"It's nothing," she said, unsure if she was ready to expose her feelings.

"Does this nothing have a name?" Lex asked.

"Mason. But it's not what you think."

"I'm not thinking anything. And, in any event, what *you* think is all that's important."

"I don't know what I think. I've got mixed emotions. I'm afraid he might be complicated."

"Are you sure you're not just still afraid—period?"

"Lex . . . must you always cut straight to the heart of the matter?"

A quiet hum sounded from Wallace's phone.

"You have your phone on? In confession?"

"Sorry, it's my 'Fess Up Online app—in case you had a really long line. I'll see you tomorrow," she said, as she slipped out of the confessional and darted for the side door of the church.

"Wallace Hartman," she whispered into her phone.

"This is David Bosso. It's playtime."

"Where?"

"The F&T on Gorman Street. And listen, it's such an old case and such a weird charge, the fucking magistrate wouldn't give us a no-knock warrant, which means you can't go busting in. So keep in mind that Stacky can be a kitten, but he knows how to play rough too. Don't let your guard down."

SEVENTEEN

After forcing Carla to record the messages, Don had tried without success to extract Matt's location from her. Apparently, she had been telling the truth when she claimed she didn't know where he was. She had been full of other useful information, though, and using that information to plot the capture of the runaway Matt Gable would be almost unfairly easy. The plan required the free use of Carla's house, which meant that anyone who might come looking for her would have to be kept away, but arranging that would be pretty simple.

With Carla bound and drugged and stowed behind the middle row of seats in his rental van, Don made his way to the abandoned subdivision he had discovered on his way into Bayou Sara. He had known, going in, that he would need a place to store Carla for a while, and one of the nearly completed houses in this defunct development—an apparent victim of the 2009 housing crash—would do very nicely. At one point, after he had revealed his name to her, he had wondered whether it might not be better just to kill her, but eventually the logic of his original plan reasserted itself. Her hostage value was simply too great to just toss away. If Gable didn't show up, or if he failed to become sufficiently cooperative, Don could use Carla as a bargaining chip to improve his situation. If Gable *did* show up, and came across with the goods, then Don could pay Carla a final, lethal visit on his way out of the area, and that would be that.

He backed into the driveway of one of the three nearly completed spec houses situated near the back of the little neighborhood.

Don discarded Carla's purse, but he kept her wallet, keys, phone, and all of her other devices—dangerous things to be caught with, but necessary tools for reeling in the big fish.

After a quick shower to refresh himself, he would start the next phase of his plan. Step one would be to send Matt the recordings using Carla's phone. Then he would have to figure out a way to deal with Mason and the detective that Mason was now in league with.

Mason's presence in Baton Rouge was an unwelcome and unforeseen complication. Don's principal reason for copying Echeverría's signature method had been to draw Mason's attention *away* from the true situation, not to draw Mason onto the stage as a player in his own right. And definitely not to draw the man into such close proximity. Mason, by himself, would have been fairly easy to handle because Don knew him so well. Even the local cop, Wallace Hartman, would have been easy to deal with, had it been just her.

But acting and thinking together, they comprised a new entity of unknown capabilities. This, Don recognized, was a very dangerous threat. But, it was also possible that the pair presented some useful opportunities. He still had the detective's card he had found among the junk in Carla's purse. And the fact that Carla's phone showed a call to the detective on Wednesday meant their connection was stronger than Don had assumed. That might prove useful.

Still, Don worried. He had become aware of this new threat only because he was lucky. A sign the gods were on his side. But he knew from long experience as a gambler that those spirits were comically fickle. He would either have to complete his mission or neutralize this new peril before the gods started rooting for the other team.

EIGHTEEN

8:30 P.M.

Stacky Vincent lived on the top floor of the F&T Hotel, a four-story redbrick affair with laundry-laden casement windows and brown-bagged liquor bottles scattered on the sidewalk out front. The place hadn't functioned as a proper hotel in ages. It was now home to a steady trudge of prostitutes, street preachers, and other assorted hustlers. The rest of the neighborhood was crammed with businesses catering to people stuck on the low rungs of the ladder—payday lenders, car title pawn emporiums, and lawyers who specialized in defending the kinds of crimes the area residents specialized in committing.

Wallace and two other officers moved quickly through the hotel lobby. Wallace rode up in the ancient elevator, while the other two, Davis and Blackwell, took the stairs. When the elevator opened on the top floor, Wallace kicked a cleated metal wedge into the door track, jamming the door open.

Stacky's room was at one end of the hall, the stairs were at the other, and the elevator was in between.

Davis and Blackwell emerged from the stairwell and moved

quickly toward Stacky's room. They positioned themselves on either side of the door. Wallace stayed by the elevator.

"Stacky Vincent," Davis called through the door. "This is the police."

A sudden chorus of flushing toilets meant party time for whatever lived in the pipes around the F&T.

"Open the door, Mr. Vincent." Davis pounded the door frame. "We have a warrant for your arrest."

"What for? I haven't done anything," Stacky hollered.

"Open the door, now, Mr. Vincent."

"Okay, okay."

"Open the door, and step into the hall with your fingers laced behind your head."

The door opened and Stacky strode confidently into the hallway. He had long brown hair and a full, neatly trimmed beard—Jesus as an outside linebacker.

"What's this about?" He took in the two officers, then looked toward the elevator and the stairs. He arched one eyebrow and a virile smile tugged at the corners of his mouth as he eyefucked Wallace.

Davis turned Stacky toward the wall and pulled his right hand down to cuff him.

"You're under arrest for the manslaughter of Farrell Macklin," Blackwell intoned. "You have the—"

"Fuck that." Spinning gracefully away from the wall, Stacky pulled Davis into Blackwell's path, sending both officers to the floor in a tangle. He sprinted toward Wallace.

She assumed a low, blocking stance.

Stacky threw his arms above his head and leaned back into a feet-first home-base slide, aiming for the stairwell behind her.

Wallace dropped, knees first, straddling and trapping him as he slid on his back beneath her. Her weight stopped his slide just as the point of his chin came to rest firmly against her pubic bone.

A suggestive smirk started spreading across his face until Wallace two-handed her 9mm into his line of vision.

"Don't even think it."

9:05 P.M.

The sound of Mason's phone yanked him from his slumber. He had fallen asleep watching the videos. He hated falling asleep when it was daylight, then waking up after dark. It left him feeling disjointed and unable to concentrate.

"It's me," Wallace said, cringing because she couldn't help thinking she sounded like a girlfriend.

"What's up?" he asked, trying to clear the fog from his head.

"We just hauled in Stacky Vincent. They're booking him as we speak. After that, we'll start the interrogation. If you still want in on it, I'll need to come get you, now."

"I'll be waiting out front," he said.

9:30 P.M.

Traffic was heavy and it was taking Don much longer than expected to drive from the dump he was staying in to Mason's much nicer accommodations. He had been calling Mason's room periodically, as he drove, but each time the call went to voicemail. If he got no answer after a few more tries, he would assume Mason was out. At that point, he would find a parking spot with a clear sight line to the front door of the hotel and wait for the boss man to return.

NINETEEN

Matt was almost to Lake Charles when one of his increasingly frequent bouts of anxiety took control. He pulled over at the first truck stop he came to and drove to the rear of the lot. He closed his eyes and breathed deeply, trying to calm down. His encounter with the red-haired man at the motel had rattled him more than he wanted to admit. The sense of dread had ratcheted up even further once he'd been able to work out the problem with his cloud storage provider and was able to view the video from the cameras outside his house. There was the red-haired man, big as day, lock-picking his way into the kitchen, right before the fire started. *Who was he?*

Maybe the fine folks at Tunica thought Matt was sharing their research secrets and the red-haired man was some sort of operative trying to put a stop to that. That might explain why the man was operating alone. But it wouldn't explain all the heavy-handed tactics.

Matt supposed his pursuer could be some sort of lawman, but it wouldn't make sense for the local police to devote this kind of effort to looking for him. They were overwhelmed with an endless flow of missing person cases, on top of the countless other demands on their time and resources. And even if the red-haired man was *with* the government, he didn't seem to be acting *for* the government. Government agents, acting under cover of legal authority, usually traveled in pairs and showed badges when trying to apprehend someone. Skulking around motels, waving guns, and threatening to hurt people didn't fit their MO.

The idea that the man might be a rogue agent was especially troubling, because such a person would have government-grade capabilities without the limitations that went along with government accountability.

It was that possibility, and that possibility alone, that convinced Matt to turn on his regular cell phone—something he had not done since the night he watched his house burn. A determined pursuer would be able to locate Matt from his phone use, but it was a risk he had to take. Plus, it was a risk that was easily managed. With such a relentless person on his tail, Matt needed every edge he could get. After all, the man had found Matt's house, so it was conceivable that he also knew about Carla. If the man had paid her a visit, perhaps she could shed some light on the man's identity.

As he listened to his voicemail, his mood went from bad to worse. Carla's earliest messages, from four nights ago, had been flirtatious. But after that they had progressed from concerned, to worried, to frightened. The ones she had left over the last few hours were beyond disturbing. It occurred to him that the red-haired man might be behind the messages. The man's presence at the warehouse meant he had become aware of Overman, so the fact that he was also dogging Matt's trail meant he had figured out the connection between Matt and Overman and possibly Carla too. How had the bastard gotten so far? And how much did he know, or think he knew? Not even Overman knew everything, because Matt hadn't told *anyone* everything.

He walked over to the truck fueling area and pretended to talk on his phone, as he listened to the truckers chat among themselves. Several were headed to points east or north. One of the northbound truckers finished fueling and pulled his rig into the parking area. When he headed into the truck stop, Matt taped his phone to the undercarriage of the man's trailer, then got back in his car and resumed his westbound route. He would find a room in Sulphur, the little town west of Lake Charles, and then start fresh in the morning.

TWENTY

The interrogation rooms were intended to induce a sense of isolation and helplessness. Wallace wondered what course in school taught architects how to design such dispiriting spaces. Stacky sat on a metal stool that was bolted to the floor, his hands cuffed to a steel ring in the center of a metal table. When she and Mason walked in, Stacky's gaze remained fixed on the table. Most people in his situation looked up when someone came in, with a trace of guarded hope on their faces. But not this guy. He wasn't feigning interest in his cuticles, or dozing, and he didn't appear to be praying. He just wasn't looking up.

Like all interrogations, this one would involve a delicate give and take, with Stacky doing most of the giving. Wallace knew she would have to strike the perfect balance between hope and despair. She would need to ignite a spark of optimism and use Stacky's cooperation to fan that spark. And she would have to use any failure to cooperate to make him fear that his dignity and emotional defenses were about to be publicly taken down. A subject's sense of distress always escalated dramatically when the interrogator and the subject were not the same gender, and Wallace intended to use this fact to her full advantage.

"Mr. Vincent . . ." Wallace began, then stopped. The slimy smirk he'd had at their initial point of contact had returned.

"Detective Hartman. Back already? We're spending so much time together, lately, people are gonna start thinking we're a couple. Grab you a chair. I'd offer you my lap but you can see I'm kinda tied up at the moment."

"What's with your little bad-boy attitude, Stacky? I don't get it."

"Oh, I think you get it. You're a good-looking woman, Detective. I think you get it whenever you want it. Is that what you're here for, stud?" Stacky shot Mason a conspiratorial wink.

"You're in serious trouble," Wallace said, slamming her palms down hard on the table, getting nose-to-nose with Stacky. "That upstanding citizen you killed? Farrell Macklin? He was related to a cop."

"If you're gonna talk like that, I'll want a lawyer."

"Play it that way and there's no room to wheel and deal. Just you against the machine," she said, trotting out the standard opening gambit.

"On a bullshit charge. I'll take my chances. Get me my lawyer."

"It'll still take time and money to grind through the system."

"That's why God created bail. Lawyer, please."

"How long will this take?" Mason asked. "I'll want to start the transfer to federal custody."

"That's largely up to Mr. Vincent."

"Federal custody?" Stacky asked. "You guys make this shit up as you go along?"

"Are you familiar with the RICO statute?" Mason asked.

"I'm familiar with my fucking right to counsel," Stacky blasted. "I'm familiar with the fact that I've asked for him three times now, but it seems he's not being summoned to my defense."

"Do you have a lawyer, or will you need a public defender?" Wallace asked.

"I got my own. I'm ready for my phone call, Detective."

Wallace had a duty officer escort Stacky to the telephone, then she left Mason in the interview room while she wound her way through the old building to the detective section. She took a few minutes to check messages and look for any new forensics that might have come in on Overman. She found a note from Mike Harrison stating that the former Tunica scientist who had originally ordered the osmosis bags had ended up not needing them, and that he hadn't taken them when he left Tunica. By the time she got back, Mason was pacing in the hallway. She showed Mason Mike's note, then looked into the interrogation room.

Stacky was back at the table, chatting with his lawyer, Hamilton Hines, also known as Hambone, because of his accomplished courtroom theatrics. From time to time, Hambone had been known to address his arguments and his questions to the spectators in the courtroom, instead of the jury. Occasionally he would sustain his own objections, if he thought the judge wasn't going to. And once, he had even brought his own gavel, in his briefcase, and banged it on the table, demanding order in the court, when the prosecutor started to make an argument he didn't want the jury to hear.

But, on a more substantive level, Hambone was every prosecutor's nightmare. He had mastered the playbook for both teams. He was a career criminal lawyer who started out as an assistant DA, then eventually got himself appointed U.S. Attorney. After that, he went into private practice as a defense lawyer. With his pasty-white complexion, his chronic halitosis, and a hair transplant that looked more like a tree farm than a hairstyle, he didn't cut an imposing figure, but he couldn't be intimidated and very few ever got the better of him.

Wallace knocked on the door and stuck her head in. "What'll it be, Counselor?"

"I've explained to my client that while this whole charade is most likely a great big steaming pile of you know what, it is, technically at least, a prosecutable offense. That being the case, it never hurts to have an Officer Friendly to speak on one's behalf, at the right time and place."

"Does that mean he's willing to answer some questions?"

"Under certain conditions."

"And what would those be?"

"You need to clear up some issues for me, first. Am I correct that your questions won't really have anything to do with the unfortunate demise of Mr. Farrell Macklin?"

"Off the record?" Wallace asked.

"Off the record."

"Macklin is not my immediate concern."

"Then Macklin is leverage for something else. Assuming as much, I've advised my client accordingly. So let me be clear. Whatever it is we're gathered here to discuss, it will not involve my client becoming an asset of this department. And this . . . whatever it is you're up to," he said, waving his hands dramatically, "it cannot involve him admitting, directly or by implication, to the commission of any other offenses that would leave him vulnerable to enhanced sentencing under the habitual offender statutes. Are we in agreement on these basic ground rules?"

"I think we can do business," Wallace said.

"Does that mean you agree to my conditions, Detective?"

"Assuming your client is truthful and forthcoming, I agree. With one stipulation. If, after tonight, I find that we need more information about the specific matters we're about to discuss, I'll expect your client to pony up."

"As long as he doesn't become a regular informant on an open-ended basis."

"Do I need to read you your Miranda warnings, Mr. Vincent, or will you waive Miranda?"

"We don't waive Miranda," Hambone said.

Wallace activated the room's recording equipment, introduced Mason, then read the Miranda warnings from a card she carried with her. After that, she and Mason spent the next few minutes explaining what they were looking for.

Despite his earlier displays of irreverence, under Hambone's watchful eye Stacky's demeanor gradually improved, and he grudgingly fell into the spirit of the interrogation.

"Listen, Ronnie didn't tell *anybody* everything," Stacky said. "For sure, not me. I was just one of a number of guys that drove him around."

"Did you drive him to the warehouse that day?"

"I drove him close. He had his own ways of getting from the car to the actual place—something that he kept to himself, for obvious reasons."

"What did he talk about on the way over there?"

"Nothing. Jimmy, one of his guns, sat in front with me, and Ronnie sat in the back with Luke, his other meathead, and one of his girls. Celeste, I think's her name."

"Did you know the name of the person he was meeting?"

"Nope."

"Ever lay eyes on him?" Wallace asked.

"I didn't know who he was meeting. How the fuck would I know if I'd ever seen him?"

"Ever seen this guy?" Wallace showed Stacky the picture of Matt on her phone.

He studied the image carefully. "No ma'am. You think that's who did Ronnie?"

"Let's get back to who Ronnie was meeting at the warehouse," Wallace said. "Do you know if he met with that particular person before?"

"That was the word."

"Always at the warehouse?"

"Don't know." He shrugged.

"What do you know about how they got connected in the first place?"

"He made a small buy from one of Ronnie's street dealers. Came back, said he wanted some more—a lot more. But he wanted to deal with the next guy up the ladder, because he didn't want the shit getting stepped on and he didn't want to keep paying retail."

"Wouldn't most dealers think he was a cop, at that point?" Mason asked.

"No cop would be dumb enough to be that obvious," Stacky said.

Hambone did a slow, God-deliver-me headshake.

"How many times did he try that routine?" Wallace prodded.

"He must've come back four or five times. Always bought a little more, always looking to go big—deal with the wholesaler."

"You got any names for the street dealers this new guy was buying from?" Wallace asked.

"Don't know, don't wanna know, wouldn't tell you if I did know. I'd be better off inside than free on the street after coughing up a name like that."

Wallace sensed it was a line Stacky wouldn't cross so she moved on. "This new guy, his plan to deal with people higher up the chain, it apparently worked," Wallace said.

"So it would seem," Stacky replied.

"Did he make the big buy?"

"Turns out, he wasn't a buyer after all. When he finally got his shot with the wholesaler, they roughed him up pretty good, looking for a wire, making sure it wasn't a setup. "

"Why check for a wire?" Mason asked. "You just said they were satisfied he wasn't a cop."

"Because cops aren't the only fuckers that use listening devices." Stacky paused. "Anyway, as I was saying, they didn't find a wire. What they found was this dude had brung a fair amount of shit with him. Said he wanted to make a donation. A good faith kinda thing. If they liked it, he could arrange for more."

"But not for free."

"Nooooooo. Definitely not for free. But he claimed he could keep delivering at a much better price than Ronnie was paying for what-ever he was moving at the moment."

"Did Ronnie go for it?" Wallace asked.

"At first he thought it was a trap—his own suppliers testing him to see if he was willing to get in bed with another outfit."

"But he eventually went for it," she said

"For all the good it did him."

"What made him decide it wasn't a trap?" Mason asked.

"Hard to say," Stacky mumbled, after a momentary hesitation. "But I can tell you this—the shit that little fuck was peddling was quite a bit more than a cut above what was coming up from Mexico. Anyway, at some point, Ronnie quit worrying this new guy was setting him up."

"But it appears that's exactly what happened," Mason said.

"My client didn't see what happened," Hambone pointed out.

"What do you *think* happened?" Wallace asked, sitting on the edge of the table and looking down at Stacky.

"Look, it's a dangerous game. Everybody's your enemy. You only last as long as you can outsmart all the motherfuckers that want to shove your ass in the ditch."

"Do you know who did it?" Mason asked.

"I just told you—" Hambone began.

"You just told us that he didn't *see* who did it. That's not the same as he doesn't *know* who did it," Mason said, cutting him off. "Was it an insider—one of Overman's own people?"

"I don't think so. But I do know that the big guys in Ronnie's crew, they didn't want him touching it. They couldn't figure it out, and it scared 'em. For a while, everybody got the impression he was leav-ing it alone, but he obviously went ahead and did it anyway."

"How many buys did he make from this new guy?"

"Several, I think. But like I say, I wasn't his only driver. I didn't know every move he made."

"Ronnie's usual supply, plus what he was getting from this new guy, that meant there was a lot of extra product on the street," Mason said. "Was Ronnie moving all of it, or were there people that Ronnie and his crew didn't know who were getting in on the new stuff?"

"As far as I know, Ronnie was moving it all. If outsiders were coming in, there'd be bodies stacking up by now. But remember, I wasn't involved in that business. I pressed a gas pedal. I pressed a brake pedal. I turned a steering wheel."

"Let's go back to these get-togethers between Ronnie and this new supplier. You only knew that the meetings took place after the fact?" Mason asked.

"Whenever he showed back up with the merchandise, that's how they'd know."

"Did anybody ever wonder where some nobody off the street could come up with so much good stuff at such a good price?" Wallace asked.

"Didn't I just say that Ronnie's guys, they couldn't figure it out? So, obviously, somebody'd been wondering about it. Two of Ronnie's best people, guys he brought up in the business, they decided they were gonna follow this fucker and see where he got the stuff, but they couldn't do it. Nobody could figure out when or where Ronnie was gonna meet the guy, so they could never get set up on him."

"You just said you drove him close to the warehouse for his last meeting? Wouldn't *you* have known that he was going to meet his new supplier?" Wallace asked.

"Don't you people listen?" Stacky said, raising his voice. "I just fucking said nobody knew when it was gonna happen. All I knew was Ronnie wanted to go from point A to point B."

"Did he have a cover story?" Wallace asked. "Like would he say he was going to church or to the opera, but he would go meet this new supplier instead?"

"Ronnie was into a lot of things. Whenever he was out in the daytime, with one of his women, it was a pretty good bet he was taking her to make a video. The studios where they make that shit tend to move around a lot. So, when he and Celeste got out of the car, we just assumed she was going for a, uh, screen test." Stacky used his cuffed hands to put air quotes around screen test.

"He was making porn?" Wallace asked.

"He was making money. Every way he could."

"We should have a chat with this young lady," Wallace said to Mason. "Maybe she can account for Overman's movements between the time they got out of the car and the time they got to the warehouse. Maybe she was there, and she could ID the guy."

"She can't help you," Stacky offered.

"Why not?" Wallace asked.

"She's already been asked all those questions. By people who know how to get answers. Trust me, she don't know shit."

"If his own people didn't know where he would be meeting this guy, how do you think the killer knew where he would be?" Mason asked.

"That's actually a damn good question. My first thought was that this new supplier was a scout, from a potential competitor, using the coke as bait. And once Ronnie let his guard down, he killed him."

"But?"

"Too complicated. Too many meetings. Too much could go wrong. Besides, if that was the play, once Ronnie was down, the new guy's people would be moving in at the top."

"Has there been any kind of overt move by someone to take Ronnie's place?" Mason asked.

"A little tussling on the inside, but nothing's settled."

"Nobody trying to move in from the outside?" Mason pressed.

"You'd be up to your ass in autopsies, if that was happening."

"Could someone outside his organization have gotten familiar enough with Overman's routine to follow him?" Mason asked, abruptly changing direction.

"Possible, but very risky. Slip up and get caught, and it's gonna be a bad day at black rock. Plus, Ronnie was hard to keep up with. A few a y'all's undercovers kept a decent watch on him, but watching places he hangs out ain't the same as sticking with him, move for move."

"So, where do you think this new supply was coming from?" Wallace asked.

"Law enforcement. Evidence inventories. I figure this new guy, whoever he was, he was fronting for a group of cops who were systematically looting every sizable drug seizure they could get their greedy little fingers on. How hard could that be?"

"Harder than you might think," Mason offered. "That's not to say it couldn't be done. But there's no central registry where the inventory for all the evidence facilities is listed."

"You ever heard of social media, Mr. DEA? Everything can be organized. There are totally private versions of all those kind of websites, devoted to things you just would not believe. Trust me, it could be done." Stacky paused a moment. "Tell me something, Detective."

"What's that?"

"Why are you two so fired up about this? In your eyes, Ronnie was just trash. You're probably glad somebody got rid of him."

"I'm a homicide detective. If this killing was an early skirmish in a turf war, there will be more homicides. The best source for whether that's happening is the killer himself."

"Well, if I knew who it was, I'd probably tell you. Ronnie was pretty good to me."

"Has this guy turned up again, since Ronnie's been out of the picture?" Wallace asked.

"Not that I know of."

"A minute ago, you said your *first* thought was that the killer knew where Ronnie would be because the new supplier was the killer, and it was a planned meeting. What was your second thought?" Mason asked.

"That the killer didn't follow Ronnie. He followed the other guy—this new supplier."

"That's interesting. Please, go on," Wallace encouraged.

"Think about it. This new guy was either trying to take Ronnie's territory or trying to supply it. And since there's no sign he's trying to *take* it, the supply angle's looking good. But for that to work, the supplier needed Ronnie alive."

"So the killer had to be someone else," Mason said.

"Bingo."

"So who would be tracking the new supplier?" Wallace asked.

"Somebody who noticed a solo operator toting a shitload of powder one way and a shitload of cash the other. And there's a million ways that could happen. The street sees a lot, and you won't always know when it's looking at you."

"But why would the killer follow this supplier into the warehouse?" Mason asked. "That seems too dangerous. Why not take him on safer ground?"

"Maybe the killer wanted to step into this new supplier's shoes. For that, he'd need to know who was on the other end of the deal. So he sneaks inside to see who's who."

"But if Ronnie was an important piece of the enterprise, why turn around and kill him?" Wallace asked.

"These situations tend to be unstable. It doesn't take much to spark off some serious shit. Somebody shows up unannounced and things come unglued. Everybody thinks the other guy set 'em up. Guns come out. Somebody starts hosing the place down with a Mac-10 and it's anybody's guess after that."

"You think Overman was just collateral damage? Caught in the crossfire?"

"That's the only thing that makes complete sense to me at this point in time."

"Excuse us a minute," Wallace said, steering Mason toward the door.

Gone were the days of one-way mirrors. Now, video cameras linked interrogation rooms to a bank of monitors in a single observation room. Wallace and Mason stood in front of the screen that showed Stacky and Hambone.

"If the new supplier was the killer's target, that supports our idea that there were at least three people in the warehouse," Wallace began. "And the motorcycle in the woods tells us the new supplier almost certainly has to be Matt Gable."

"But now we have to assume they weren't all there at the same time," Mason said. "The killer must've showed up after the money and drugs had changed hands and Matt was already gone—gone on a crotch rocket—otherwise we'd have found him dead in the warehouse, along with Overman."

"And the killer decides that if he can only have one—Ronnie or the new supplier—the new supplier is worth more. So he wrings information about the new supplier out of Ronnie, then kills him." Wallace flopped into one of the chairs and stared at the ceiling.

"If we could just figure out where Matt was getting his merchandise," Mason said.

"What about Stacky's evidence-locker theory? He said this new stuff was better than what was coming from Echeverría. If Matt was fronting for a group that was getting high grade goods to begin with, and getting it free, from police inventory, they could afford to pretty it up a bit to get a competitive advantage. In comes our good friend Matt Gable, the chemist."

"Something about that doesn't feel kosher, but I can't say it's not what's happening."

"Can you see a downside to telling Stacky how Ronnie Overman died?" she asked, changing direction.

"Is there an upside?"

"His whole perception is based on it being accidental. If he knew the truth, things might look different to him. He might have an idea about who could do such a thing."

"It's worth a gamble." He started toward the hallway, but Wallace stayed in the observation room, still staring at the ceiling. "You having second thoughts?" he asked.

"Just sifting back through everything. Something's there, I just can't get it to gel." She pushed up out of the chair and moved toward the door, then stopped, her attention held by a monitor showing one of the other rooms.

Mason followed her gaze.

"See the man on the hot seat?" she said, pointing at the monitor. "That's Arthur Staples, the man who found Overman in the warehouse."

Staples's hands rested free on the table. A bandage covered two fingers on his left hand. "Should we pay him a visit?" Mason asked.

"After we're done with our guest of honor."

"Just for the sake of conversation, let's say your theory is correct, that the killer wanted to step into the shoes of this new supplier," Wallace said, after she and Mason had rejoined Stacky and Hambone. "If he succeeded, how would he stay connected to the source of the new supplier's merchandise?"

"Maybe the killer *was* the source. Once he and his buddies got the goods out of evidence, they'd need to hook up to a distribution system—a *very* dangerous maneuver. So, they have this guy, the one we've been calling the new supplier, they have him take that risk and make the connection. Once that's done, they decide they'll get rid of him and deal with Ronnie directly. But the deal blows up and Ronnie ends up getting shot, instead."

"We don't currently assign a high probability to that scenario," Mason replied.

"Why's that?" Stacky asked.

"Ronnie's cause of death would seem to indicate otherwise," Wallace said, resuming her seat on the edge of the table.

"I'm not followin'," Stacky said, with a puzzled look.

"You're not about to inform my client that he's a suspect in the Ronnie Overman homicide, are you?" Hambone asked.

"Should I?" Wallace asked.

"Don't waste your time. He's alibied. Airtight."

"Do you know how Overman was killed?" Wallace asked, returning her attention to Stacky.

"I just assumed he was shot. But now that I think about it, it was never specifically reported in the news so no, I guess I don't really know."

"It was nothing so quick as a stray bullet," Wallace said. "His fingertips were crushed with pliers, then somebody slit open his abdomen and sewed a live snake inside."

"Motherfuck," Stacky hissed. He jerked back, his eyes rimmed white like a frightened horse.

"The killer was after information and wanted it very badly," Wallace continued. "If the new supplier worked for the killer, the killer would already know the supplier's identity and wouldn't need to torture it out of anyone. No, the killer had to be after something else."

"Think, Stacky. This is the important part. Who could do something like this?" Mason asked.

"Motherfuck," Stacky repeated, shaking his head in disbelief. He slumped forward, resting his head on his hands. "I don't fucking know. Somebody who knew what they were doing. This had to be a pro job. Maybe it *was* an inside job."

"Think hard," Mason pressed. "What could the killer possibly want to know so badly?"

"I swear to God I don't—"

Something clicked in Wallace's head and she interrupted. "What made Ronnie stop thinking his regular suppliers were no longer trying to trap him?" Wallace asked, in a quiet voice, derailing Mason's line of questioning.

Mason shot her an irritated look. He opened his mouth to re-ask his question, but Stacky's sudden turn toward Hambone stopped him.

"Hey. I'm talking to you." Wallace raised her voice, getting up in Stacky's face.

"My client obviously wishes not to answer that question," the lawyer intoned.

Sensing pay dirt, she tried again. "What made Ronnie think his higher-ups didn't give a shit if this new supplier stepped into the picture?"

"Detective Hartman," Hambone blared, rocketing from his chair and extending a hand in her direction.

Wallace shrugged out of reach. "Come on, Stacky. If it looks bad, I'll give you immunity."

"Bullshit," Hambone yelled. "Stay quiet, Stacky. She can't offer you immunity. Only the prosecutor can do that and she knows it." He rounded on Wallace. "I can't believe you're pimping my client like this, with me right here telling you not to."

"It's money, isn't it?" she said, ignoring the outburst. "Ronnie was a businessman. He wasn't going to risk everything for a few more bucks, not even quite a few more bucks, unless he had the boss's blessing—which he evidently got. For a price. Am I close?"

"Stacky, not a word," Hambone barked.

Wallace turned to Mason. A sense of calm settled over her in the wake of her flash of insight. "Ronnie's higher-ups were okay with him peddling the new guy's product as long as they got their cut."

"How does that threaten *him*?" Mason pointed at Stacky.

"Perhaps you'd like to take over as counsel for my client," Hambone gibed.

"You are way too plugged in for being just a driver, Mr. Vincent." Wallace circled the table and stood next to Stacky, bending to speak into his ear. "But then you weren't driving just *people*, were you? You were driving the money. Handing it off to the bigger fish up the line. Is that what's got you so tongue-tied?"

"Don't answer that, Stacky," Hambone said. "No more questions."

"Is that all you're worried about?" Mason asked. "Getting pinned as a money runner?"

"Speaking entirely hypothetically, the knowing transportation of anything of value in furtherance of a criminal enterprise is itself a crime. In fact, it's a felony if the underlying crime was a felony," Hambone lectured. "And if the enterprise happens to cross a state line, it becomes a separately prosecutable *federal* felony. So, if you think my client's gonna stick his dick into a trap like that, on the off chance you might soft-pedal this bullshit manslaughter charge, please feel free to think again."

"Look, this has been fun and all, but I've been about as useful as I believe I can be," Stacky said. "When are you nice people gonna let me out of here?"

"Some other folks have questions about other cases, first," Wallace said.

"What?"

"After that, you're out as soon as you make bail or the DA decides not to prosecute."

"You're fucking kidding me."

"Be helpful and maybe the DA will recommend low bail."

"We don't want that," Hambone said. "I want my client bonded out the regular way and I want your people to argue hard for something substantial," he said, woodpeckering a fingertip on the tabletop.

"Goddamn," Stacky shouted. "Whose side are you on, you fuckin'—"

"I'm saving your ass, big boy. You waltz outta here smelling like a deal, your people are gonna think you bought your way out by talking pretty with the police lady. Next thing you know, they're feeding you feet-first through a wood chipper."

"Just remember," Wallace said, getting up in Stacky's face again. "When I come calling . . . you be ready with a story to tell or I'll reel you back in."

"This way," Wallace said, as soon as they were in the hallway. "Arthur Staples. Remember?"

"Right," Mason said, hanging back.

Wallace was visibly excited. "We still don't know who killed Overman, but I think we know who didn't. Echeverría was getting his cut from whatever Matt was pushing, so he would have no motive to kill Overman."

"You should have let me know you were going to cut me off like that."

A startled look flashed across her face. She had expected a thank-you, not a slap, for solving the Echeverría riddle. "I didn't know I was going to. Everything just suddenly fell into place."

"Well . . . it seemed a bit calculated."

"Well . . . it wasn't," she insisted.

"I looked like a stooge in there, five steps behind everyone else in the room." He gave her a wry look, hands in his pockets.

"Mason, please. We're starting to sound like an old married couple." His flinty expression told her that her breezy manner wasn't going to defuse his annoyance. She leaned back against the wall, exhausted but still keyed up from the interrogation. "Okay, look. Do you remember when we were sitting in the woods, babysitting Matt's motorcycle?"

"I remember," he said, rocking lazily from the balls of his feet to his heels.

"And David Bosso walked us through how Stacky got hooked up with Overman by doing Overman a favor—something Overman didn't want any of his regulars to see?"

They resumed walking toward the room with Arthur Staples.

"That was years ago."

"The point is, it meant that even way back then he trusted Stacky. So, once it clicked that Stacky knew more than someone who was just a chauffeur would know, things . . . you know."

Mason shook his head and gave her a grudging smile. "Damn. Nicely done."

"Thank you," she said, blushing at his compliment. "One more thing. I think we can eliminate Stacky's evidence-locker theory as the source of the new supply."

"Why's that?"

"Those cocaine inventories are all over the country. For a supply that spread out to have the effect your analysts saw right here, it would all have to be shipped here and sold here. It makes more sense to just sell it back into the markets it was seized from."

They stopped outside the room Staples was in.

"For all the good I've done, I could have stayed in DC and just faxed you my list of questions," Mason said.

"Don't be so modest. If it weren't for you—"

"If it weren't for you, I wouldn't have an officer in the hospital, getting his goddamn brains put back together."

Wallace and Mason turned back toward the voice. It was Wallace's boss, Chief of Detectives Jason Burley, coming up the hall behind them. He positioned himself between Wallace and the door to the interrogation room. His face had fresh bed creases, he looked hastily dressed, and his stony glare darted back and forth between Wallace and Mason.

"What is Arthur Staples doing in there?" Wallace asked, springing up on her toes to look over Burley's shoulder into the room.

Staples was still sitting at the table. His clothes were torn, but other than the bandage on his fingers, he appeared to be in good shape. He turned at the sound of Wallace's voice, giving her his trademark dead-faced stare.

Burley folded his arms across his chest. "Where is your partner, Detective Hartman? Not your hotshot DEA buddy here, your partner—the one I put you with?"

"How should I know? Every time—"

"He's your partner. That's how," he bellowed.

"It's the middle of the night," Wallace protested. "We're partners. We don't live together."

"Don't you get a smart mouth with me. *You're* here, in the middle of the night. Your *partner* should be in on this, unless there's a damn good reason otherwise. It is never 'how should I know,' while you're out squiring around—"

"I'm not squiring around anybody. We've been—"

"*I know* where you've been. Do you know where your partner's been?"

Wallace started to speak. Her face crumpled when the answer hit her. "I told him to research Staples. I never said to tail him."

"Did you tell him not to? Did you?"

"What happened?" She shouldered past Burley into the room with Staples.

"He beat Mike Harrison into a coma," Burley shouted after her. "That's what happened."

Wallace turned to look at Burley, as her stomach dropped. "Oh, God. Is he going to be okay?"

"Too soon to tell." He closed his eyes and took a deep breath.

"Where did they take him?"

"Your sudden, but belated concern is commendable, but it doesn't erase the fact that this should never have happened."

"I'm not trying to erase anything," Wallace said, her voice rising. "I just want to know where he is."

"General. He's in surgery and, from there . . ." Burley pursed his lips and shook his head.

"Mr. Staples," she said, sitting in the chair across from him. "Look, I know you and I got off to a rocky start, but I'm not your enemy. Let me help you."

Staples remained mute, no longer even looking at Wallace, so she walked out of the room and pulled the door closed behind her.

"Your partner was prowling around behind the Staples residence, alone, in street clothes," Burley said. "Staples thought he was a burglar. Decided to teach him a lesson."

Wallace could feel herself getting ready to explode. "I don't understand why you even brought him here," she said, pointing back at Staples, her voice rising. "Any of us would have done what he did. And since when is it okay for a plainclothes to be lurking around a private residence alone at night?"

"Exactly," Burley said, throwing his arms up. "How is it you didn't know Mike was gonna pull a stunt like that?"

"Because the partner you put me with won't return my calls, he misses meetings, he makes a point of being here only when I'm not." When it looked as if Burley was going to argue the point, Wallace cut him off. "Mike's not a rookie. He knew better than to do what he did. I've had him driving a desk because that's where he belonged." She looked back toward the interrogation room.

"Three o'clock, Hartman. By three o'clock tomorrow, you make sure everything you got on this investigation is in the books. After that, you stand down."

"You're taking me off the case?" She moved away from Mason and stepped into Burley's personal space. "Are you kidding me?"

"Mike was new to detectives. You should have supervised him better," Burley said, looking down his nose at Wallace.

"Don't tell me I didn't do my job. I gave him what he could

handle. Things he needed to learn. He wasn't ready to be back on the line."

"Maybe you shouldn't have been so quick to make up your mind on that point."

"I don't think that was the problem here." She stepped back and folded her arms across her chest.

"Enough from you," Burley said, his eyes slitted and his right hand came up like a stop sign. "Consider yourself lucky I don't initiate a disciplinary action. Three o'clock. You be in my office, ready to answer questions from the new team."

11:00 P.M.

Wallace and Mason exited the building, Wallace silently fuming as they made their way toward her car until she couldn't hold in her rage anymore.

"Burley knows this wasn't my fault. He knew Mike was a loose cannon when he gave him to me, he just doesn't want to admit it because it would put his own ass on the line." She stopped, hugging her arms around her body and stared at the ground. After a few seconds she looked up at Mason. "Sorry you had to see that."

"Don't be. Until now, I was starting to think of you as a real pushover." He gave her a look of such bemused admiration that she burst out laughing.

"Stop doing that," she said.

"Doing what?"

"That. That goofy look you have whenever something intense happens. That's the second time today. I'm a serious detective."

"You're right," he chuckled. "It's unseemly for you to go around . . . laughing like that."

"So, where does all this leave you?" she asked, once she regained her composure.

"Back to Washington. I'm satisfied that Echeverría wasn't the mastermind behind this, even though Stacky wouldn't come right out and say he was running the money."

"I'm happy to introduce you to whoever this case gets handed off to," she said.

"Actually, I think I've got what I came for. Since Overman's dealers are moving all the new stuff and Echeverría didn't kill him, the whole idea of a cartel war gets pretty wobbly. First thing in the morning, I'll cancel the meetings I had with the sheriff's investigators and the FBI."

"Shall I drop you at your hotel, then?" she asked, looking down, scuffing the toe of her boot against the asphalt.

"Alright," he said after several seconds of silence. "I had hoped to do a little sightseeing, before I went back to DC. But it's so late. Another time?" he asked, studying her face.

"There are things to be seen, even at this hour."

"Really?"

"Yes, really." She felt like a teenager asking for a first date, and his decision to pack up and leave was making her feel untethered. They had quickly fallen into the kind of easy, almost playful give-and-take that made it feel as if they had known each other for ages. It had the feel of something familiar and important, and she wasn't ready for it to be over.

"Have you had dinner?" she asked.

"So long ago I'm starving again. Do you think that place we went to yesterday is still open?"

"I have a better idea," she said. Her phone buzzed. "It's Chief Whitlock. Wallace Hartman," she answered, and stopped walking. "That is strange. Anything we can act on?" She listened for a while longer, then ended the call.

"What was that?" Mason asked.

"Matt Gable's phone lit up for a couple of minutes, went dark for a while, and then lit up again, moving steadily northeast from a point somewhere near Lake Charles."

"Can we have him picked up?" Mason asked, excitedly.

"The phone's been recovered, but Matt wasn't with it. Whitlock got the State Police to home in on it, and they found it duct-taped to the underside of a long-haul truck. But then, why do I care? It's not my case anymore."

TWENTY-ONE

11:05 P.M.

I thought your car was in the lot over there," Mason said, pointing in the direction where they had left her cruiser.

"That's my official ride. My personal vehicle is over here."

They walked without speaking until they arrived at a restored late sixties Oldsmobile convertible. "Hop in." She slid behind the wheel and started the car. "Let's go celebrate my humiliation while the wound is still fresh."

"And where will this celebration take place?" he asked, easing into the passenger seat.

"The Bridge City Diner. It's not far." She lowered the top, then pulled out of the parking deck, heading west toward the river.

"Cop hangout?"

"Nope. You wanted to see the sights, remember? We're going where the locals go. When I was a kid we'd go for lunch on Sundays. After ten it turns into a blues club."

"Sad music? In your condition?"

"My cousin Jeff is playing tonight. He's worth the risk."

"Just him, or does he have a band?"

"The Closet Kings. They're all straight sons of gay parents who came out at a time when that was more difficult. They see the name of the band as a salute to their parents' courage." Wallace looked over at him to gauge his reaction. "My mother's brother is gay," she injected into the momentary silence. "In case you're wondering. Which I know you were."

"How do you know I was wondering?"

"Because everybody always does. Even today."

"So, what instrument does he play? Your cousin, I mean. Not your gay uncle. In case you're wondering. Which I know you were."

She smiled at his wordplay. "Guitar and piano."

They rode quietly for the next few minutes, then she pulled into a spot right in front of the diner. The restaurant was near the Mississippi River, about a mile south of the mammoth bridge that spanned the giant waterway.

They took one of the few remaining tables. Within seconds two male hands landed on Wallace's shoulders from behind and a ponytailed head of blond hair moved in alongside her right ear.

"I couldn't help noticing that you're not noticing me."

"Only because first cousins are still against the law—even in Louisiana," Wallace replied dreamily, tilting her head to accept a kiss on the cheek.

"So who's this man at the table with you? He looks like the fuzz."

"He is. A big-time federal something or other." Wallace introduced Jeff to Mason, and they chatted for a few minutes. When a waiter arrived to take their dinner orders, Jeff excused himself and headed for the stage.

After a few drumbeats to set the rhythm, the band launched into a slow, heavy, slit-your-wrist blues number. A throaty harmonica dragged in the bass and, after several bars, the rest of the players moved in one at a time.

"They're good," Mason said.

"Mmm," Wallace nodded, letting herself get carried into the music. When she glanced over at Mason, his eyes were closed and his head moved gently with the melody.

By her count they had already had four fights and then made up four times in the thirty-six hours he had been in Baton Rouge. And twice in one day he had pulled her out of herself and made her laugh when she had felt like murdering someone instead. Twice. In one day.

It had been a long time since anyone had so handily and expertly defused her anger and it felt good. Wonderful, in fact. He hadn't passed judgment on her wrath. He had just been there, pointing out the shortest route to safer ground. It occurred to her that people didn't do things like that for people they didn't know well or care about.

Once their food arrived, brief bursts of chatter about the case alternated with stretches of companionable silence as they ate and listened to the band play a blistering rendition of Kenny Wayne Shepherd's "Blue on Black"—one of Wallace's favorites.

"Now that we've had time to catch our breath, tell me—what's your story?" Wallace asked, after the meal was done.

"Sad music *and* a dull story. You're a glutton for punishment. Well . . . let's see . . . I've been doing this drug policy gig with the government since . . . what?" he asked, when he noticed Wallace trying to suppress an impish smile.

"Oh, nothing. This is fascinating." She propped one elbow on the table and rested her chin on her upturned palm, the tip of her little finger jittering against the corner of her mouth, in time to the music.

Mason gave her a sidelong glance, then tried a new tack. "I grew up in Maryland, on the coast. I left after high school. Worked my way through college—the first in my family to go—then went to work for the DEA as a border patrol . . . what?"

"I was asking about *you*," she said, laughing. "Not your résumé."

"Sorry," he mumbled, trying to sound like a good sport. "Why don't you just ask me some really specific questions and I'll try to answer as truthfully as I can."

"You don't have to be truthful. We don't know each other that well."

"Fine," he said, laughing self-consciously. "Then just ask what you want to know, and I'll at least try to be intriguing."

"Mmmm . . . the old bad-cop-and-the-cagey-suspect routine? With or without Miranda?"

"Now you're just laughing at me."

"I am not. I'm laughing *near* you." She covered her smile with the back of her hand.

"Okay, fine," he said. "With Miranda, but only if she's good-looking."

"Well played." She grabbed his hand and flashed a playful look. "So, how many times have you been married?"

"Zero," he said, flinching at her directness.

"Please, let the witness respond only to the question asked, without amplification or elaboration," she said, lazily baton-twirling the swizzle stick from her drink through the fingers of her free hand.

"You're the master interrogator. You're the one who asked a question that only required a one-word answer," he poked back.

"What was growing up like, way up there where you're from?"

He stared off into the middle-distance, obviously trying to connect with something, started to speak, then stopped.

"Sorry," she said, although she wasn't. "Was that too . . ."

"No, it's okay. It's just not a story I tell very often."

"I could have been more tactful."

"I'll take your word for that," he said, turning to look directly at her. "My father was quite a bit older than my mother, and I was the last of four children, with a big gap between me and the first three—the proverbial accident. He worked in one of the big shipyards. One of those men who was so sure his importance was far greater than anyone else ever suspected."

"Mason, I wasn't trying to be nosey. Really. If this is—"

"I'm not letting you off the hook so easily," he said, giving her a gentle smile. "Anyway, dear old dad got pushed out. Forced retirement. The very last year it was legal to do that." Mason looked into his glass, swirling the remnants of his drink, his lower lip pushed out. "Every morning for a month after that he pulled on his coveralls and his boots and waited out on the front porch—grinning like *he* knew something *they* were about to find out the hard way. He was absolutely convinced that any minute they'd be sending someone over to pick him up and rush him back down to the yard. You know, just as soon as they realized they couldn't build the boats without him. Of course, no one ever showed up. He was forgotten the minute he walked off his last shift. After that, you couldn't so much as crack a smile in front of the man. You might have just heard the funniest joke on earth, but he'd assume you were laughing at him, and that fist would come flying."

"Oh, Mason." She studied his face like a nurse examining an accident victim.

He gave her a rueful smile but didn't elaborate.

"Are you close to your siblings?" she asked, hoping to find a bright spot.

"I keep in touch with my sister." He turned to watch the musicians.

Wallace had other questions, but she could tell from his posture and expression that story time was over. He still hadn't asked her a single thing about herself. Maybe his wounded childhood made him overly cautious in that regard. She knew, from her years as a cop, that rising above the crippling effects of an abusive family was never easy, but Mason had clearly done it. If the only lasting effect was a reluctance to dig into others' lives for fear of bringing up unwelcome memories, then he had achieved something rare and heroic.

The band finished their set, and the musicians left the stage. Mason remained motionless, staring vacantly across the room. Wallace gently poked him with the swizzle stick.

"Sorry," he started, turning to face her. "You caught me daydreaming. Are we ready to go?"

She smiled and nodded. A sweet expression warmed his face when he realized she was still holding his hand.

FRIDAY 1:00 A.M.

"One more thing worth seeing in the nighttime," she said, as she started the car and dropped the top. They pulled away from the diner and she quickly made her way to River Road and headed south for several blocks.

"Have you ever seen the river . . . up close, I mean?"

"Once, up in Minnesota, right near the source."

"That doesn't count," she said with a dismissive wave. She pulled onto an access road that took them to the top of the levee, and then turned back to the north and stopped the car on a level spot just below the crest on the river side.

The bridge was straight ahead. The river, down to their left, was over half a mile wide. Oceangoing vessels steamed past each other through the center of the channel. Rafts of barges shoved around by tugs glided sedately through the water closer in. Everything on the river moved in slow motion. The bridge lights formed a huge cantilevered constellation floating above a skyline backlit by the hazy glow rising like radiation off the factories stretching far to the north along the river.

Wallace left the car and moved lightly down the slope toward the water, along a footpath barely visible in the light from the ships. Mason gamely followed. She stopped a few feet above the water line.

"It feels dangerous this close to the water."

"It is," she said, looking at him, then turning to look toward the far bank.

Whirlpools spun off by the passing river traffic wheeled through the murky shallows in front of them. The only sound was the low thrum of marine engines. Mason stood perfectly still. Wallace couldn't tell whether he was petrified or mesmerized. After a few minutes she led them back toward the car. As they reached the top of the levee, Mason snapped a picture of the bridge and the city behind it. Wallace turned at the sound. He raised his phone again and snapped a shot of her in the gauzy light from just a few feet away.

"Give," she said, pulling the phone from his hand.

She held it at arm's length, then pulled him into the frame with her and took a selfie.

"How's that one?" she asked, handing the phone back to him.

He studied the shot. *He* had been looking into the camera. *She* had been looking at *him*.

She relaxed against the car, her eyes locked on his. The moment was heavy with possibility, and she could see him struggling. Maybe trying to think of something clever to say that would close the remaining space between them—and wrestling with whether to say it.

"It's okay," she said, breaking the spell. "Words can be so awkward at this point. Just come close." She pulled open the door and climbed into the backseat.

They were wrong-footed from the start. After a frenzied shedding of clothes, Mason became slow and deliberate. Wallace wanted to give in to the moment, but all of the turmoil and upheaval of the last twenty-four hours were reasserting themselves. She felt distracted and combative, like she was about to jump out of her skin. The more unhurried Mason became, the more feverish she felt.

"Feels like we're fighting," he whispered.

"I need you to fight back."

He moved with greater urgency, but she needed something more. Again and again she got close to the edge, then her thoughts would intrude. Her heart was in it but her mind wouldn't shut up and her body refused to cooperate. She hoped he wouldn't take it personally. She also hoped he wasn't one of those men who needed a lot of post-game commentary.

After a few minutes of awkward silence, Wallace squirmed into a sitting position, facing him with her back against the door. She covered herself with his shirt and watched him as he struggled back into his pants. He leaned against the opposite door, looking at her, his knees drawn up.

"The backseat of a car makes me feel like a teenager," Mason said.

"Was your first time in a backseat?" she asked, taking the bait, trying to separate her thoughts from her emotions.

"Yes. I'm that cliché," he admitted. "You?"

How odd, she thought, that this would be the very first real question he asked about her. "I'm shocked you would just assume this wasn't my first time?" She smiled, thinking maybe a little verbal jousting would chip away some of her physical discontent.

"Sometimes I can be an idiot."

Extra points for honesty, she thought. "So . . . I've wasted my first time on a caveman? I'm late to the game and I've chosen poorly. This may have to be my last time." His expression told her he was unsure of the tenor of her response. She studied him carefully for several seconds, before deciding to continue. "My first time was the most embarrassing moment of my life. I had just turned seventeen. We got caught . . . in my room . . . by my dad."

"Do we jump-cut to Daddy walking down the aisle with you on his left arm and a twelve-gauge in his right?"

"You've been reading too much Faulkner. Actually it was nothing like that. He gave us two minutes to make ourselves presentable, then he explained himself very thoughtfully. He didn't object to what we were doing, only when we were doing it."

"As in, before that walk down the aisle?"

"He was very old-fashioned about some things."

"Was that the end of that boyfriend?"

"My father was a realist. He liked Kenny quite a lot and our little bit of monkeyshine didn't change that. He encouraged us to pursue the emotional side of the romance, but on the physical side he laid down the law. If any player attempted to advance beyond second base, the game would be called on account of injury."

"He actually used those words—second base?"

"It got the point across." She raked her hair back with both hands.

"You know . . . I can't even fathom having a father like that."

"They don't make men like him anymore," she said reverently.

"So, was Kenny content to . . . uh . . . hit doubles, after that?"

"He tried so hard to be good, but I just couldn't keep my hands off him." She smiled self-consciously at the recollection.

"Poor guy. Do you know where he is now?"

"Row 88, plot C."

"Jeez. I seem to be stepping wrong every chance I get." He hung his head and squeezed the bridge of his nose.

"We eventually got married and life was truly lovely. Then one day, a few years ago, he and my dad and Martin, my older brother, they were headed off on a hunting trip when they got zeroed out by a serial drunk driver."

"My God," he whispered, wide-eyed, shaking his head. "Wallace, I have no idea what to even say."

"No one does."

"You still have close family nearby?" he asked.

"My mother. She teaches English at a private girls' school here in Baton Rouge. And my little brother, Lex, who's a priest. A Catholic priest."

"Religion wasn't part of my upbringing. I don't think I would even recognize what would get someone headed down a path like that."

"Lex was desperately in love during college. The girl, Angela, was beautiful, smart, from a good family, the perfect mate in almost every way."

"Almost?"

"By accident, one day, Lex discovered she had a little side business turning tricks in the parking lots between classes."

"And that drove him to become a priest?"

"He lost faith in his ability to judge women, so he committed himself to a faith where he felt he wasn't likely to be deceived."

"Has that worked out for him?"

"He's making progress. He's gone from naïve idealism to informed disillusion. Whether he can make the final step to mature belief . . . only time will tell."

Mason's eyes were closed. A gentle lapping sound drifted up from the river as the wake from a passing boat washed onto the bank. The faint warble of a police siren sounded in the distance.

"I could have saved him," she said.

"Your brother?" Mason chuckled. "From the priesthood?"

"Kenny. My husband. I could have saved him. All of them."

Mason opened his eyes, a fearful expression rising in his face.

"We argued about something that morning, just before they left. I can't even remember what, anymore. But we had a way of handling things like that. It wasn't anything we had consciously agreed to, it just came naturally to us. Whenever we fought we made up—right then, right there. Always, always, always."

"Except that day," Mason said quietly.

Wallace nodded, quiet tears flowing freely. She ran the sole of one foot along Mason's shin, her eyes squeezed shut. "He tried, but I turned him down. I walked away. Just one kiss, one word, one anything, and they would have been a few seconds later leaving. That drunk driver would have run the red light and they wouldn't have been there to meet him." She looked at Mason. "I know you want to say something. That I couldn't have known. It wasn't my fault. Kenny could've forced the issue. But don't. I know all those things. I've always known all those things, and they don't make any difference. I *should* have done what I *could* have done, but I let my stubborn ego get in the way, so I didn't."

She closed her eyes and pressed her lips together and continued to cry. After a few minutes, she looked up at Mason. He was looking at her with the same sweet expression he'd had just before they left the restaurant.

"You probably think I'm a mess."

"What I think is that you must be unbelievably strong."

"I'm not playing that part very well," she murmured, wiping her face with the sleeve of his shirt.

"Not so." He put his feet on top of hers, then reached toward her. "You bear it with a great deal of grace." He took one of her hands in both of his. "We've spent a lot of time pretty close together over the last few days, and I never had an inkling you were carrying something so heavy. You can be so lighthearted and funny and gentle."

"I shouldn't have thrown all this at you," she said. "We were supposed to be celebrating."

"Actually, I'm glad you told me. I have to confess I've been so curious about you."

"Well, you sure have a funny way of dealing with your curiosity," she said, with a disbelieving smile. "It wasn't until after you had your way with me, in the backseat of my car, that you asked even one question about me."

Mason chuckled at her attempt to cast him as the playmaker. "To be perfectly honest, you frighten me just a little. You're . . . intricate . . . unexpected . . . a lot to hope for in one person."

Wallace hadn't anticipated as much revelation and feeling as Mason's words implied, but she wanted to hear what else he had to say. She waited for him to speak again.

"I'm not explaining myself very well."

"But I'm enjoying it," she said, with a soft smile.

Mason's gaze traveled meticulously from her face to her toes, then back.

Wallace watched him, his eyes making her feel naked, despite the shirt draped over her body. She blushed.

Mason cocked his head and raised an eyebrow.

"I think that's my shirt you've got there," he said with a straight face.

"You can't have it back, just yet." She laughed and crinkled her nose, tucking the shirt protectively around her. Her face heated up with unaccustomed modesty.

"I'm afraid you can't keep it. That would be theft. And you being an officer of the law and all . . ." With a raffish look, he extended his hand toward her, palm up, crooking his fingers in a slow hand-it-over gesture.

"Fine. Be that way." She balled up the shirt and tossed it over his head toward the darkness beyond. As he reached high to catch it, she crawled on top of him, her hands quick and sure as they unfastened the button on his pants.

2:30 A.M.

They were mostly quiet on the ride back to Mason's hotel. It felt like an intimate silence, if not completely comfortable. She could tell Mason didn't want the evening to end, and she didn't either, but she also needed to be alone for a while. A lot had happened in the past few days and she needed time to think through everything without more variables getting added to the equation. They agreed to talk in the morning.

She stared after him for a few seconds, as he walked from her car to the front door of the hotel, then she pulled away and headed toward home—a small bungalow in the Garden District that she shared with Lulu and Boy Howdy, a pair of overweight black-and-white cats.

2:45 A.M.

The detective certainly had good taste in cars, Don thought, when Wallace's convertible pulled in front of the hotel. He couldn't be absolutely sure, but the expression on Mason's face as he exited the car made Don think that their being out so late together on a school night might have involved more than police work. And while he couldn't see the detective's expression as clearly, there was no doubt that her eyes followed Mason from the car to the front door of the hotel.

The big convertible was easy to follow as she drove off and the traffic around the hotel was heavy enough to give him cover. As they approached a residential area, however, most of the traffic evaporated. Don hung back a ways, losing sight of the Oldsmobile as it rounded a corner into a quiet, leafy neighborhood. When he turned the corner, her car was nowhere to be seen.

TWENTY-TWO

FRIDAY 3:00 A.M.

During the drive home, Wallace tried hard to understand the implications of her frolic on the levee. In general, she was good at knowing the difference between the things that made her happy and the things that made her feel good, and sex, rare though it was these days, usually accomplished at least one or the other. Tonight it had eventually accomplished both. But it had also left her feeling exposed and vulnerable, as if there were an uninvited, unexpected stranger in the midst of her emotions. And the sense of unfinished business she had felt earlier, when Mason had told her he would be going back to Washington in the morning, had intensified.

She entered her house through the carport door and looked around for the cats. As usual, Boy Howdy was home, but Lulu appeared to be out. Boy Howdy was a momma's boy. Lulu was a slut.

Don drove slowly down the street, rubbernecking from side to side, looking for some sign of her. The pecan and oak trees lining the street were so big and their branches hung so low that a number of the streetlights were lost among the leaves, giving a murky green cast to the light that filtered down to the pavement. Just when Don was beginning to wonder whether he would be able to find her, a pair of headlights burst on, spearing him like a fish. A millisecond of fear arced across his nerves. Instinctively his hand went up, palm outward, to shield his eyes.

He quickly got his fright under control when he realized that even if she saw him, she wouldn't know who he was. But it wasn't her, and the car pulled into the street and sped away.

Several houses farther down the street, he spotted her car—the only vehicle in a two-car carport and she had parked dead center. That meant she was used to having the whole carport to herself. She lived alone.

Driving aimlessly through the neighborhood, he pondered his next move. Attempting to deal with the detective by entering her house seemed too risky. Cops carried guns and she might be the type who kept hers handy, even when she was off duty. As a female cop, living alone, she probably slept with her gun. Plus, she might be more valuable alive. She might even lead him to Matt Gable.

Don wound his way back onto Wallace's street and drove past her house again. Her car was still there. Pulling to the curb about fifty yards away, facing toward her house, he killed the engine. Then he tried to find a position that was bearable, but not comfortable enough to send him into dreamland. He didn't need to make his next move in pursuit of Matt until lunchtime tomorrow. For now, he would watch the detective, trying to figure out whether she would be a threat or an opportunity and how to deal with either eventuality. He would also fuck with Matt Gable's head some more. He pulled Carla's phone from his bag.

After putting down food for the cats, Wallace wandered into the den and lay down on the couch, once again letting her mind page back through the last several hours. She hadn't talked about Kenny, her late husband, in a long time. But tonight her usual list of reasons for remaining tight-lipped seemed inconsequential and hard to bring into focus. Without warning, a brief sadness clutched at her. Something old and comfortable was slipping through her fingers. A feeble nostalgia glimmered around the edges of her memories, but it faded quickly.

She wanted to talk to Mason—to find out more about what he was thinking and feeling. But tomorrow would be soon enough, after she had a bit of distance from the events.

Boy Howdy circled by within easy reach, nonchalantly playing for affection. She hauled the massive cat onto her chest, intending to confide the secrets of her day to the purring, wide-eyed creature, but his heft and his warmth were almost instantly narcotic.

TWENTY-THREE

7:30 A.M.

The ringing startled her awake. She was still on the couch. Boy Howdy had deserted her in favor of the top of the backrest. He stared down at her as she felt around for her phone.

"Hello," she rasped.

"It's Mason. Sorry to call so early, but my office just called. Things have changed. I know this won't be your case much longer, but I think you need to know this."

"I'm listening."

"It was from someone in our recon section. They do satellite photo analysis."

"Don't tell me. They got shots of us on the levee last night."

"I hadn't thought of that," he laughed. "But no, that's not it. Do you remember me telling you about the supply analysis one of my guys did?" Mason asked.

"Sure. That drove your theory that the Overman killing might be the start of a turf war."

"If an analysis reveals something that might require a change in tactics, as a precaution we have a second analyst attempt to replicate the result. It's a top-to-bottom redo. Everything gets looked at again."

"And?"

"The second analyst got the same results."

"That's good, isn't it? It means we were operating under the correct assumptions, right?"

"Yes, but this person from the recon section, where some of our data came from, she was helping the second analyst. She started to question the data itself. It didn't look right to her. It was too symmetrical. Naturally occurring data has a certain randomness to it, but this didn't, so she ran a data integrity analysis, thinking that somehow the information had become corrupted."

"Had it?"

"It was tampered with."

"Before or after the original analysis?"

"Before. Months before."

"Is there any way to know who did this?"

"So far, all we know is that it was done from an unassigned terminal, using the login ID of an employee who couldn't possibly have had anything to do with it."

"Who would do such a thing? And why?" she asked.

"Good question. I've tried to contact the original analyst, but he's been out sick, and he's not answering his phone or email."

"Is there any way to restore the original data?"

"That's already been done."

"So, what's the bottom line? Where does this leave things?"

"At a minimum, it means that someone wanted me, the Intelligence Division, to believe a turf war was brewing, when it wasn't . . . that distribution patterns were changing in ways that they weren't. That the increase in the street supply of cocaine in south Louisiana was due to an influx from surrounding states, but that's not the case either."

"So what data was changed?" Wallace asked.

"The direction that some of the cocaine was moving when it was seized. In fact, unusually large amounts were seized moving *out* of Louisiana into Mississippi, but the data was modified to make it look like it was moving *into* Louisiana, instead."

"Why would anyone bother to do that?"

"To make it look like the rival cartels that were operating in those other states were moving their product into Louisiana because it was becoming more profitable here. Hence, our cartel war theory. In fact, the overabundance we saw appears to somehow be originating *in* Louisiana and some of it is being moved *out* into the surrounding states."

"So we're still wrestling with the same question," she said. "Where is it coming from?"

"And still no answers. Plus a new question—who altered the data, then covered their tracks?"

"Let's go back over what we have so far," she said, now fully alert. "A spike in supply in south Louisiana, a missing . . . hang on," she said, when her phone signaled an incoming call.

"Detective Hartman," she answered.

"Detective," a reedy woman's voice began, "this is Louise Mautner. You sent me the picture a that motorbike."

With all that had happened in the last thirty-six hours, Wallace had forgotten about sending the picture. "Thanks for calling back. Does it look like the . . . uh . . . crotch rocket you all saw?"

"I showed it around. That's what took me s' long to call you back. Not everybody agrees, but there's more says it is than it idn't. Me? I know it is. There's a scrape mark along the rear fender kinda looks like a lopsided arrowhead. Forgot all about that 'til I saw it again in your picture."

"Thank you, Louise. This is very helpful. If you think of anything else, please, you have my number, don't hesitate to call."

"Alright, Detective. Good luck."

"Oh, and by the way, we never got back to our little discussion about Officer Marcels, your friendly neighborhood shakedown artist."

When Louise neither spoke up nor hung up, Wallace took it as confirmation that Marcels was indeed the creep involved.

"As I was sayin', Detective, good luck with your investigation," Louise said, hanging up.

"Mason, are you still there?" she asked, reconnecting.

"Yeah. Everything okay?"

"That was Louise Mautner, the woman we met under the power lines. I sent her the picture of Matt Gable's motorcycle and she's positively identified it as the one they saw the day Overman was killed."

"So unless someone else was riding that motorcycle, the connection between Gable and Overman now seems pretty solid," Mason said.

"And it puts them at the warehouse at approximately the same time. But we're still no closer to knowing where all this unaccounted-for cocaine is coming from. Now that we know some as-yet-to-be-identified employee in your office is involved, are you still leaving today, or will you be staying?" Wallace asked.

"I don't see how I can leave until I find out how my outfit is involved in what's going on. We obviously didn't know as much as we thought we did. When will we know what's in the stuff from Gable's lab?"

"I'll call Connie at the lab, the minute we hang up. Any luck on the camera feeds from Matt's house?"

"We've both got homework. I'll call you back."

"From eleven to one, I have an appointment, but I'll try to call you before that," she said. Their plan to find a quiet part of the morning to talk about the previous night had crumbled before the day even started. She hurried through breakfast and a shower, put down food for the cats, and headed out. She needed to stop at Colley's to let him know about getting booted off the case. She was terrified that he would be disappointed.

After that, she would switch out her personal car for her police cruiser and then drive to the crime lab to check the progress on setting up the materials from Matt Gable's lab.

8:45 A.M.

She cruised through her neighborhood, taking in the sounds and smells of the Garden District. At least one member of her immediate family had lived in this part of town for over seventy-five years. Until she was about seven or eight, though, she couldn't get her mind around the idea that a house that had once belonged to someone in the family could ever belong to anyone else. It just didn't seem right. Capitalizing on her oddball notion, her ever-enterprising brothers had concocted a mission to "get inside" the house their uncle Raymond had at one time owned, and for once, they were going to let Wallace take the lead.

Standing on the front porch, the home's then-owner had listened patiently to Wallace's pitch about how the house belonged to their uncle and that she and her brothers just needed to see inside to make sure everything was still okay. Wallace had burst into tears of frustration when it became obvious that the lady of the house wasn't going to throw open her home to inspection by a posse of pint-sized rascals. Wallace's frustration quickly turned into hurt when she looked toward her brothers for moral support and saw them hooting and high-fiving at the curb, just before they tore out on their bikes, leaving her behind.

The memory was so vivid and so encompassing that Wallace failed to notice the van that was following her.

Colley and Stella lived near the old Bocage area of town, several minutes from Wallace's house. Most of the homes had been built in the sixties and the neighborhood had matured nicely. Their home had a deep porch that ran across almost the entire front of the house and wrapped around the right side. He and Stella had spent a small fortune unburdening the house of all of the architecturally appalling upgrades inflicted on it by previous owners. Period bathroom fixtures had been purchased from dealers in antique building materials and re-enameled in their original but now out-of-fashion pastel shades. And after years of carting around two rotary dial telephones from her childhood home, Stella had made Colley put them back into service. Installing and hiding the converters that made the phones function on a digital line had taxed Colley's craftsmanship, but the phones worked perfectly.

Colley was sitting on the front porch in a white wicker chair, drinking coffee and reading a magazine, when Wallace stopped at the curb. She saw a tiny current of worry cross his face as she walked up to the house.

9:06 A.M.

Well, isn't she the dutiful daughter, Don thought as he rolled past the house and saw Wallace and the older man chatting on the front porch. How touching, that she would put a visit to Daddy ahead of getting to work on time. Mason had been correct—she *was* nice-looking, very nice-looking.

As he reached the end of the block, Don pushed those thoughts aside and focused on the next steps in his plan to capture the elusive Matt Gable. For that, he would need to keep his meddlesome boss and the pretty detective running in the wrong direction for a little while longer. That would not be a problem. He turned in the direction of the freeway, and Bayou Sara, wondering how Carla was adjusting to life in captivity. Before the day's festivities got underway, he would need to pop in on her to make sure she was still sufficiently zonked out.

———————

"You did right," Colley said, after Wallace told him about her confrontation with Jason Burley. "I'd have handled Mike Harrison exactly the way you did. And Burley is a shithead for pushing him on anybody."

"But it's so humiliating to be yanked off a case," she said.

"Only if you fucked up . . . which you did not do."

"It still looks so shitty."

"Which is why you have to set the record straight. You have to file a formal grievance over this. Not just what Burley did, but how he did it. It should never be a public spectacle like he made it. But you have to have clean hands to do this, so don't leave any loose ends. Make sure you follow up everything you've got working on this case, right up to the minute you hand it over."

She wanted to tell him about Mason's call regarding the data change and the cover-up, but Colley's expression told her his thinking had shifted gears. "What is it?" she asked.

"Stella doesn't want me to go back."

"Well, what do you think?" she asked, unable to hide her alarm.

"She's probably right," he said, quietly, not looking at her.

"She probably is," Wallace said, trying to sound calm. She knew the chances of Colley coming back to work became more remote with every advance of his condition, but she hadn't expected him to pull back so soon. She certainly hadn't expected to get the news like this. When she tried to change the subject, Colley pressed the issue for a few more exchanges.

"I can't talk about this anymore, right now," she protested when it became clear that Colley had made up his mind. "You should have given me some kind of warning."

"I know. I'm sorry. But look, last night was the first time Stella even hinted in this direction. I could tell she'd been thinking about

206 • Roger Johns

it for a long time, but she never said anything until last night. She's just scared, and I understand that. We were up most of the night, going round and round about it. So what can I say?"

"Listen, I have to go. I'll come back later . . . this afternoon." She leaned over to hug him, pressing her eyes against his shirt to blot her tears.

The walk from the porch to her car was agonizing. She forced herself not to turn and look back. She was afraid he would look sad . . . and a million miles away. *Just drive to the lab to check on how Carla is coming along, close out the case, then come back in the afternoon.*

TWENTY-FOUR

9:40 A.M.

Matt was starting to sweat, as he stared at his tablet. The voice-mails from Carla that he had listened to yesterday were alarming enough, but the emails that had arrived late in the night, while he was sleeping, felt menacing. Someone claiming to be with the federal government had visited Carla at her home and had become agitated when she couldn't produce Matt. The man had shown her a badge. He said he might return with other government agents. Carla's description of her visitor made Matt fairly certain it had been the red-haired man.

The final email left Matt angry and frightened. She related that she had found something at Matt's house when she had been there recently. Matt was already at work, and she was getting ready to leave when she was overcome by a fit of nosiness. She was ashamed, but she snooped anyway. She only wanted to get to know him a little better, so she had gone poking through his stuff—and found something. It looked work-related—the kind of thing that was forbidden to take outside of the Tunica facility. The kind of thing that could get one fired . . . or even arrested.

From: Carla Chapman 3:00 a.m.
To: Matt Gable

... so I was going to sneak it back into the lab and give it back to you there along with a teensy-weensy lecture on the evils of taking research documentation outside, but I chickened out. It would be just my luck the day I brought it back in would be my day for a random bag search. Can't you just see me trying to explain my way out of that one without implicating you know who? But by the time I decided to just put it back where I found it and forget I ever saw it your house had gone up in smoke—just like you, apparently, which I don't understand why you haven't at least let me know you're okay. In any event, I've still got it and it's scaring the crap out of me, because now I don't know what to do. In case it's somehow a clue to where you are or if you're in trouble and we could use it to buy your way back, I don't want to destroy it. But what if Mr. Government Drone comes back with more questions? Or a search warrant? He wasn't so friendly the first time so I don't think having to do a second go-around will improve his attitude. What if they get the idea you and I were up to something together? Something besides ... you know. Ha-ha. I might have to turn this thing over to them just to save my own skin. I absolutely don't want to do that but I also don't see myself holding up all that well under the search light in the face routine. I'm flying home today—family emergency—and I don't know when I'll be back so I have to make a quick stop at my house in Bayou Sara, at one o'clock, to pack a bag. If you want this thing back this would be a good time to get it.

Matt couldn't decide whether Carla's message was a threat or an invitation or a trap. She hadn't signed off with any of her usual gooey stuff, but he actually viewed that as a welcome development. If nothing else, the email confirmed that he should never have gotten involved with her, but his ego and his libido had taken turns pummeling his better judgment into submission. Regardless, he had to reclaim his property.

How she had found his hiding place, he would never know, but there was nothing to be gained by trying to figure that out. If she had only minded her own business, all of the things he had hidden in the house would have burned, and his exit would have been clean and final. Now there was a loose end that had to be clipped. Grudgingly, he decided to return to Bayou Sara.

His paranoia-honed instincts were telling him not to reply to Carla's emails, that he should just show up. If he hurried, he could get there in time to find a safe place to watch and wait.

It was hard to believe his career as a scientist—for that matter, his entire life up to this point—was drawing to a close. It had been only four days since he was last in Bayou Sara, but already the town was feeling like part of his distant past. He had never integrated himself into the community, even though he had lived in the little town for nearly three years. Once, during his senior year of high school, he had driven out to a ranch where he worked the summer before, just to yuck it up with the guys like he did when he worked there. But it hadn't been the same. Everyone was polite and friendly, but nothing felt the way it had the previous summer. He had moved on, and they were still there. He was going places, they were not. After an awkward half hour, he left. He never even considered doing something like that again.

That same sense of no longer belonging that he had felt back then was strong now and it made his skin crawl. He needed to retrieve what was his and get the hell out of Dodge—permanently.

9:50 A.M.

"Ms. Chapman hasn't come back to finish putting all this together," the evidence tech said.

"Have you called?" Wallace surveyed the neatly laid out glassware and other devices.

"I don't have her number."

"How much was left for her to do?" She called Carla's number.

"I'm not sure. We laid it all out, according to her labels and diagrams, so maybe it was only a matter of putting everything up on the racks and hooking the setup together."

"Who's going over all this once it's put together?" Wallace asked, as Carla's number rang.

"Dr. Hardison. He's a consulting chemist from the university. He's supposed to be here pretty soon. I was hoping we would have everything ready before he got here."

"I need some of whatever is in the piece from the very end, the output end, made available to Connie Butterworth," she said, hanging up when Carla's outgoing message started to play.

"She took it already. She was waiting for me when I showed up this morning."

"Perfect. I'll keep trying to get in touch with Carla and see if I can get her over here. Could this stuff be put back together without her?"

"Maybe. Whether everything's correct depends on how good her notes were. I'd rather wait."

Just as Wallace was about to head back to her car, her phone signaled an incoming text. "Call me." It was from Connie Butterworth.

"Connie, it's Wallace. I'm in the building, but I was just about to take off. Do you need me to wait?"

"I'll be right down."

Two minutes later Wallace and Connie were leaning against her car in the parking lot.

"Listen. I found a few things and they're all kind of blowing my mind," Connie said.

"In a good way or a bad way?"

"In a weird way. First of all, the cocaine from the Overman homicide had none of those homegrown extraction traces that Colley was telling you about. It's not just that there was very little—there was nothing."

"Is that unusual?"

"Nobody with a profit motive would spend the money just to get street drugs that clean."

"What else did you find?"

"Remember our little science lesson about alkaloids and isotope ratios?"

"Sure."

"Well, the ratios don't match any known patterns."

"What would account for that?" Wallace asked.

"A new growing region, maybe, that nobody knows about. Some radical change in growing conditions. There could be other explanations. I just don't know."

"I'm afraid to ask what else you found."

"The stuff from Gable's lab is just like the Overman stuff."

"I don't get this," Wallace said. "Wherever this stuff comes from, why would anyone purify it to the point that it's uneconomical, then hand it off to street dealers who will just cut it back down to street grade?"

"I've got a feeling the answer to those questions are the solution to your case. Listen, I gotta go. I'll email you my formal reports later today."

Wallace sat for quite a while in the parking lot, mulling over what Connie had told her. She sensed some deep invisible thought process struggling to surface. It was as if she had everything she needed to understand the case, but she just wasn't seeing it the right way. Maybe when three o'clock rolled around, instead of handing things off to another team of detectives, she could rub Burley's nose in a fully solved case.

Despite trying to make sense of everything, the answer never came. Her only breakthrough was a bit of inspiration about how to stop all the ugliness her colleague Officer Marcels was inflicting on

Louise Mautner and her fellow gardeners out on Choctaw Ridge. Wallace pulled out of the parking lot, headed toward her brother's house. When she saw a supermarket up ahead, she stopped and picked up a sack full of produce. As soon as she and Marcels had a bit of face time, hopefully later today even, she would use the vegetables to drive home her point.

11:05 A.M.

Wallace pulled into Lex's driveway. As she was getting out of the car, a text came from Carla's number, letting Wallace know that after she had gotten home from the lab the night before, a friend had called to tell her about a job opportunity. A minor position in a small company on the East Coast had come open unexpectedly and she had managed to arrange an interview. The quickest flight was from New Orleans, so she had driven there, late last night, and she had just boarded. She would return as quickly as she could, to finish their little project at the crime lab.

"I'm sorry I'm a few minutes late," Wallace said, as Lex opened the front door.

"I'm just glad you got here before Father Rudanski got too liquored up," he said, standing aside as she stepped into the living room.

The other priest tried to eye roll past Lex's sophomoric conversational gambit, but Lex pushed on, trotting out gentle barbs, one after another, to provoke conversation. After a few minutes, Lex led them into the kitchen. He was fixing something involving ducks he had killed himself. Things had been moving so fast over the last few days, and with Colley's bombshell about not returning to work, she needed to let her mind just coast for a while. The chitchat with her brother and his fellow priest, along with the simple chores Lex gave her, felt relaxing and therapeutic.

"You can easily see that Father Rudanski is a whole lot older than me," Lex gibed. "So you're probably wondering how we could have gone to seminary together."

"I really hadn't given it much thought," Wallace lied.

"He always does this," the other priest said with another eye roll. "And call me Jack, please."

"Jack was married and had a career before he became a priest. He has two kids—grown kids," Lex said.

"You're a widower?" Wallace asked, expertly rocking a chopping knife up and down along the curve of the blade, reducing a carrot to precisely segmented discs.

"My wife died when our kids—twin girls, by the way—were just a few months old."

"I'm so sorry. What did you do, before you became a priest?" She scraped the pieces of carrot into the salad bowl.

"Chemical engineer. I worked in the petrochemical plants along the Mississippi."

"Becoming a priest seems like a radical shift from engineering," Wallace replied.

"The priesthood was my original career choice but I fell in love during high school. After my wife died, I knew I'd eventually make good on those intentions but I had two girls to raise first."

"What does a chemical engineer actually do?" Wallace asked.

"Unbelievably boring stuff," Jack said. "In my case it was the ultra-exciting world of polymer synthesis. I designed processes that industrial companies would use to produce specific products—mostly soft plastics and things like that."

"I've been trying to get Jack to see if he could synthesize a consecrated host in the lab," Lex said. "It would put an end to the Vatican monopoly on transubstantiation."

"Your brother must have been a handful, as a kid," Jack said. He raised a glass of wine to his nose and inhaled slowly before taking a sip.

"As a little boy he had a lot of mischief in him, but during his teenage years he went through a goody-two-shoes phase," Wallace reminisced. "Our mother used to joke that he came dangerously close to burning the candle at one end. He didn't become a wiseass until he went off to the seminary."

11:30 A.M.

Nearly four hours after Mason had finished his call to let Wallace know about the data tampering, he received the password that would allow him to access the videos from the other camera—the front camera—that they had found at Matt Gable's house. He set up the video from both cameras to run side by side at three times normal speed, then sat down to watch. Even at the faster speed, the long stretches of nothing happening caused Mason's mind to wander. He found his attention consumed by thoughts of the previous night. He couldn't stop thinking about her.

Their first phone conversation, the day he had called to set up his trip to Baton Rouge had left him intrigued. She was a quick thinker and refreshingly unimpressed by his federal pedigree. After their first morning on the job together, he had gone from intrigued to captivated, but he and Wallace lived different lives, hundreds of miles apart. If he got too attached, going back to his life in Washington would be painful. But if he passed up the chance to get to know her, he knew he would regret it forever. With some difficulty, he had decided to choose regret over pain, so he promised himself he would just stick to business. But things hadn't worked out that way. Even after he had realized that she was going to overpower his resolve, he hadn't expected to discover that they would both have tender feelings in play.

A change in the video caught his attention. Someone had moved across the frame and was standing at the door, facing away from the camera. Mason rewound to just before that point, then played it forward. He froze as he watched the grainy image of Don Brindl move across the screen. A cold sweat erupted over his entire body. With a trembling finger, he stopped the video and called Whitlock.

"I just got back to the office, Mr. Cunningham, and I was just about to call you to say thanks for keeping your word."

"Carla Chapman is in serious danger," Mason blurted.

"Come again."

"I know who burned Matt Gable's house."

"You've seen the videos?"

"I have. But listen, you need to get someone to her place as soon as possible. I have to make another call. I'll get back to you as soon as I can."

"Mr. Cunningham, you're gonna—" Whitlock began, but Mason was gone.

BAYOU SARA 11:50 A.M.

Mason's call had seemed frantic enough that Whitlock decided to check out Carla's house himself. He parked in front and did a slow walk around, looking carefully at all the windows. He tried the front door, but it was locked. His knock went unanswered. There was a locked gate at the end of the driveway, just off the garage, at the rear corner of the house. Through the gate Whitlock could see a fenced-in yard shaded by an ancient sycamore near the back. A metal storage shed sat off to one side, in the shade of the big tree. The six-foot chain-link fence along the rear property line was completely covered by a thick ligustrum hedge, except in the center where a padlocked gate opened onto a central alley that ran behind all the houses.

After a couple of minutes of rooting around in the collection of flowerpots flanking the garage door, he found the gate key and let himself into the backyard. He tried the back door. It was unlocked. He pushed it open a few inches and called Carla's name. There was no answer. He listened carefully for the sound of a television or a shower, something that might drown out the sound of his voice, but the house was quiet. He pushed the door all the way open and moved slowly through a small utility room into the kitchen, identifying himself and continuing to call her name as he moved deeper into the house. He looked in every room, but no one was home.

If Carla was in some sort of jeopardy because of her connection to the missing scientist, her troubles were playing out elsewhere. The house showed no signs of a struggle.

Whitlock left through the back door. He would call the skittish DEA agent to let him know that, as far as he could tell, nothing was amiss. The thought of having to spend time hand-holding the man was irritating, but the thought of having to field even more calls about the situation seemed worse. Whitlock was about to exit the backyard when he decided, instead, to take a quick peek inside the storage shed. Nobody was home there, either.

TWENTY-FIVE

12:10 P.M.

Don flinched at the sight of the police car parked in front of Carla's house. He immediately turned off her street and meandered through the neighborhood. Why would the police be here? He knew Carla hadn't escaped or been discovered. He had stopped to check on her, not fifteen minutes ago. She was still in the attic in the abandoned house and she was still completely out of it from the sedatives he had fed her last night. If his calculations were correct, she should be out for at least another six hours.

As far as he could tell, no one knew he was in the picture, so he couldn't think of a reason why anything that had happened so far could be connected to him. And there was precious little in the house that he needed to worry about. He had been careful to put things back the way he found them in the dining area where he and Carla had spent their time together.

A forensic examination of the house would reveal that someone other than Carla had been there, but it would be a long time, if ever, before anyone could link that sort of evidence to him. No official samples of his hair or genetic material existed. His fingerprints were part of his profile at DEA, but he hadn't left any prints behind—of that he was certain.

Perhaps the police car out front was just the local constable doing his due diligence on Matt's missing person report. Don would circle back every so often until the car was gone. Then he would leave his own vehicle close enough to allow a speedy getaway and go the rest of the way on foot. If need be, he could always commandeer whatever vehicle Matt arrived in. Assuming Matt even showed up.

On his second drive-by, the police car was gone. On his third drive-by, with no other obvious busybodies in sight, Don assumed the coast was clear. He parked two blocks away, then walked briskly toward the entrance to the central alley behind Carla's house. The collection of devices he had taken from Carla on his earlier visit rattled around inside his shoulder bag.

He checked his watch, then picked up his pace. Time was running short. He had wanted to be in position long before Gable arrived, but the presence of the police car had chewed away some of his margin of safety.

Just as he turned into the alley, an elderly woman emerged from a gate farther down and waddled slowly up the alley in Don's direction. She wore a ratty flower-print house coat and dingy white terry cloth slippers that barely contained a pair of record-setting bunions. A bleary-eyed basset hound that looked older than the woman lollygagged alongside on a retractable leash, sniffing out a place to relieve itself.

Don didn't have enough time to saunter past the woman and out the other end of the alley and then come back after she was gone. But he couldn't afford to register on the old woman's radar, either. He wanted to be invisible, so he acted as if he belonged there and strode confidently to the fence line at the back of Carla's yard and used her key to unlock the gate. The woman showed no interest in him. She seemed concerned only with her dog, muttering impatiently to the animal—probably some practiced incantation intended to hasten the evacuation of its bowels.

Once inside the fence, Don went straight into the house, then shot a quick glance back at the alley through the window in the door. The old woman with the dog was nowhere in sight. A quick survey of the rooms told him the house was empty. He made sure all the windows were locked and that the front door was bolted and chained. Matt might have a key and, if he showed up, he might try to enter through the front. Don needed to funnel him toward the back door.

On his way back out, Don applied a strip of duct tape across the striker plate to keep the spring bolt from latching. The tape also provided enough bulk to barely hold the door shut. A gentle touch was all it took to push it open.

Don hurried down the back steps and across the yard. He gently slid open the door to the storage shed and ducked inside. The little window in the side wall of the shed offered a view of the gate and the sycamore tree at the back of the lot. He left the door open so he would also have a clear view of the back of the house, then he settled in behind a lawn mower. Even with the door open, it was sweltering inside the shed. He would have preferred to wait in the house, where it was cooler, but he couldn't afford to get cornered in the event the nosy policeman returned or Matt showed up with company.

By making it impossible for Matt to communicate with Carla or to even determine whether it was actually her who was sending him the ominous emails, Don had left Matt no choice but to return to Bayou Sara if he wanted to reclaim what he believed Carla had taken from him.

He knew Matt would suspect a trap, and that Matt would want to study the situation before making a commitment—as he had done with his two-motel scheme in Baton Rouge. But he felt confident that Matt wouldn't want to watch from in front of the house. Inquisitive neighbors or Carla herself might see him. The tree and the shed in the back were the only real options. But Matt would avoid the shed. It would be too difficult to abort the mission if he had to exit the shed, run across the open backyard, and then get through a locked gate. From the tree, however, Matt could simply drop over the fence into the alley, leaving any pursuers to wrestle with the locked gate.

Ever the thinker, though, Don acknowledged the gentle tug of anxiety. Sometimes people behaved in unexpected ways. Mason had been reliably habit-bound for years, keeping his nose in the numbers and his butt glued to his office chair. But then, very much against the odds, Mason unexpectedly broke his usual pattern and showed up in Baton Rouge. Don hoped he would not be similarly disappointed by Matt Gable.

TWENTY-SIX

Wallace was trying hard to keep her mind on the conversation with Lex and Jack, but she couldn't stop thinking about Colley and Mason and the things Connie had told her.

"Jack's writing a book that he's too shy to mention. You should ask him about it," Lex prodded, evidently noticing the drift in Wallace's attention.

"So," Wallace said, without skipping a beat, "how's your book going?"

"Like a tortoise on Prozac. But I persevere because I think it's an important topic."

"Which is . . . ?" Wallace asked.

"The problems I see with the very antiscientific notion of Intelligent Design."

"One of the arguments against Darwin and evolution?" Wallace asked.

"Many in the religious community find it appealing because they believe it eliminates the need to consider evolution. But, in the end it will prove very damaging to religion in general and to its supporters in specific."

"How so?" Wallace asked. She turned toward the priest, giving him her undivided attention.

"Well, you know, it rests on the idea that life simply could not have arisen from the blind obedience of matter and energy to the fundamental forces that govern the universe."

"It does seem rather insulting to God to say that he couldn't have designed a system that would produce his intended results over some enormously long period of time."

"Beyond that there's a practical flaw in the whole idea. Before long, some scientist somewhere is going to cook up a living organism in the lab from completely inert ingredients. It'll be primitive, but it'll be able to sustain itself by extracting molecules from its environment and modifying them to meet its metabolic needs. After that, it will be absolutely indisputable that mere human intelligence is sufficient to the task of intelligent design. That permanently crowds out the idea that a supernatural intelligence is required to create life. The whole concept of intelligent design is a theological cul-de-sac."

"Do you really believe that humans will discover a way to synthesize a living creature?" Lex asked, dishing some salad onto his plate.

"Many are close, as we speak," Jack said. "And, of course, as soon as the first one's done, just like computers, and cars, and cell phones, improvements will be rapid."

"Won't that undermine all religion, not just the idea of intelligent design?" Wallace asked.

"I don't think so," Jack said. "And, it's a question of scale and order, really. It's one thing to be able to replicate a feature of your universe—like living creatures. It's quite another to be able to create the universe itself. An existing egg may produce a new chicken, but that existing egg can't produce the preceding chicken that laid it."

Wallace laid her fork on the side of her plate. "Lex, I'm sorry, but I have to go." Her eyes were focused on some faraway point.

"Was it something I said?" Lex asked, trying to be funny.

"No, it was something Jack said."

"Wallace, please, I hope I didn't offend—"

"Far from it. You've actually helped me. I'll explain, later," she said, hurrying for the door. "Jack, it was wonderful to meet you. Have a safe trip. Lex, I'll call, I promise," she said, her thoughts already miles away.

Wallace tried to remain calm, as everything tumbled into place. She dialed Connie's number as she hustled down the front steps of the house.

"That lab setup you tested already," Wallace began, the moment Connie answered, "you tested something from the output end of the process, right?"

"That's what you said you wanted." Connie sounded exasperated.

"Well, now I need you to test something from the very beginning, from the input end."

"Okay, but I can tell you right now what I'm going to find."

"I don't think so. And listen, keep this quiet. Not one word to a blessed soul," she said, slipping into her car and pulling away from Lex's.

"Why all this cloak-and-dagger?"

"Sometimes just knowing something is risky, especially if other people know you know."

As soon as she hung up, Wallace called the evidence tech who was handling the reassembly of Matt's lab apparatus to let him know that Connie Butterworth would be coming down to collect a sample and that Carla would not be returning any time soon.

"It doesn't matter that she won't be back" the tech said. "Her contribution would be moot, at this point, anyway."

"You got it up and running without her?" Wallace asked.

"We've got nothing at all. After you left this morning, a change of custody order arrived. We had to pack up everything and make it available for a transfer into federal custody."

"What? Where did that order come from?"

"Hang on," he said. "The Intelligence Division in the DEA."

"Whose name is on the order?" Wallace snapped.

"No name. Just the agency. But the order was authenticated before it came to me."

"That bastard. I can't believe he would do this to me. Where is everything now?"

"In the evidence room."

"Transfer me."

As the transfer rang through she hoped that Monica Simon, the head of the evidence room, would be out and that one of her assistants would pick up instead. Monica had an uncanny sense of how to get under the skin of virtually anyone who pressed her too hard. She was tone deaf to the idea of pleasant cooperation, but she had perfect pitch when it came to the line between irritation and insubordination. And Wallace, like others on the force, had gotten crossways with Monica when time constraints led to demands that Monica deemed uncongenial to her preferred style and pace of work. The phone seemed to ring forever. Wallace pictured the custodians being too busy to answer the phone because they were politely and carefully handing over all of her evidence to Mason and his comrades.

"Evidence. This is Monica Simon."

"Monica, this is Detective Hartman. I hope I'm not catching you at a bad time."

"Well, to tell you the truth, Detective Hartman, it seems like every time we talk there's a bit of a dustup comin', if you know what I mean. But, I'm willin' to let bygones be bygones. What can I do for you?"

"I'm calling about a batch of evidence that was subject to a change of custody order just this morning. It was glassware and other

laboratory items that were taken into evidence on the Ronald Overman homicide. The case number—"

"I know the items you're talking about," Monica interrupted.

"Is the evidence still in your possession?"

"Technically, it's in the possession of the State Police, not me personally, but it's still within the physical confines of the evidence
room, if that's what you're asking," Monica drawled.

Wallace could sense a lecture coming on about the fine points of
state-to-federal evidence transfer regulations.

"But you gotta understand. Once we got that order, things
changed," Monica continued, never one to underdeliver when it came
to doling out the greatest amount of information when one had the
least amount of time to listen. "We may presently maintain *actual*
possession, but the material subject to that order falls within the
constructive possession of the federal government. You see what I'm
sayin'? As a consequence, we hold it strictly as their agent."

"Who issued the order? Not the agency, the person?"

"I don't have that information."

"Can you find out?" Wallace asked, struggling to keep her composure.

"There's no standard procedure for doing somethin' like that.
That doesn't necessarily mean it couldn't be done, but—"

"Does the order state when the feds are going to pick it up?" Wallace asked.

"It does."

Monica was going to make Wallace drag it out of her piece by
piece. Breeding frustration in others seemed to be Monica's drug of
choice, and once she sensed that she had it, she worked it like a mor-
phine drip.

"When, then?" Wallace asked, offering up a quick prayer to the
patron saint of patience.

"Noon."

"It's already past that."

"Well, the order specifies a must-be-ready-by time, not the time the pickup will happen. It's always possible, of course, that those times could be—"

"I need you to keep the pickup from happening," Wallace said.

"Say what?"

"I need you to unpack everything."

"Oh Jesus God in heaven," Monica spewed. "How did I know something like this was gunna happen just the minute I heard your voice when I picked up the phone?"

Just as she was wondering if there was a patron saint of justifiable homicide, her phone signaled an incoming call from Mason. "Monica, please—"

"You know I can't stop it just on your say-so. And besides, have you got any idea how long it takes to pack up about a bajillion little pieces a glass and other assorted gizmos, all done in the strictest adherence to state and federal evidentiary chain-of-custody protocols? And now it's got to be unpacked and returned to inventory without breaking the chain?"

"The paperwork will be on your desk as soon as I can get it there. I'm headed your way now. I just need you to make sure nothing leaves the building."

"As you wish, Detective Hartman, although I gotta say, this is not gunna go a long way toward building a strong sense a comma roddery between us. And I'm just sayin' . . . if the federal marshal gets here before your stop order does, I'm gunna have to turn the stuff over. I got no authority to do otherwise."

"And I'm just sayin', unpack the goddamn crates," Wallace hissed into the phone. "Your job is to do what needs to be done. This isn't about what suits you. Got it?"

"Loud and clear, Detective, loud and clear."

TWENTY-SEVEN

12:18 P.M.

As soon as Mason had hung up on Whitlock, he had called his own boss to tell him what he knew about Don. From there, a notification was sent to the FBI, and a plan for apprehending Don set in motion. But it was going to take time. The first thing they would do was see if they could track Don's phone. The special agent in charge of the Baton Rouge office called Mason and gave him the name of a contact in the office and set up a communication protocol in case Mason came into possession of useful information.

As for tracking down Carla, that would be a matter for the local authorities. Neither the FBI nor the DEA had jurisdictional authority to act—something Mason already knew. He had not intended to call Wallace unless Whitlock reported that something was definitely wrong. But sitting and waiting was causing his anxiety to lurch into overdrive, so he called her anyway. When she didn't answer, he thought about getting a rental car, but the man at the desk downstairs told him it would take two hours to have a car sent over. Mason was on the verge of calling a taxi when Whitlock finally called back.

"Is she okay?" Mason asked.

"Don't know," Whitlock responded. "She's not home. The back door was unlocked, so I went in for a quick look-see. The place appears to be a normally occupied residence. No sign of foul play. And lots of folks around here aren't compulsive door-lockers, so the open back door may not mean much. Looks to me like she's just out."

"I've got a really bad feeling about this."

"We'll start checking with her employer . . ."

"Former employer," Mason interjected. "She was fired yesterday."

"Okay. Former employer. We'll check with the neighbors, see if we can locate any friends she might be with. I've got her telephone number from the missing person report she filed on Gable, and we've been calling it. So far there's no response."

"What about her car? Have you—"

"It wasn't at her place, but that by itself doesn't mean anything either. As I'm sure you're well aware, when people are at Point A but find they need to go to Point B, they have been known to make use of their automobile to accomplish that type of task. So, are you gonna tell me what's got your hair on fire over this? We're a small department and you folks are stretching us a bit thin. Even *I'm* gonna be out of pocket starting in about ten minutes. Now I'm guessing this has something to do with whatever it was you saw in those videos, so you can start right there."

"Sorry, Chief. That will have to wait." Mason hung up on Whitlock, when his phone signaled a call from Wallace.

"I don't know what kind of game you're think you're playing with me, pal, but I don't like it," Wallace said, not even trying to hide her anger.

"What are you talking about?" Mason asked.

"I'm talking about that evidence transfer that came from your office. The one ordering our people to pack up everything from Matt's lab and make it available for a federal pickup."

"I didn't do that. But, listen, we've got a bigger problem on our hands. We'll straighten out this evidence thing in a minute. In the meantime, I need you to pick me up at my hotel."

"Mason, I'm not your chauffeur. Don't just assume that I'll drop whatever I'm doing to come drive you around."

"And I'm not asking you to just drive me around. Please. I need your help."

"I'm on my way," she said, cooling off a bit. "Wait for me out front."

As Wallace pulled up to the front of the hotel, she saw Mason pacing near the bell captain's podium. He looked haggard and anxious.

"I stopped the evidence grab, just like I said I would, so don't even ask about that," he said, as he pulled open the door and slid into the car. He looked ready for more of the conflict their last call had stirred up.

"Thank you," she said, meeting his gaze with a vague smile. "I'm sorry I yelled at you. I was caught off guard by that transfer order and I was still in the grip of an ugly exchange with the woman who runs the evidence room. I should've known you wouldn't go behind my back like that. I'm sorry."

"It's okay. I might've reacted the same way," he said, returning her smile.

As he leaned forward to set his bag on the floor, Wallace could make out the straps of a shoulder harness crisscrossing under the back of his jacket. "Are we expecting trouble?" She reached over and snapped the harness like a bra strap. "The shooting kind of trouble?" she asked playfully.

For a second, his face brightened, then a dense cloud of worry moved in. "We need to be prepared."

"For what? And look, I'm not questioning your capabilities, but guns are serious business. Exactly when was the last time your job put you in harm's way?"

"I did my time toting guns on the border as a DEA agent—"

"Right after the Mexican-American War."

"That's actually pretty funny," he said without smiling. "We should get going?"

"You haven't told me where, yet."

"Bayou Sara." He pulled his tablet from his bag, then sat back, staring straight ahead. He started to speak, then stopped.

Wallace pulled away from the hotel heading north toward the I-110. When she looked over at him, she saw deep lines creasing his forehead. "Mason?" she said softly, her hand on his shoulder.

Her phone rang. It was Connie Butterworth.

"Hi, Con. I need some good news." She listened for several seconds. "Sorry you had to wrestle with Monica Simon. I would have warned you, but things have been galloping." She listened for a while longer. "Keep this to yourself, for the time being. I think the victim in this homicide was killed for knowing what you just told me."

She ended the call, then looked over at Mason, to check his reaction to what she had just said, but he was still staring through the windshield. Apparently he hadn't been listening. "Mason, what's going on?"

"I know who burned down Matt Gable's house."

"Really?"

"Mmm hmm."

"Neither of us is in the mood to do this cross-examination style, so why don't you just tell it?"

"Remember me telling you about the analyst that first identified the data patterns that made us think we were looking at a cartel war?"

"Of course," she said.

"His name is Don Brindl. The videos show him lock-picking his way into the back of Matt's house just before the fire started."

"One of your own people is behind all this?"

"Behind it all? I don't know. Involved? So it would seem."

"How does this put Carla in danger?"

"I spoke to Don, yesterday."

"So?"

"So, this was before I saw him on the videos—before I knew he was the one who burned Matt's house," he said, typing and touching his way to the video of Don. "I told him about what we found in Matt's lab and I told him about Carla. How she was his girlfriend but that she was also a scientist who worked with Matt, and how she was going to help us figure out what the stuff in the lab was all about. This is him," Mason said, holding the screen so she could see the frozen image of Don approaching the door to what had been Matt Gable's house.

"And you think Don has been hunting Gable and now he'll be going after Carla too?"

"He might have already found Gable, which may be why we can't. But in any event, if Don thinks Carla can help him get to Gable, he will certainly go after her. All I know at the moment, and this is from Whitlock, is that she's not home and she doesn't answer her phone. He's looking but he doesn't have the manpower to do this right."

Wallace had been right. Mason's hard-case federal lawman attitude was an act after all. To his credit, it was a role he played well, but even more to his credit he knew how and when to let it go, to let the real man step forward.

"I wish you had said this sooner. Here, look at this." She thumbed open Carla's text about going on a job interview and handed her phone to Mason.

"And you know for a fact that this is from her?" Mason asked, as they passed the tall white limestone spire of the state capital building off to their left.

"It's from the number I've called her at before," Wallace said.

Mason visibly relaxed. "I need to let Whitlock know. He's going to think I'm an idiot."

"Maybe he won't," she said.

Mason spent the next few minutes on the phone with Whitlock, explaining about the text and eating crow.

"Since the heat is off on the Carla rescue, I need to run a quick errand. Do you mind?" she asked, after he ended his call with Whitlock.

"Not at all."

They were moving through an area that had been cut in half by the building of the freeway. Fragments of residential zones segued into stretches of sparse woodland and swampy patches. The airport appeared off to the right. A jet flying low and slow on approach lumbered over the car as they sped north.

"After my errand, you can bear witness to my humiliation as I hand off what little is left of this case."

Mason looked over at Wallace. She was just staring at him, a huge smile spreading across her face. "What do you mean by 'what little is left'?"

"Do you know why Don was breaking into Matt's house?" she asked.

"No, but I've got a funny feeling you're about to tell me?"

"My friend Connie, who works at the crime lab, has made some rather interesting discoveries."

"Such as?"

"Such as . . . the cocaine we found in the warehouse with Overman has none of the traditional purification traces, no contaminants, nothing."

"If that's what your lab found, then I'm sorry I called off the evidence transfer."

"Before you climb all the way up on that high federal horse of yours, you might want to know the rest of the story."

"I'm listening," he said, giving her an impatient get-on-with-it finger twirl.

"The residue from the product end of Matt Gable's lab setups was tested and it's not just any old blow. It's identical to what we found with Overman—also, clean as a whistle."

"Well, that just makes no sense at all. Why would Gable or Overman, or anyone else for that matter, waste money cleaning up wholesale-grade product just so downstream sellers in the States could recontaminate it when they cut it back down to street grade?"

"I had the same question."

"Wallace, look—"

"Just wait. Connie also compared the coke from Gable's lab and from Overman, looking at the alkaloid and isotope ratios."

"I'm impressed," Mason said.

"Don't be smug. It's unbecoming."

"Just tell it already, would you? I can see you're dying to lord this over me."

"That's true. I am. But tell me something first—and this is probably something you would know. Why is the cocaine business exclusively an import business?"

"Because the coca plant grows only in the Andean highlands of South America."

"Rubber trees don't grow here, but we don't import all the rubber we use," she countered.

"Well, that's because we can make synthetic rubber from petroleum. We cannot, however, synthesize the cocaine molecule in the lab—at least not the psychoactive left-handed version."

"We can't?" she asked.

"Back in the late 1800s, someone discovered a method, but it produces almost entirely the wrong version along with lots of contaminants and by-products. The yield of L-cocaine hydrochloride is so low that the cost of a gram of street-grade would be thousands of times higher than what the imported stuff sells for. Many have tried but, so far, none have succeeded."

"But if some chemically savvy Rumpelstiltskin did figure out how to spin the straw of ordinary chemicals into cocaine gold, do you think you would have heard about it at the exact instant it was discovered?" Wallace asked, exiting the freeway.

"Well, no, of course not. I'm just saying. . . ." Mason's voice trailed off.

"When Connie called just a minute ago, she had just finished testing the glassware from the *input* end of Matt's process. Wanna know what she found?" Wallace asked.

"Not cocaine."

"Not cocaine," she echoed.

"Un-fucking-believable," he murmured. "What made you think to test the input end?"

Wallace told him about her lunch with her brother and his fellow priest. She recounted their discussion about the priest's forthcoming book and how it touched on the idea of synthesizing living organisms in a lab—something no one had done before—and how that suddenly got her wondering why the cartels went through all the trouble of growing coca way down in South America, then extracting the drug from the leaves, and then purifying it and shipping it to markets across thousands of very dangerous miles.

"Why don't they just make it in a lab, like they do meth, I wondered? Then it hit me."

"Is it possible Connie made a mistake? That the stuff on the input end was just a really low grade of cocaine? So low her tests missed it? And that for some reason we can't yet figure out, Matt was trying to bring it up to sellable grade?"

"She said she ran the test twice and both times it came back negative. It will take time to identify exactly what the chemicals were that Matt was feeding into his process but, for the moment, all we really need to know, and the thing she called to tell me a few minutes ago is that, whatever those chemicals are—"

"—they're not cocaine," Mason finished. He was stunned. She had figured out, over lunch, what he had been unable to do with a Ph.D. in statistics and a platoon of analysts armed with big-time computers.

No wonder she had gotten past his defenses so easily, the night before. She hadn't been just listening to his story, she had been taking him apart, decoding the patterns in his life, just like she deciphered everything else.

"Where did you go?" Wallace asked, breaking into his thoughts.

"Just thinking. You are seriously good at what you do."

"Thank you," she said.

"I still can't believe Gable figured this out," Mason said. "Since he was making it cheap enough for Overman to sell on the street, his process obviously has a high yield and it uses inexpensive inputs. In my world this is equivalent to discovering cold fusion."

"Is it too much of a stretch to say this is what Don was doing in Matt's house? Trying to get his hands on Matt's process?"

"I think it's obvious that's what Don was after. And it explains who fiddled with the data in my office—he did. And now we know why."

"But what made him think someone discovered how to make cocaine in a lab? I mean, how did he know the extra supply here wasn't coming from some other source, the way you and I first thought?"

"My guess is that he didn't know. The most likely scenario is that he started going over the data and saw there was a great deal more cocaine in Louisiana than could be accounted for by any realistic shift in existing supplies, and that none of the other U.S. markets were being starved for product. From there, he would have dug deeper and seen that Overman had actually become an exporter instead of just an importer, and that Overman was using new routes to move stuff *out* of Louisiana into the surrounding states. That would make the existence of a new source almost a certainty. So he massaged the data to throw the rest of us off, then started coming down here to do a bit of fieldwork."

"But how did he zero in so precisely on Baton Rouge? On Ronnie Overman?"

"There was a cholera outbreak in London in 1854. John Snow, a physician, used the statistical tools of his day to map the location of every known case. In almost perfect concentric circles, the number of cases increased the closer he got to one particular neighborhood and to one particular water well. He disabled the well by removing the pump handle and the epidemic came to a screeching halt. Put a hundred and sixty years of improvements in statistical methods together with the massive computing power we have today, and it wouldn't surprise me if Don had figured out Overman's blood type."

"Okay, he figured out Overman was the distribution point, but what about where Overman was getting the new stuff?"

"That's where the field work would have come in. He would have to come down here and find that out the hard way."

"By torturing it out of Overman?" she asked.

"So it would seem."

"Clearly, though, he had to already be tuned into the idea that synthetic cocaine was a possibility."

"It's been a subject of speculation and worry for a long time."

"Would Don have known how to make it look like Echeverría's handiwork?" Wallace asked.

"He was fascinated by the personalities that pulled the big levers in the cartels. He studied them like most guys study the stats of their favorite sports figures."

"What happened to Overman was pretty gruesome, though. Could Don have actually done it himself, or do you think he had help?"

"Good question."

"What was Whitlock's reaction to Don in the videos?"

"Skepticism is definitely the man's strong suit. He was willing to concede that we now have a suspect in the arson case."

"Did he think there was a connection between Don and Gable's disappearance?"

"What he said was, and this is pretty close to an exact quote, 'Agent Cunningham, I know to a certainty that you, and probably Detective Hartman too, are already holding this Brindl fella responsible for Gable's disappearance, and I am equally certain that there's nothing I can say that'll pry you loose from that idea, but I'm reserving judgment on that until I can get my hands on a bit more corroborating evidence.'"

Wallace laughed at Mason's off-key attempt to mimic Whitlock's southern accent. "I don't know why he had to lump me in with you."

"Probably to make one of us feel good."

She smiled at his lame joke, happy that he had worked his way into a better humor. "There's one last thing I don't understand."

"What's that?" Mason asked.

"If he is, in fact, the one who killed Overman, why did he do it in a way that was calculated to catch your attention? Why not just make it look like an accident, or a run-of-the-mill homicide?"

"Even before Don presented his faked-up analysis that made it look like a turf war was brewing, the raw data from this area was heating up, so to speak. I knew something unusual was going on. But we weren't going to know exactly what it meant until the data was analyzed. Don knew attention was focusing on south Louisiana and he knew things were going to be looked at pretty closely, so he skewed his analysis—"

"—to reinforce the bogus cartel war idea and get everyone looking the wrong way," Wallace finished. "I get that. But still he could have ginned up some totally benign explanation and kept you miles and miles away from all this. And I would have gone on my merry way and worked it as just another drug-related killing."

"Once Don figured out Overman was the epicenter, he knew he'd eventually have to kill him. The death or disappearance of such a major drug figure would tell me something was wrong here. And if it came on the heels of some innocent explanation of the quirky data, that would have looked like a contradiction. Don would know something like that would just beg for intense scrutiny."

"So he concocted his cartel war idea, doctored the data, then made Overman's death look consistent with that, figuring you'd accept it for what it appeared to be." Wallace shook her head and drummed her fingers on the steering wheel.

"The bigger the lie, the bigger the buy-in," Mason agreed. "The oldest propaganda trick in the book."

"A brilliant plan."

"From a brilliant man and a master game player," Mason finished. "And, he wouldn't need us looking the wrong way forever—just long enough for him to get his hands on the magic method. It didn't hurt that Echeverría happened to get killed when he did. Just a lucky coincidence but, since dead men tell no tales, it meant we might never be able to prove Echeverría wasn't behind it all."

"I guess Don's mistake was his assumption you would never come down here to investigate."

"A safe assumption. In my shop, I'm famous as the geek who never leaves the office. I'm a number jockey," Mason said.

"I would never have guessed," she laughed. "So why *did* you decide to come down here?"

"I almost didn't, but it was just too disturbing not to take a firsthand look. If I just went with the data, and got it wrong, the cost in money and lives would have been too great." Mason shifted in his seat, turning away from Wallace, and stared out his window.

"What are you thinking?" Wallace asked, after nearly a full minute of silence.

"You have no idea how foolish I feel. Don and I have been colleagues for years. How could I have missed something this malignant right under my nose?"

"Parents miss things with their kids who still live at home with them. What chance would you have against an evil-genius colleague who was determined to keep things below the radar?"

"This thing has got to be contained. Once it gets loose, the response from the cartels is going to be extreme. People will be sent to steal the method and snuff out anyone who even looks like competition. Killing in the cities, in the most lucrative markets, is going to skyrocket. This is going to be a disaster." He shook his head, still obviously stunned by the developments. "He must have left signs along the way. I just missed them, plain and simple."

"Do you think that Don suspects you know he's here?"

"No. He thinks I think he's home sick."

"Then he won't be worried about being tracked, so there's a chance he's still in Bayou Sara and that his cell phone is still on. Call Whitlock, and tell him to get the phone company to look for it."

"The FBI's already doing that," Mason said, then filled her in on his call with his boss. "By the way, where are we going?" he asked, noticing they were in an area they had not been in before.

"I need to deliver the stuff in that bag," she said, pointing to the grocery bag in the footwell behind her seat.

Mason turned to look at the produce-filled bag. He waited for her to explain further but she remained focused on the road ahead. "To whom?" he asked, his curiosity getting the better of him.

"One of the men in that car, right over there. The one facing us." She pointed toward a police car idling in the parking lot of a crummy strip center. *One-oh-seven* was stenciled on the front left fender. During the drive, she had remained alert for one-oh-seven's periodic location broadcast.

The driver-side window of one-oh-seven was positioned alongside the driver's window of a second police car facing in the opposite direction. The windows were down and the drivers appeared to be engaged in animated conversation across the three-foot space between their cars. The driver of the car Wallace pointed to was resting a muscular forearm on the bottom of the window frame. He was a beefy, thick-wristed man, with a see-through comb-over hair style. Long-timers on a beat tended to claim the driver's seat, so Wallace assumed the man behind the wheel was Marcels.

"Please tell me you're not about to do what I think you're about to do," Mason groaned.

"You don't have to be here, if you don't want to. See that little coffee shop at the end of the parking lot? If you don't have the stomach for this, you can wait for me in the ladies' room."

"Wallace, this doesn't seem wise."

"Look, this shit heel has it coming. He's been terrorizing those elderly people on Choctaw Ridge. It stops today." With one hand, she hauled the bag over the seatback into her lap as she steered the car with her other hand.

When it looked like Mason was about to say something, she cut him off. "Is this where you insist on coming along as my backup?" she asked.

"This is where I stroll on over to that ladies' room you mentioned."

She reached in the bag and pulled out the receipt and dropped it into the console cup holder next to Mason's phone. She brought the car to a stop, nose-to-nose with the car driven by her intended target and waited until a what-the-fuck-do-you-think-you're-doing expression hardened onto the driver's face. Then she opened her door.

"Wallace?" Mason asked, as she put one foot out of the car.

"Yes?" she drawled, afraid he had succumbed to an impulse to either try to talk her out of it or to go along as her protector.

"If this thing goes south, is there next of kin you want me to notify?" he deadpanned.

She was about to give him a dirty look, but laughed, instead, when she realized he was playing with her. Shaking her head, she climbed out of the car with the bag in her hands and moved into the space between the two cars in front of her.

The driver's name tag confirmed that he was her man.

"Officer Marcels, I'm so glad I found you," she said, noting his pasty complexion and his small furtive eyes.

"I need you to move your vehicle," Marcels said in the tone they all used to assert control of a situation. Every eye in both cars was riveted on Wallace.

"I'm Detective Wallace Hartman," she said, showing her badge. "I brought you something. I think you're gonna love it." She flashed a saucy smile at the other men in both cars.

"What I'd love, is for you to move your car, like I told you, okay, sweety? Now just—"

"I heard you the first time," she interrupted, keeping a gentle quality to her voice. "Here you go," she said, shoving the bag through the open window onto his lap. "Now you won't have to steal from the poor. Plus, you can get a little more fiber in your diet. You could stand to drop a few pounds."

An anxious quiet fell over the group.

"What's in the sack?" Marcels's partner asked, craning in for a look.

"Fuck off," Marcels snapped, as he peered into the bag and realized what was happening.

He tried to ram the bag out through his window, but he hit the top of the frame. Some of the vegetables scattered back into his car while others flew onto the ground around Wallace's feet. A tomato burst against the top of the window frame and gobbets of pink sludge slopped onto the inside of his door.

"What the fuck is this?" the driver of the other car asked, laughing.

"All a y'all just fuck off," Marcels bellowed. He shoved his door open, trying to pin Wallace between his door and the other car but Wallace shoved back, slamming the door closed and rocking Marcels down into his seat. Shreds of tomato splattered from the window frame onto his uniform shirt.

"What's the matter? Did I bring the wrong stuff?" she taunted. "Isn't this what you usually shake them down for?"

Uneasy laughter came from the other officers.

"You fuckin' bitch," he hissed, trying to heave his door open again, with the same result as before. "You don't know who you're messin' with."

"You're wrong. I do know," Wallace countered, then waited a beat. "You look like you want to hit me. Go ahead. Hit me, little man." She leaned forward, hands on her knees, her face looming in his open window. "Go ahead. I won't tell."

Marcels just stared at her, his face was crimson with rage.

"What's the matter? Afraid you'll get your ass kicked by a girl? And with so many eyes watching." She paused. "Hey, we're all brothers in arms. No tattletales out here. Come on," she said in a quiet, singsong voice. "Hit me, you fucking coward."

"Stay cool, bubba," his partner urged. "Don't let this ragged-out bitch make you do nothing stupid. It's just noise. Just a buncha bullshit yappin'."

"Oh, I can just see the wheels turning in that mean little gorilla brain of yours," Wallace said, her face still framed by his window. "Just remember this. If a dark cloud of any kind should sail into the lives of those people you've been thieving from, behind Choctaw Ridge . . . if any one of them should so much as get a headache . . . I won't bother looking for who . . . I'll come looking for you." She waited a few seconds to see if he would respond. When it became clear he wasn't going to, she stared at each of the other three men in turn. When no one offered a challenging stare she strolled back to her cruiser.

1:10 P.M.

"Remind me not to get on your bad side," Mason said, as Wallace started the car.

She waited several seconds, letting her elevated emotions shed some altitude, then turned toward him. "Consider yourself reminded."

"Aren't you worried he'll make a move against you?"

She gave him a quizzical look, as if his question didn't make sense. "Did you call Whitlock yet?"

Mason was about to respond, when his phone rang. "That's him, now. Yes, Chief," he answered. "I'm in the car with Detective Hartman and I'm putting this on speaker."

"Okay, you two. We got trouble in paradise, so listen up. After your hysterical call this mornin', Agent Cunningham, I got one of my people to do a little look-see with the phone company, on the off chance Ms. Chapman's phone might be visible. After your next call, letting me know she appeared to be on some kind of job interview, I should have canceled the lookup on her phone, but it slipped my mind. And, wouldn't you know, they just got back to me."

"With what?" Mason asked, impatient with the chief's round-about way of speaking.

"Well, long story short, it turns out Carla Chapman's phone was right here in Bayou Sara as of late this morning. We don't know where it is now. It's been turned off. But the triangulation gurus at the phone company tell us a transmission from her phone very definitely originated from here right around eleven o'clock, when you said she would have been in New Orleans getting on a plane."

"What's your next move, Chief?" Wallace asked. She glanced over at Mason. The look of dread was back on his face.

"My next move is some heavy-duty dream time. I'm having a colonoscopy. In fact, I'm prepped and on the table, and they're about to start pumping the happy gas. And my doctor is giving me the same hurry-it-up look I get when he thinks I'm taking too long to sink a putt."

"Chief, we just finished some business here, and we can be in Bayou Sara in about twenty minutes. Do you mind if we take a look around?" Wallace asked, heading north and pressing hard on the accelerator.

"If you want anything done in the next hour, you'll *have* to do it yourself. That's why I'm calling you now, instead of *after* this scope job. There's only three other officers on my force and they're all committed on some pretty serious stuff. Sophie and Jake are doing a prisoner escort two parishes away, and my only other one, if all's going according to plan, is eyeballing a pretty nasty group of highly dedicated automobile thieves. At the moment, I haven't got a spare body to put on this. Just remember. Usual conditions—I get everything you find, and don't screw anything up. And one more thing. If you end up at Carla's house, the key to the gate by the garage is in the peonies."

"Thanks, Chief," Mason said, ending the call. They rode in silence for a few minutes.

"I know we already went over this but are you *sure* you want to be in on this?" she asked.

"I'm the cause of this problem. What else would I be doing?" He turned to look out the window. "Any ideas on where we should start looking?"

"Carla's house, of course."

"Whitlock looked already," Mason protested. "She isn't there."

"Wasn't there," Wallace corrected. "But, forget Carla for a second. Focus on Don. He either sent, or forced Carla to send, that bogus job interview message from *her phone*. And Whitlock just told us that her phone was in Bayou Sara when the message was sent. That means Don was in Bayou Sara as recently as a few hours ago."

"But it doesn't pinpoint his location."

"It does. There are only two places I would know to look for Carla, once she failed to show up today—her house and the Tunica lab. The phony interview message presumed I knew she was no longer at Tunica. That leaves only one place I'd be sure to look—her house. And since the message was intended to keep me from looking for Carla at all, and since her house was the only place the sender assumed I would know to look, it's clear to me that the real purpose of the message was to keep me away from Carla's house, because there's still something important that's going to happen there."

"Someday you'll have to teach me how you do that," Mason said. "Are you always so clever?"

"Couldn't be a local detective, otherwise," she smiled. "And look, if Don had control of her phone, he had control of *her*. So he's not looking for her, he's looking for Matt."

"And she's the bait," Mason said.

"That means, as recently as two hours ago, Don still didn't have what he came for."

"Which means Matt's still alive. And hopefully Carla, as well."

"From your lips to God's ears," she said, as they closed in on Bayou Sara.

Mason called his contact in the Baton Rouge FBI office to let him know Don was probably still in Bayou Sara and that Carla Chapman's house was a likely location. He gave the man Carla's address, then he leaned back and closed his eyes.

BAYOU SARA 12:50 P.M.

Carla could barely keep her mind focused on one thought. Whatever Don had given her was powerful and still in her system. Her body had always been resistant to sedatives, but this was something else entirely. Every time she tried to gather her wits she found herself drifting off. Once, though, she had heard him next to her. It seemed like it was just a few minutes ago, but it could have been hours. Her sense of time was too disjointed to tell. She had had enough sense, however, to know that she needed to remain motionless and appear to be still unconscious. Playing possum had been easy. She just let herself slide back down into the darkness. But not all the way.

He had nudged her with his foot, and shined a light in her face, to see if she might be coming around, but she had hidden from him in the welcoming embrace of the drug itself.

Now it felt like he was no longer there. She tried hard to focus on listening, to see if he was nearby, but she could no longer hear him. At least she didn't think so. After a few minutes, she allowed her eyelids to open just a hair, but for a second, she couldn't remember why she needed to do that. Then she remembered. She opened her eyes wider and turned her head from side to side. Wherever she was, it was gloomy. She was flat on her back, and she could feel the strapping tape that bound her arms straight at her sides and she could feel more of the tape wound around her ankles. A strip of tape covered her mouth. She tried to raise her head so she could look around, but her head felt like it weighed a ton. All of her did.

Her back ached and the floor was hard. She tried to raise her knees to take the pressure off her lower back, but she couldn't. She rolled onto her side and looked toward her feet. Don had tethered her feet to a standpipe that ran up through the floor and continued up through the roof above. Slowly, she turned her head and looked around. She was inside a small, closet-sized room. She moved her head some more. The small slatted fanlight in the wall behind her was the source of the gray light. She was in an attic.

She felt herself slipping back into unconsciousness. The effort of rolling onto her side and looking around had been exhausting. No, she had to stay awake. She had to clear her head. She had to get away before Don came back.

Slow, deep breaths. Her shallow breathing while she had been unconscious would have slowed her metabolism of the drug. She had to get it out of her system. Deep, steady breaths. That would speed things up. But soon her rhythmic breathing began to feel hypnotic and she felt herself slipping away again. She switched to sharp heaving inhales, but when that brought on a bout of nausea, she was forced to dial it back.

Finally, the clouds in her thoughts receded a bit. If she could keep her eyes open, she might make it.

Turning her head, again, she spied salvation—a nail head, just barely visible, was protruding from one of the studs in the wall to her left. It was only a few inches above the floor.

Summoning all of her strength, she sidled over to the wall and squirmed until she was up against the nail head. She could feel the tape near her left wrist catch against it. As she wiggled, she felt the tape start to tear against the sharp metal. She moved as fast as the tape and the remnants of the drug allowed her to.

Matt jogged up the alley behind Carla's house. His small pack contained a pistol, a throwaway phone, and a pair of binoculars. He hoped his gimme cap and the heavy-framed sunglasses made him look different enough that neighbors who had seen him in the past wouldn't recognize him now. He called Carla's landline. Her outgoing message came on.

"It's me," he said in a low voice. "Pick up." No one answered. Maybe she hadn't arrived yet. Maybe she had come and gone already. Wouldn't that be just like her? She'd probably show up early for her own funeral.

Matt counted gates as he moved up the alleyway. Carla's was the fourth house on the right. He checked the gate to make sure it was locked, then turned his attention to the huge sycamore tree in her backyard. A thick branch ran almost parallel to the fence, extending a foot or so over the top, into the alley. It was too high to reach from the ground, so he pulled a neighbor's heavy plastic dumpster against the fence and climbed onto the lid. The branch was still nearly two feet beyond his reach. Looking carefully for a spot to grab hold, Matt leapt. He wrapped his hands around the thick branch and swung free for a few seconds.

His jump unbalanced the dumpster. It fell noisily into the alleyway, leaving him swinging about six feet above the ground. He swung his right foot up and over the limb, then wrangled his torso up as well. From there, he stood on the branch, steadied himself, and then walked tightrope style to the massive trunk of the tree. He climbed a few feet higher until he found a place that provided a reasonably sheltered view of the back of the house. Once he knew Carla was inside, he would use his key to get in through the back door. He would strike quickly, recover his property, and move on.

Through the partially blocked window in the shed, Don could see Matt standing on the limb several feet above. He watched Matt take a phone from his pack and place a call—probably to Carla's cell phone. After several seconds he saw Matt end the call and make a second call. When that call also went unanswered, Matt stowed the phone and brought out a pair of binoculars and began scanning the back of the house.

Don watched the time change from 12:59 to 1:00. If he sprang the trap at exactly one o'clock it might seem too pat and Matt's survival instinct could take control, causing him to run—so Don waited.

Don watched as Matt checked the time, then raised his binoculars to scan the house again. He watched as the nervous chemist shifted from foot to foot on the branch, checked his watch again, and turned to scan the alley.

As the time changed from 1:01 to 1:02, Don saw Matt look toward the house, then back at the alley. At 1:03, the tempo of Matt's jittery movements sped up. At 1:05, Matt stowed his binoculars and looked in the direction of the alley, then started his descent toward the branch that overhung the alley. Don reached into his bag and pushed the button.

Just when he had decided Carla would be a no-show, Matt heard the heavy hum and rattle of her garage door going up. He quickly climbed down and dropped into the yard, wanting to catch Carla just as she was entering the house from the garage. He accelerated past the shed, reaching into his pocket for the key to the back door.

Don pressed the remote again, sending the garage door back down. The noise covered the sound of his footsteps as he darted from the shed, closing the distance between himself and Matt. Just before Matt reached the back door, Don fired his Taser and Matt collapsed in the grass. Don yanked the Taser darts from Matt's neck and shoved the device into his pack. He skipped lightly around Matt's deflated body, grabbed the puzzled-looking scientist's wrists, and dragged him to the back door. Don bumped the door open with his backside and hauled Matt through the small utility room, into the kitchen.

"Hello, hello," Don crowed.

Matt was on his back on the kitchen floor, his flaccid muscles useless.

"Remember me?" Like a rodeo calf roper, Don rolled Matt onto his stomach, then duct-taped Matt's ankles and wrists into a single package behind his back.

"Almost done," Don intoned. He dragged the hog-tied Matt down the hallway and into the bathroom, then heaved him into the tub. Don wedged Matt down on his side, so that Matt's arms and legs pressed against the far side of the tub and his face was mashed into the near side. Don reached down and turned Matt's head until he was facing upward, looking directly at Don.

Matt tried to speak, but a mewling whimper was all he could manage.

"Won't be long, and you'll be fit as a fiddle," Don said. He stopped and stared down at Matt. "You know why we're here, and you know what I want, so here's the deal. Sooner is better. More is better. I ask the questions. You give the answers. If you're clear, complete, and, most important, if you're quick about it, you'll live to tell the tale."

Don pulled the Taser from his bag and gently jabbed the darts into Matt's face, one on each side of his nose, just beneath his lower eyelids. He brandished the control box in front of Matt.

"Do I need to explain?" Don asked.

"Uh-uh," Matt croaked.

"Wonderful. Then let's get underway. First things first. Tell me where your car is. Just in case we need it."

"We?" Matt whispered.

"I'm not an unreasonable man," Don said. "There could be a place for you in the enterprise I'm going to set up around your little discovery. Your skills are obviously very unusual, not to mention very valuable. Think about it. Now, where's the car?"

As Matt gave directions to the car, Don produced a box cutter and thumbed the blade to full extension. He reached into the tub and cut the straps of Matt's backpack and hauled it onto his lap. The unmistakable weight of a gun inside made Don smile. He emptied the contents of Matt's pockets and backpack into his own pack.

A quick pat down revealed a nylon pouch taped to the small of Matt's back. Don cut it free and pulled it open. It contained a small notebook and a couple of flash drives. Don paged quickly through the notebook, seeing sketches of laboratory setups and diagrams of chemical reaction sequences.

"I'll assume these flash drives amplify what's in the notebook."

"Just copies," Matt rasped.

"Good man," Don said. "Now tell me—and I'll be watching your face very closely, so you don't want me to get the impression that you're lying—where else is this information stored?"

Don admired Matt's scheme for hiding his work. The process had been broken into several sequences and each sequence was stored in several different files in the cloud. The proper order for the sequences was hidden in yet another file. All of the files were stored in obscure places and the passwords were lengthy. Don carefully wrote everything Matt told him onto the back pages of the little notebook in which Matt's discovery was written. He considered using the digital recorder he used to record Carla's messages, but if it malfunctioned he would be out of luck, so he opted for the safety of hard copy.

"I know you're holding back," Don said, trotting out the standard interrogator's ploy. "Everyone does, and I don't blame you. The psychology, you know, the game-theory aspect of it is easy to understand. But listen to me. This is no time to play your cards close to the vest. I'm good at this. I'm also a bit impatient." Don fired the Taser.

Matt seized. His eyes bulged. Strings of spit bloomed from between his lips. Despite Don's continued cajoling, though, once Matt recovered enough to speak he produced nothing more of value.

"Maybe you weren't holding back after all," Don said matter-of-factly, the way one would apologize for jostling a fellow passenger on a crowded subway. "So, have you given my offer of employment the serious consideration it deserves?" he asked. "You do realize your options are limited."

Matt opened his mouth to speak, but the hoarse laughter of crows and the slam of a car door caused them both to cut their eyes in the direction of the sounds. Don saw a glimmer of hope flash into Matt's eyes. Hope that the slamming door signaled the arrival of the cavalry. Don shouldered his pack and shoved the little pouch with the notebook and the flash drives down the front of his pants. He might get separated from his pack, but it was unlikely he would get separated from his pants.

The crows suddenly sounded louder. The back door had opened.

"Too slow. Maybe next time." In one quick motion Don drew the blade across Matt's throat, then hurried toward the front of the house. Footsteps sounded faintly from the utility room, behind him. The chain and bolt locks were still engaged on the front door, just as he had left them. He wouldn't be able to open them in time. Besides, there might be others out front.

TWENTY-EIGHT

1:35 P.M.

A fast-moving cloud deck replaced the afternoon glare with an overlay of shadowless gray, as Wallace and Mason entered Carla's neighborhood. The entire area was in decline and some of the houses had bars on the windows, Carla's included. Wallace pulled to the curb in front of the house. After donning body armor vests over their clothes, they walked to the front door. It was locked. They walked around to the side of the house. Using the key Whitlock had told them about, Wallace removed the lock and pushed open the gate. They moved slowly to the back door. Wallace extended her hand toward the knob, then stopped. She raised her finger to her lips, signaling for silence, then pointed at the tape over the striker plate.

Mason reached inside his jacket and freed his weapon from its spring-loaded clamshell holster. Wallace motioned for him to crouch low against the outside wall to the right of the door frame. She assumed the same stance on the left side. Gun in hand, she gently pushed on the door and it swung slowly inward. Using a small hand mirror, she peered inside. Nothing.

A stab of doubt ran through Wallace as Mason started to move past her. She placed a restraining hand firmly against his chest and gave him a hard, questioning look. He continued past her with a dismissive shake of his head, moving into a spacious utility room. There was a door to the right and a doorway straight ahead that led into a kitchen. They could see yet another doorway beyond that, that opened onto a hallway.

Using hand signals, Wallace motioned for Mason to take the door on his right and then to go right at the hallway and search the front of the house. She would take the kitchen, and then move leftward down the hallway into the rear of the house.

As Wallace entered the kitchen, Mason carefully opened the door to his right. It led into a garage. He peered carefully around the door frame, then went in. An anemic shaft of light shone through the slit window in the louvered metal door, illuminating a dust-covered splotch of oil on the concrete. A hot water heater stood in one corner and metal shelves with stacks of old newspapers and plastic bottles of insecticide were attached to one of the side walls. But there was no car. He backed out into the utility room in time to see Wallace disappear leftward down the hall.

A quick look in the under-counter cabinets, the refrigerator, and the open pantry had told Wallace the kitchen was clear. She entered the dark hallway. The living room was to her right, but she turned her attention to the hallway on her left. Two doors opened off the right side of the hallway and one off the left. With her back to the wall, gun in a high, two-handed grip, she sidestepped down the hall to the door on the left. A bedroom.

Even in the low light she could see the room was empty, except for a few boxes stacked against one wall. She checked the closet.

Nothing. The window was closed and latched from the inside. She crossed the room, crouched just inside the door, then looked left and right into the hallway. Empty. She pushed the knob lock and pulled the door closed as she stepped into the hall.

Mason locked the garage door behind him, then strode quickly through the kitchen. He stood at the doorway to the hall, listening. He could hear Wallace moving through the back of the house. Crouching low, he turned right into the living room. A couch, against the wall to his left, faced the rest of the room across a coffee table covered with books and magazines. In the far corner a heavy club chair sat catty-corner, facing obliquely toward the couch and the hallway. Further to his right the room opened into a dining area that connected to the kitchen by way of a pass-through window. He walked between the couch and the coffee table to check the space between the far end of the couch and the wall. A floor lamp stood in the space, alongside a pair of sneakers.

Wallace crossed the hall and opened the first door. The master bedroom. She entered, keeping her back against the wall. Two doors opened off the bedroom. One was open. It led to a closet. She inched around the room to the closet and turned on the light. No one inside. The faint smell of dirty laundry was mixed with the sharp scent of dry cleaning. She locked the closet door. The remaining door would lead to the bathroom.

The dining area was open and clearly unoccupied. One end of the dining table was covered with piles of bills and other household paperwork. An unfinished jigsaw puzzle took up most of the center of the table. Mason studied the room for some clue as to what had happened after Whitlock had been here. Other than the tape on the back door, nothing even looked out of order. Perhaps whatever was going to happen here had not yet taken place. Perhaps they were too late. A door clicked shut, deep in the house. He recalled the shed he had seen in the backyard. He would check that next. He did a slow turn, running his eyes over everything—the table, the couch, the heavy club chair in the corner. Nothing. Confident the front of the house was clear, he holstered his weapon.

Wallace checked the bedroom windows. Closed and locked from the inside. Standing to the side of the bathroom door, she gently pushed it open. It swung silently on its hinges until it rebounded against a rubber-tipped doorstop inside. Crouching low, she used the mirror again, to look around the doorframe. Empty. But as she crossed the threshold the meaty butcher-shop smell of unspoiled blood thickened the air. The fresh violence it implied clashed with the fruity shampoo smell and the tranquil gauzy light filtering in through the closed blinds.

She squatted down by the tub. The corpse's face and chest were covered with blood. She touched one of his hands. Still warm. Then she heard it—the faint plinking sound as a droplet of blood hit the bottom of the tub. A fresh kill—less than two minutes. Don was still in the house. Just not back here.

Mason heard a low tapping sound. He looked back over his shoulder toward the hallway. Wallace was halfway up the hall, wide-eyed, gently drumming her fingers against the wall to get his attention. She beckoned him toward her, then stabbed her finger furiously toward the front of the house. She was mouthing something—but the light was too low for him to read her lips. Did she want him to go out the front? He turned back toward the front door.

Don was standing in the shadow behind the big club chair—gun raised. He fired before Mason could draw his weapon.

Mason staggered toward the dining table, bracing himself with his right hand on the back of one of the chairs. As Don moved deftly into the room, Mason laced his fingers through the handhold at the top of the chair and flung it into Don's path. Don became entangled in the chair and fell forward. His gun flew free into a corner of the dining room.

Mason stumbled backward into the kitchen. He slid to his knees, struggling to maintain awareness. Blurry gray crowded in from the edges of his vision. He slewed back onto his haunches, then flopped onto his back.

Wallace could hear Don scrambling to his feet in the living room, but there were no sounds from the kitchen where Mason had fallen—a very bad sign. She knew Don wouldn't leave the house without at least *trying* to eliminate her, because she could tie him to the killings. But she had to help Mason.

As she hurried the last few steps to the kitchen doorway, Don rushed her. He seized her gun hand with both of his and yanked her arm high, exposing her belly, before smashing his heel against her rib cage.

Wallace twisted sideways to shield herself from another blow. Still gripping her gun hand, Don wrenched her violently from side to side, slamming the back of her hand against the frame of the kitchen door. Her gun discharged and fell from her hand. With a quick sweep of his foot he kicked it into the dining area where it slid beneath a heavy buffet. Still holding her wrist, he whipped her around and bashed her against the sharp edge of the corner.

The pain was blinding.

She twisted back to face him, cupped her left hand and swiped at his head, trying to box his ear, but he drew back and the blow didn't land flush.

"Stupid girl," he roared, then spat in her face.

With both hands, he grabbed Wallace by her shirtfront. He lifted her off the floor and propelled her backward down the murky hallway. She got a glimpse of Mason. The bullet had ripped through his left armpit and his entire left side was slicked with blood. Wallace had seen wounds like that before. They could quickly be fatal. Over Don's shoulder she saw Mason's legs twitching.

She swung furiously with both hands, swarming blows to the sides of his head. As he lowered his head to avoid her fists, Don pitched forward just enough for Wallace to get her toes on the floor and halt their backward movement.

She spread her feet wide, then with her left hand, she hugged his wrists against her chest. Swinging her right arm over both of his, she coiled tightly to her left, then spun back, driving the point of her elbow into the side of his head. Instantly, her right arm went numb all the way to her fingertips, but Don wobbled and his grip loosened.

Wallace skipped back half a step, then snapped a toes-up kick to Don's groin. As he crumpled forward, Wallace brought her knee up to meet his rapidly descending chin. A groan sounded deep in his throat and he fell facedown in the hallway.

She leapt past Don and raced toward Mason. His breathing was shallow and ragged. His eyes were open but they held a vacant stare. A gentle pulse of blood rippled beneath his body armor.

"Hang on, Mason. Hang on. I've got you," she whispered, as she slid to her knees beside him. She tore off one of his shoes and rammed it sole-first deep into his bleeding armpit, then pushed his arm tight against his side, pinching off the torn artery with the hard edge of the sole. She slid him forcefully against the wall, using the wall to hold his left arm firmly against his body. She sat on the floor facing him and gently pushed with her feet against the right side of his rib cage, keeping him steady, and maintaining the pressure.

With her right hand still feeling fat and barely responsive, she wrestled her phone from her pocket and dialed nine-one-one.

From the hallway, a bullet plowed through the sheetrock wall near her head. She flattened herself against the floor. Don knew she was not going to desert Mason and that, without her weapon, she would be an easy kill. They would both be easy to pick off. Wallace looked down at Mason and her heart started to break. Not yet, she told herself. Not yet. She looked around for some way to improve the odds. There was a heavy butcher block table behind her in the center of the kitchen floor. With her left hand, she reached for it, but it was just beyond her grasp.

Her call was ringing. As she leaned back farther toward the table, her phone slipped from her still-tingling right hand and tumbled into the gloom somewhere near Mason's head. She could hear the tinny voice of the nine-one-one operator asking for the nature of her emergency.

"Officer down," she shouted over the operator's attempt to go through her checklist of questions. Twice more she repeated "officer down" and recited Carla's address, then she went quiet—listening.

She could hear Don dragging himself up the hallway in her direction. Each movement brought forth gasps of pain that betrayed his progress. He fired another shot through the wall, but this one went high, slamming into the cabinets across the room.

Once more, she reached back toward the table, until she was almost completely stretched out along the kitchen floor—a defenseless target. She looped her fingers around the nearest leg of the butcher block and pulled, but it was heavy and dried mop grime had bonded its feet to the floor. The sounds from the hallway marked Don's quickening progress.

With the leg barely within her grasp, Wallace jerked. The table snapped free and tottered toward her. Once it was close enough, she toppled it and dragged it close enough that she could use it to help hold Mason steady and to shield him from further gunfire.

Sirens howled in the distance.

Carefully, she probed under Mason's jacket, feeling for his gun, hoping he still had it. She found the straps of his shoulder harness, but it was twisted around his body. She traced the harness around his blood-soaked chest. The holster was pulled out of position. It was underneath him.

Wallace gently lifted his right shoulder, feeling beneath him for the holster, which was wedged under his left shoulder. The weight of his body was keeping the gun from springing free. She pulled the holster toward her, but stopped when the sliding strap started to dislodge the shoe that was stanching the flow of blood.

Inch by inch Wallace spider-walked both of her hands beneath Mason's shoulders, trying to get his weight off the holster without disturbing the shoe. Her gaze toggled between Mason and the door to the hall. She felt the gun. The mouth of the holster was facing to her left. She tented her aching right hand over the mouth of the holster—just enough to shift his weight off the gun without moving the shoe. Noise from the hallway drew her attention. Don was on his knees in the doorway. Mason's gun sprang free into her left hand. Don raised his weapon.

In a single motion, she leaned right to draw fire away from Mason and slid the gun from beneath his limp torso. Left-handed, she fired. The bullet grazed Don's head, scoring a shallow furrow into the scalp above his left ear.

Loud voices came from the front of the house. Someone banged on the front door. The door frame splintered and voices called from the living room.

Wallace switched the gun to her right hand, as Don lunged past her through the kitchen, toward the utility room. She turned, tracking him. She fired, but missed, when Don stumbled and sprawled near the door. She frantically checked to make sure her movement hadn't caused Mason to start bleeding again. The back door banged open and Don's footsteps scraped across the concrete slab at the bottom of the steps.

TWENTY-NINE

Don slipped from the house and scuttled toward the fence. His mind was racing. After he had safely stowed the notebook and flash drives, he would return and take care of the detective. Using Carla's key, he unlocked the gate and hustled into the alley in the direction of Matt's car. Now that his identity was known, he would have to abandon his rental vehicle. If it wasn't already the subject of an APB it was certain to be within the hour. But nobody would be looking for Matt's car for a while.

Prudence dictated that he vacate the area as quickly and as surreptitiously as possible. He hated having to leave without getting rid of Carla first. But, with Gable dead, she was no longer useful as bait. And with the frenzy of law enforcement activity that was about to erupt in this little burg—foot patrols, roadblocks, maybe even door-to-door searches—any value she had as a bargaining chip was outweighed by the risk of getting caught as he dragged her out of the house. He needed to be gone before the net closed around him.

A heavy vomitus feeling blossomed up from his groin where the detective had kicked him. She had hurt him, but he had won the prize. He reached down to pat the little package stuck in the front of his pants—but it was gone.

She must have knocked it loose when she booted him in the groin. In all the commotion, he hadn't noticed that it had slipped from its hiding place. What a goddamn disaster. What an unmitigated disaster.

Mounting rage blotted out the pain in his head and the ache between his legs. Holding a blood-soaked handkerchief to the gash above his left ear, Don peered back through the gate, raking his eyes along the path he had taken from the back door to the alley. It wasn't there. It must still be in the house.

As Don continued his survey, a stocky man carrying a gun and wearing body armor with "FBI" stenciled in yellow capitals across the front stepped out of the back door. The agent studied the blood spatters on the concrete slab at the base of the steps, trying to gauge the direction of whoever had left them. Then he systematically scanned the yard, his head slowly moving in short methodical arcs. Before the agent's gaze could find him, Don ducked behind the hedgerow lining the fence.

As Don hustled toward the car, Plan B formed in his mind. Even before it fully manifested itself, he fell in love with the idea. He would kill two birds with one stone. He would recover what he had snatched, at such great cost, from Matt Gable and he would punish the detective who had taken it from him.

A paramedic pulled Wallace away from Mason so they could get to work. Her thoughts turned completely inward. She barely felt the hand on her arm, ushering her into the hall.

"I'm okay," she kept saying. "I'm okay, I'm okay, I'm okay."

She heard the paramedics calling out the steps in their procedures. Sporadic bursts of static from shoulder-mounted radios punctuated their chatter with some faraway ER doc. She heard these things, but none of them registered. Shameful, terrifying thoughts and images seized control of her—Mason's juddering legs as she battled Don in the hallway, the ridiculous amount of blood soaking through Mason's shirt and pooling around him as she fought to stop the bleeding, the flubbed wrong-handed shot at Don from less than six feet away. Mostly, though, she thought that she should never have let him enter the house with her. She had listened to him and ignored her instincts and Mason was paying the price for her failure of judgment.

From the bathroom, Wallace heard someone radio in the corpse in the tub—the missing Matt Gable she was willing to bet. The blood on the corpse's face had kept her from positively identifying him earlier.

As she turned toward the front of the house, looking for a place to sit and recover her equilibrium, she felt something under her left boot. She felt it, but it almost didn't cut through the blizzard of sensory input clamoring through the air around her. Almost. It made just enough of an impression to sneak past a fast-rising wall of worry that was trying to fence off the rational part of her mind. She looked down, but she couldn't tell what it was. She made a conscious effort to focus her mind on what her eyes were seeing.

It was a nylon pouch with strips of tape stuck to one side. She recalled the cut ends of tape she had seen on the body in the tub. Opening the pouch, she poured the contents into her hand—a small, leather-bound notebook and two flash drives. She thumbed through the notebook, then returned the items to the pouch and slid it into a cargo pocket on the outside of her pants leg.

The FBI and the paramedics had arrived at almost the same time. Not long after that, Whitlock arrived and started lecturing the feds about some arcane aspect of crime-scene management. Mason was stretchered out the front door and into an ambulance. Light bars atop the responder vehicles strobed into the darkening sky and small knots of people from the neighborhood gathered on the sidewalk.

There was a tense moment between Wallace and the FBI agents when they tried to debrief her on the spot. The ambulance was leaving, so unless they intended to arrest her, she intended to follow it. But Wallace didn't fight Whitlock when he insisted on taking custody of both her and Mason's weapons. Both had been fired by an officer in the line of duty, and she knew he was required to keep them.

On the way to the hospital it began to rain—the kind of slow, steady, steamy rain that could go on for hours. Tire-spray from the road coated everything with a thin film of grime, and deepening cloud cover fooled some of the streetlights into coming on early.

BATON ROUGE 3:00 P.M.

Just as she was pulling up to the hospital, Jason Burley called to remind her that it was three o'clock and to find out why she wasn't in his office handing over the case. He blew a fuse, when she told him what had happened. He went completely ape-shit when she told him she wouldn't be coming back to headquarters until Mason was out of surgery. She knew it was a poor career move to hang up on Burley when he was in mid-scream, but she had bigger worries at the moment. When he didn't call back, she assumed he had either accepted her decision or he was busy preparing her termination papers.

Not to be deterred, the FBI agents followed Wallace to the hospital. They cornered her in the hallway outside the ER, then they all trooped down to a vacant office for a friendly game of twenty million questions. Once they established to their satisfaction that Wallace didn't know any more about where Don might have gone than they did, they left the hospital.

When Wallace returned to the waiting room outside the ER, she learned that Mason had been taken into surgery and she was directed to the surgical waiting room.

Despite her exhaustion and the slow march of the hours, she knew she wouldn't be able to sleep. She was hungry but she couldn't eat. And she didn't even try to stop her mind from going over and over her decision to let Mason go into Carla's house with her. She felt ashamed and guilty and desolate. She had spent years carefully avoiding the kind of man who might provoke such deep feelings so that her mistakes wouldn't—couldn't—put someone she cared about in danger again. Yet, somehow, that was exactly what had happened.

The place on her abdomen where Don had kicked her was sore and bruised. Her right hand was swollen and tender, and she felt pretty sure something was fractured. The triage nurse had asked if she wanted to have it looked at, but Wallace declined. She didn't want to think about her hand because that made her think about Don and the rest of the miserable situation. She had no interest in being distracted from wallowing in her personal miseries.

When it finally dawned on her that she should probably try to contact Mason's family, she retrieved his satchel from her car and looked through it for names and phone numbers. She felt strange looking through his things. Unable to find anything helpful, she was about to give up when she spied an envelope shoved into a divider pocket. Her initials were scrawled on the front.

She was momentarily mystified by the odds and ends inside. Then it hit her. The receipt from the vegetables she used on Marcels, the swizzle stick from the Bridge City Diner, a matchbook from the restaurant where they shared their first meal the day he arrived, their temporary visitor badges from the Tunica lab. Souvenirs from their adventures together. Had he planned to present them to her? What would that little scene have been like? A tiny smile jockeyed her bleak expression aside as she played with the possibilities.

Her phone rang.

It was Colley's landline. Shit. She had promised to return during the afternoon to continue her protest against his decision to retire.

"Colley, I'm so sorry—"

"I'll tell him you said so."

It was Don.

THIRTY

L et me talk to Colley," she demanded. "I have to know they're okay."

"I've misjudged you," Don said, playfully. "After that spirited fight you put up in the Chapman woman's home, this afternoon, I expected a good deal more bluster from you. I had steeled myself for the onslaught of your righteous indignation, armored my fragile ego against a string of frightful threats. Instead, you come with this boring, no-nonsense approach."

"Just tell me what you want, then," Wallace countered. She grabbed Mason's bag and sprinted for the exit.

"You don't give the orders," Don said flatly. "And you need to understand something. Until this business we have together is concluded, you will speak only and always to me. You will not attempt to communicate with anyone else. You will not hang up. And you better pray to all the gods you know that this call doesn't drop, because if it ends for any reason, or if I think you're stepping out on me, I'll put a whole lot of dearly beloved blood on the walls . . . and on your conscience. Now, back to what I'm after. I want the thing you somehow took from me during our little lovers' quarrel. It was a thoughtful parting gift from the former Matt Gable and it has a lot of sentimental value to me."

"And what exactly would it be that you lost?"

"I didn't lose it. That would imply that I'm careless and I assure you I am not. You managed to deprive me of my little treasure, undoubtedly when you tried to emasculate me."

Wallace recognized his technique. Lots of hostage-takers used it. They toyed with you. They mixed glib humor and a cavalier attitude toward the situation with the nastier elements of their endeavor, hoping to convey the idea that they were unstable and capable of inappropriate, unpredictable actions. The whole idea, of course, was to put you in the mood to meet their demands, lest they be provoked to give in to their inappropriate, unpredictable impulses. She had been trained to see past this, to maintain control of the situation and her capacity to reason, but that only worked well when the hostages were strangers.

As soon as she cleared the exit, she raced to her car, which was parked only a few yards from the building, in a space reserved for law enforcement vehicles.

"The sounds coming through your phone just changed," Don said, the instant she stepped outside the hospital. "You were indoors, and now it sounds like you're outside. What are you doing, Detective?"

"I was getting out of my car," she lied, "but I'll stay where I am. What do you want me to be doing?" she asked, sliding behind the wheel and slamming the door hard to make sure he heard it. Little demons of fear were starting to swarm over the wall. She focused on the fact that Don was winding her up, and she told herself not to fall for it. As she fought to remain unaffected, her thoughts flashed to Mason who was fighting a battle of his own. She grabbed her Bluetooth headset that was stashed above the visor.

"We're going to make a trade, Detective . . . your precious little friends for you and the package that remained behind when you forced me to flee the scene earlier. And you better be able to deliver."

Wallace buttoned her phone inside her shirt pocket as she switched on the headset.

"What makes you think I could even get whatever this thing is that you want?" she asked. "If it stayed behind after you left, it's probably been taken into evidence by now. The place was crawling with police and crime-scene techs. Nothing of any consequence would go unnoticed."

Wallace coughed to cover the sound of her car starting.

"If, as you say, it was certain to be found, then I'll assume that it *was* found," Don insisted. "And that would have been a big deal. Everyone in the place would have heard about it right then and there, including you. And I know *you* were there. You were there for a good long while because I was halfway to Baton Rouge by the time the fucking ambulance nearly ran me off that God-forsaken road on its way to the hospital. And then there you were in your little Barney Fife squad car, in hot pursuit, all lathered up about your new best friend Mason. Simple logic tells me that if the police found it, then you heard about it, and if you heard about it, you would know what it is. And you wouldn't need to keep asking me what I'm after."

Wallace remained quiet, afraid anything she said, even her tone of voice, would give her away. She moved quickly into the traffic pattern around the hospital.

"Sorry, Detective, but your claims of ignorance just don't add up. You're a liar, and not a very good one. You should have just said you knew what it was and that you knew it was bagged as evidence. *That* I would have believed. But claiming ignorance when we both know my property would have been the belle of the ball is implausible. In fact, I'm willing to bet my badly bruised testicles that *you* are the one who found it and that you've still got it. So you can give your little charade a rest. Having my property with you is going to make matters a lot simpler."

Again, Wallace remained quiet. She focused on the road ahead. Traffic was easing up, but a lot of thoughts were competing for her attention. She turned on her police flasher and pushed the pedal down as hard as she dared.

"We can always test my little theory, Detective. We can see how much pain the lovely Mrs. Greenberg can take, and how much humiliation you're willing to put your excellent partner Mr. Officer Greenberg through as he sits helplessly by and watches me beat the shit out of his lovely bride. That sort of thing can seriously damage a relationship, as I'm sure you can imagine."

"No need for that. Enough people have been hurt already. What makes you think I didn't turn it over to the police or the FBI?"

"Because I shot your boy Mason, and it's just possible you'll want payback. I saw the way he looked at you when you dropped him off at his hotel so late last night, in that fancy car of yours. I saw the way you stared so longingly after him, as he strode into the lobby like the conquering hero. Didn't look like police business to me. No, you wouldn't give up the one thing you could use to lure me into your crosshairs."

The streets into her neighborhood were usually quiet on Friday evenings, and tonight was no exception. She turned in, slowing, to keep her tires from squealing on the damp pavement.

"What's the stuff in the little book about, anyway? And the flash drives?" Wallace asked, trying to steer their conversation into an area she hoped Don would not find agitating.

"Is this another of your lies, Detective? Cleverly concealed in the form of an interrogatory sentence? Do you really not know?"

"I know that at least two people are dead because of what's in the little book. I recognize chemical notation when I see it, but what does it all mean? What could be so important?"

"Let's table that question for the moment, shall we? I'm more interested in why you would begin our little dance with a false step.

Given that the stakes are so high, I would think you'd be entirely forthcoming from the get-go."

"If you thought I didn't have what you're after—that it would take me time to get it—I would have more time to arrange a rescue. Just trying to buy time. As you say, the stakes are high. I can't afford to make any mistakes."

"You're absolutely correct about that. You cannot afford to make any mistakes. Not any mistakes at all. And do you know what's the single worst mistake you could possibly make, at this stage of the game? Hmmmm?"

"Getting anyone else involved. I assume you want me, just me, to meet you somewhere to make the exchange."

"You must be the pride of your department. So quick you are. And that's exactly what it will be—an exchange. Put all thoughts of a rescue out of your mind. If I think, even for a moment, that a hostage rescue is in the works, there will be no hostages left to rescue."

The rain had stopped but the streets were still sloppy, and it was hot and dark.

"Fine. What's my next move?"

"Where are you?"

"I told you. In my car."

"You're sounding a bit uppity, Detective. Remember, whatever hand you think you're playing . . . I'm holding the trump cards."

"I'm in my car, in the hospital parking lot," she said, as she backed into the driveway of her bungalow.

"Which hospital?"

"Baton Rouge General."

"Get out of your car and walk to the rear, then read off the license plate," he commanded.

Wallace pressed the trunk release button, as she exited her cruiser. She left the door open and the engine running. She stepped past the rear of her cruiser, reciting the number as she headed for the door to her house.

"Now sit tight, for just a second, while I check something on Google Maps. Just one second. Okay. This incredible piece of technology is telling me that, under current traffic conditions, it should take you no more than fourteen minutes to arrive at the Greenberg residence. Let's just make it an even fifteen. I wouldn't want you to feel unduly nervous. Here's your route, so listen up. Take Government Street east, Jefferson Highway southeast, then regular neighborhood streets from there. Got it?"

"I know the route," she said, as she entered her house through the carport door.

"Good. Don't be late."

"Why don't you let my wife go?" she heard Colley ask in the background. "One hostage is easier to manage than two, anyway."

"Why don't you shut the fuck up, Grandpa? Why don't I slap your fucking bitch, instead?"

Wallace had heard a lot of people hurl a lot of abuse at Colley in the time they had been partners, and it never bothered her—it was just part of the noise on the street. It came with the job. But hearing him threaten Stella wasn't the same thing. That was personal. Don kept talking, but the fury in her chest drowned out his words.

"I said, can you believe this asshole?" Don repeated.

"Don't hurt them," she murmured, realizing that Don had been talking to her—that his antics were shredding her focus.

"Entirely in your hands, Detective. Entirely in your hands. Although, for the life of me, I can't see what's got you so attached to these losers."

On her first night walking a beat, a gigantic, iced-out meth head went berserk when she and her partner confronted him, trying to defuse an escalating situation. He had head-butted her partner, knocking him out, then turned his attention to Wallace. She eventually subdued him, but not before he roughed her up, taunted her, and put his hands on every inch of her. He'd left her shaking with rage—a dangerous state of mind she swore she'd stay away from. But Colley and Stella's present circumstances were testing her resolve on that point. First things first, she kept telling herself. First things first.

"When you get here, back into the driveway until your rear driver's-side door is even with the side door of the house. If I see a plate number coming up the drive that's different from the one you just read me, Mr. and Mrs. Greenberg will become the late Mr. and Mrs. Greenberg before you can even finish backing up. Clear?"

"Very. And then what?" she asked, moving silently through her house.

"Then, you're going to take us for a ride," he said. "And in the meantime, you and I will continue our discussion. Turn off your police radio. If I hear even a hint of a squawk . . ."

"I understand," Wallace said, unplugging her landline telephone as she passed it. She didn't want the ring from some random incoming call to give her away.

"Now . . ." Don began.

Wallace could tell by his tone that he was gearing up for a bragfest. *Excellent. Just keep him jabbering away,* she thought.

"We have a few minutes, so let's get back to your question about what's in the little book."

"I know Gable was a government scientist," she said. "Are you selling secrets?" She walked to the back of her closet. "Is this some kind of industrial espionage?" she continued, trying not to sound distracted, as she knelt in front of a large, old-fashioned gun safe and quietly spun in the combination.

"Nothing nearly so mundane as that. No, the ineffable Matt Gable was kind enough to discover something that's going to change the world."

"Like what?" She looked at her watch. Fourteen minutes.

"I think you already know that, Detective. Our late friend

Mr. Gable found a way to make the most popular drug since the invention of organized religion."

"Ah. Cocaine," she said, pulling open the safe door. Soundlessly, she unshelved one of her rifles—a Holland & Holland 240. "Everything else, we can already make." She chambered a round, then stuffed a foam block with six more rounds into one of her pockets. The gun had belonged to her older brother Martin—custom made at great expense, for his twelfth birthday. Even at seven and a half pounds, it was so perfectly balanced it felt nearly weightless. "Won't this upset a lot of our neighbors to the south?" she asked, sliding the weapon into a soft-side case. "Like the ones in Colombia and Peru?" She strapped on an eight-shot Ruger pistol in an ankle holster and pulled her pants leg down to cover it. The pistol made her feel anxious.

"It will, indeed," Don said. "But that's a very high-class problem to have. And, in any event, it's my problem, not yours."

She knew she would have exactly one shot to rescue Colley and Stella, and it wouldn't be with the pistol. The rifle was for the rescue. The Ruger was for revenge. However things turned out, she was pretty sure she would lose her badge for what the Monday morning quarterbacks in Internal Affairs would see as a cowboy operation—even though Don was leaving her no alternatives. She pushed the door to the safe closed, then grabbed a hoodie off a shelf and pulled it on, leaving the hood down for the time being.

She moved back through the silent house to the soundtrack of Don's endless self-congratulations. Twelve and a half minutes, plenty of time. She just had to keep him talking.

"Are you going to sell this magic formula to the highest bidder, or will you try to make the drug and sell it yourself?"

As she exited the house, she pulled the hood up so it would muffle the change in sound from indoors to out. She covered the distance from the house to the car in tiny, quiet steps.

"I haven't decided that yet," he replied.

She laid the rifle case on a folded tarp in the trunk and pushed the lid down, pressing her butt against the lock to muffle the click of the latch.

"Why? Would you like to make a bid?" he laughed. "By the way, where are you, Detective? Give me the intersection you're approaching. Do it now."

Wallace checked her watch. Just over twelve minutes remaining. If she had actually been driving from the hospital, she would have traveled almost a quarter of the distance to Colley's.

"I'm just passing Steele Boulevard." She slid into the driver's seat. With her right hand she pulled the hood back off her head and with her left she pulled the car door quietly shut as she headed down her driveway.

"Making good time, I see. Maybe a touch ahead of schedule, by my calculation, but very good, Detective."

Wallace sped toward the end of her block.

"I'll interpret your punctuality as a sign of your earnestness," Don continued.

With her dash-mounted flasher still going, she turned onto Government Street and put the pedal down. Without her siren she still had to slow for intersections, but by not having to stop she was covering ground rapidly and she could shave minutes off her travel time, assuming nothing got in her way.

"May I speak to Colley now?"

"No, Detective, you may not. I'm not completely stupid, as you should know by now. Why would I give the two of you an opportunity to plot against me? When I followed you to his house this morning, I thought he was your daddy. Imagine my surprise when I found out he's your partner. I can only imagine what sort of secret signs and signals the two of you could cram into hello and good-bye. Sorry, but you'll have to content yourself with little old me.

"Have you ever noticed, Detective, how some people just aren't cut out to play in the big game? They mistake one clever little tech-

nical idea for something bigger. More often it's the case that the bea-
vering little inventor only invents. It takes someone who can see the
bigger picture to properly introduce something to the wider world.
Wouldn't you agree?"

Wallace worked hard to split her focus between negotiating traffic at breakneck speed and listening to Don's endless prattling.

"Well, I can tell you," he said, "Matt Gable had no vision. He was
just a grubby little toiler."

Wallace started thinking about Mason. Over and over, she re-
played that moment at the back door to Carla's house. Her hand on
his chest. The shake of his head as he shouldered past her through
the door. Her failure to make the right choice.

She killed her flashers as she made the turn off Jefferson.

"Nope," Don continued, "Gable was just a test tube juggler. Nothing more. He was never going to be the one to steal fire from heaven.
But I give the devil his due—when it was his turn to get lucky, he
made the most of it. But he also made stupid mistakes. Which was
how I became aware of him. How I tracked him down. Do you want
to know what his biggest blunder was?"

As he veered into a lecture on some kind of statistical gobbledy-
gook, Wallace turned right onto Colley's street, extinguishing her
headlights before she made the turn. Just as Don's lecture was getting
into full swing, she glided to a stop near a line of trees and flowering
shrubs that stretched from the curb to the Greenbergs' backyard. Her
car was just out of sight of Colley's house. She was eight minutes
early. If things didn't work out, she would need three minutes to return to her car and then back the car into the driveway. That left five
minutes.

"So what I still don't understand," Wallace said, when Don seemed
to be winding down, "is how you knew the numbers you were looking at pointed to this discovery. Couldn't there have been a lot of
ways to explain this?"

"There could, indeed, Detective, but as any fan of deductive reasoning can tell you, if you eliminate all the possibilities but one, the one that's left is the explanation."

Wallace popped the trunk, pulled up her hood, and got out of the car.

"Wasn't it your mythical forebear, the famed Sherlock Holmes, who put it so eloquently—after you eliminate the impossible, whatever's left, however unlikely, that must be the answer?"

She hurried to the rear of the car and slid the Holland & Holland from its case. She prayed the nightlike gloom would let her get from her car to the trees without being seen.

"I never read Sherlock Holmes," she said, making her way into the trees. "But wouldn't you have to already be tuned into the idea, before you would even start to focus on possible explanations for what you were seeing?"

"Speaking of what one is seeing, I remember passing Ted Pico's Diner, on my way over here. No doubt one of this city's most illustrious five-turd dining establishments. You should be approaching it momentarily. What's the advertised special, Detective?"

The area around the trees was littered with leaves and dry twigs, forcing her to move slowly as she painstakingly swept the dark ground with her eyes, searching for safe, noiseless spots to place her feet. It took her a moment to drag her focus back to what Don was saying.

"I've already passed it. An employee was out with one of those long poles, changing the letters on the sign out front, so I don't know. Shall I go back?"

She moved cautiously, her left hand extended for balance as she tiptoed through the brush, her swollen right hand gripping the rifle. Despite its balance, the weight of the gun was starting to make her hand throb.

"Don't be stupid," he spat. "Where are you . . . exactly?"

"I'm approaching Audubon Avenue," she said, hoping her estimate of time and distance was reasonably close to what he would expect.

"Good girl. Steady as she goes."

A twig snapped underfoot. She slowed further, unwilling to risk another noise.

The wind picked up and the sky darkened further as evening fell. It was getting hot inside the hoodie, so the breeze felt good.

"You don't want to fumble this close to the goal line. T-minus seven minutes and counting."

Like a deer that senses the hunter nearby, Wallace moved with excruciating precision.

"So tell me, Detective. What's our good buddy Mason like in the sack? The betting line at the office is that he has a little dick and even less imagination. Or maybe it's the other way around, I can't remember."

"I know you killed Matt and I assume you killed Overman and Carla. How do you go about deciding that some amount of money is worth killing people for?" Wallace asked, ignoring his taunt.

"Cocaine is a bloody game. If I put the cartels out of business, maybe the body count drops and I'm a benefactor to the human race. In any event, maybe you should just worry about getting here on time."

THIRTY-ONE

Wallace had been in the Greenbergs' house more times than she could count. She could probably walk it end-to-end with her eyes closed. In fact, if she closed her eyes now, she could visualize the layout and its furnishings, room-by-room.

"But I am sincerely curious . . . what made you even think of looking for this?" she asked, hoping her open-ended question would trigger another of bout of self-aggrandizing speechifying. She needed to free herself of the need to contribute to the conversation.

"Don't jerk me off. I can tell you're trying to keep me talking so you don't have to. If you're trying to think up some heroic stunt to save the day, forget it. I'm several moves ahead of you, so don't get the idea you'll outsmart me. Ain't gonna happen. Now start counting backward from a hundred."

She made it to seventy-nine before Don had enough.

"Very good. You know your numbers pretty well. Wanna try the alphabet now?"

"Forward or backward?" she asked, scrambling to reassemble her scattered thoughts.

"Fuck you. Just pay attention to what you're doing. I don't want you crashing into something because you were trying to drive and chew gum at the same time."

Wallace waited for Don to continue with his chatter, but he remained quiet. A wave of panic washed through her as he let the silence stretch. Perhaps he had suddenly seen through her.

"Penny for your thoughts," he said, with a casual chuckle, as if he had sensed the effect his silence was having on her.

"Just focusing on the road." She exhaled loudly, realizing she had been holding her breath.

"I'm curious about something. In all of your time policing this fair city, did you ever actually cross paths with Ronnie Overman? Meet him face-to-face."

"No. I never had the pleasure."

"Too bad. Gable wasn't much to write home about, but Ronnie Overman was actually quite impressive. He had a nose for opportunity and an uncommonly strong sense of initiative. Who knows, under different circumstances, he and I might have been able to join forces. In the end, though, he crumbled. He became eager to give up the goods on Gable, especially after feeling the gentle caress of the snake and the nasty pinch of the pliers."

Wallace heard a car on the street behind her. Its windows must have been open. Faint strains of happy forties swing music drifted in her direction, then trailed off as the car continued deeper into the neighborhood. Unconsciously, she pressed the thick fabric of her hoodie against her earpiece.

"After their first meeting, Overman had been impressed enough with Gable that he had been ready to sign the boy up, but not before he checked him out," Don said. "One never knows when a narc might be running that done-to-death scam of posing as a rogue government chemist with grand ideas and an axe to grind, so Overman hired a private investigator to check Gable out. Doesn't that strike you as hilarious, Detective? A career criminal hiring a legitimate detective to help him make his criminal enterprise more profitable. I stand in awe of the man . . . well, of his memory, anyway. That right there saved me a ton of time and effort, because good old Ron Ron was able to share Gable's name and home address with me."

As Don's soliloquy continued, Wallace worked her way through the maze of shrubbery along the side of the house, one careful step at a time, until she reached the gate that led through the fence into the backyard. At the same time, she continued her mental walk around through the Greenberg house.

She struggled to recall the details of what she would be able to see out of the rear-facing windows if she were sitting at the little bistro table in the kitchen, or leaning against the counter watching Colley fix dinner, or lounging on the couch against the back wall of the TV room upstairs, or sitting on the wicker stool under the built-in desk near the side door off the kitchen. From each of these places, Wallace focused on the part of the view through windows that included the roof of the gazebo near the back of the lot.

Once she had the view from inside to outside fixed in her mind, she transposed her point of view onto the gazebo rooftop and turned her mental images around so she could look from outside to inside—from the gazebo rooftop into the back of the house.

A low-hanging branch scratched her forehead above her right eye, and a swell of blood started collecting in her eyebrow. She used the strap to hang the Holland & Holland across her back, then lifted the ladder that lived in the space between the gazebo and the fence. As she did, her hood slipped back a bit.

"The sounds from your phone are different again, Detective," Don said.

"I opened my window. It's getting claustrophobic in here, and the AC isn't helping," she said, as she laid the ladder gently against the roof.

"Well, roll it up again. How do I know you're not waving for help, like some lunatic?"

Wallace pulled the hood back into place as she silently climbed the ladder.

The back of the house was in total darkness, just like the front, but Wallace knew to a certainty there were only two places Don could be—one was upstairs and one was down. And, as near as she could remember, the roof of the gazebo was the only spot from which she would have a clear view of both. Depending on how she situated herself, she would have a better shot at one than the other. Don's statement that he would be reading her license plate when she backed up the driveway gave her a bit of confidence that he would select the downstairs option. Plus, that would keep things simpler when the time came to hustle his hostages from the house to the car.

"Gonna make it on time?" Don asked.

Wallace assumed a prone posture along a spine of the gazebo roof. "I think so," she said coolly, even though her heart was hammering.

"Remember . . . if you're late . . . I'll have to thin the herd."

"Please don't." The accumulation of blood in her right eyebrow broke free and the blood tickled as it arced through the crease above her right eyelid.

"You really are such a devoted friend. What does that feel like?" Don asked.

"It hurts," Wallace replied. "Right now, it hurts."

"So why do it?" he asked, then resumed his saga.

While the downstairs target had better sight lines, it presented a special challenge—one where Wallace felt her skills fell a bit short. In Stella's lone concession to authenticity, during the restoration of their house, she had consented to double-paned windows across the back, on the ground floor. During certain times of day in certain seasons, sunlight coming in made the rooms unbearably hot.

"You know, Detective, you and I have got a score to settle," Don said, switching subjects.

"Yes, I know."

"I can't let that go unanswered. All those injuries you inflicted back at the Chapman woman's shitty little house."

"I understand," Wallace said, blotting out Don's threats to focus on a tricky bit of math. Window glass, like all transparent materials, had a refractive index—an amount by which it bent the light that passed through it. That meant the true location of an object beyond the glass was slightly different from where it appeared to be. The thinner the glass, the smaller the shift, but two panes, with a layer of argon in between, made things complicated. Wallace remembered the rule of thumb one of the department sharpshooters had told her—for every fifty feet between the shooter and the target, each degree of refraction produces a ten-point-five-inch difference between where one sees the target and where it really is. He had also told her that normal window glass threw things off by about a tenth of a degree. Her margin for error would be small under the best of circumstances. Double-pane windows were not the best of circumstances. Nor was gusting wind. Nor was the fact that the average human head was just a little over eight inches wide.

"So, once the Greenbergs have served their purpose, and I'm in the clear, it's going to be just you and me, kiddo. And it won't be the tender cooing and billing like we did earlier."

"I expected as much," she responded.

"You know, Detective Hartman, despite the occasional pain, this experience has had certain very significant pleasures, but I think *our* time together is going to top the charts."

"It's always good to have something to look forward to."

"You can be smug now, but you won't be later."

He continued taunting her as she adjusted her position. She could just make out the right-most window on the ground floor. The branches of the ancient mimosa that grew between the gazebo and the house were starting to lash around in the gathering wind. Had the lights been on inside the house, she would have gotten fleeting glimpses of the little built-in desk off to the side of the breakfast area. The window was a simple four-pane affair, and Wallace estimated that her target would appear behind the upper-right pane.

"I'm here," she said.

"Where, exactly?"

"Turning the corner on what would be your left, if you were looking through the living room windows toward the street." She dragged the back of her hand across her right eyebrow to wipe away the blood that had begun to accumulate again, then she twined her arm through the strap of the rifle to hold it steady against her. The sky had gone black and it was raining again.

"Turn off your headlights when you get close. Leave your running lights on, then back into the driveway, just like I told you."

"I'm in front, but everything's dark," she said, a few seconds later. "With the house dark I'm not sure I'll be able to back up all that way without crashing into something. Can you turn on the light under the carport for a few seconds, so I can at least get my bearings?"

She brought her right eye to the scope. In the darkness, the crosshairs and their hash marks were only faintly visible. She centered the crosshairs over the upper-right pane.

Her heart beat furiously. The accumulated stress and exhaustion of the last two days were fraying her composure. She summoned that day with her older brother Martin—the day he taught her how to shoot, when she was just a girl. "Think it slow, little sister, and it'll slow down," he had told her as her heartbeat galloped, causing the gun to pitch and yaw. She had pestered him for weeks to take her shooting, but when he finally gave in she tried to chicken out. The loud bang would make her deaf. The kick would dislocate her shoulder.

Her memory of that day and Martin's calm, steady voice slowed the hammering in her chest. The roaring rush of blood in her ears became a faint throb. She could barely feel the rhythmic pulse of her right carotid artery against the smooth cool stock of the rifle. Like a musician falling in behind the drummer, she put a count to the rhythm.

"Pay attention," Don said. "You get only a couple of seconds, and then the light goes off. Ready?"

"I am." Her heart rate slipped into automatic, pulling her respiration alongside.

She heard Don speak to someone else—someone in the room with him. Where was the switch for the outside light? he wanted to know.

"It's there, where you're sitting, right there on the wall," Stella said, in the background.

Wallace divided her attention between the whipping branches and her recollection of which part of the interior would be framed by the upper-right pane, praying that she remembered correctly. The bulb in the carport lit up. A faint glow bled back into the kitchen through the side door, revealing Don at the built-in desk. His back was to her, his right hand poised over the light switch, his left holding the handset of Stella's old rotary dial telephone.

She had guessed wrong. Don was framed by the upper left, not the upper right.

She started to realign, but Don rose from the desk, turning to face in her direction. He was moving out of the frame. She was losing the shot.

Again, she cast her mind back to her first day holding the gun. She felt Martin kneeling beside her, his arms along her arms, his hands on her hands, then she slipped into the magic space where time slows to a crawl. Thought fled. The whipping branches were edited out and the ache in her swollen right hand was noted but not felt. Instinct calculated the speed and line of Don's movement and accounted for the displacement of the glass. Instinct machined the crosshairs onto the target.

She squeezed the trigger.

The rifle gave up a sensuous shudder. Don twitched, then dropped from sight. Wallace heard the shell explode. Then she heard the brittle fracture of the window glass, as the sharp scent of burnt gunpowder filled the air.

THIRTY-TWO

It was nearly midnight when the last of the police vehicles cleared out of the Greenbergs' driveway. For the second time in one night, Wallace was forced to hand over her weapons.

Questions would be raised about the circumstances of Don's death, but she felt fairly confident she would be able to justify her failure to alert the proper individuals inside the department that a hostage situation existed. She also felt good that she could defend the circumstances that led to her taking the situation entirely into her own hands.

Stella and Colley drove Wallace home. She kept saying she was sorry. Stella kept telling her it wasn't her fault, there was no way she could have known. Don had ambushed them as they were walking back from visiting their next-door neighbor.

Mason had lost a lot of blood, but Wallace's trick with the shoe had saved him. Not only had the main artery that supplied his arm been damaged, but the brachial plexus, the complex network of nerves that controlled the arm was also compromised. Full recovery was possible, but not a sure thing.

Mason spent the next several days in intensive care, drifting in and out of consciousness. On his third day there, Wallace was allowed a short visit. Successive days brought increasing coherence and strength, and longer visits. Occasional words were exchanged, but mostly he slept while Wallace sat next to his bed and worried.

Calls from Washington came in, and she fielded them as best she could, but none of his colleagues came to see him. The sister Mason mentioned the day he arrived in Baton Rouge called to say she and her husband were *deeply* concerned, and she thanked Wallace for saving Mason's life. She said she would do her best to make the trek to Baton Rouge, while Mason was in the hospital, but she never came.

Even though Matt Gable's apparatus was eventually reassembled, it turned out to be useless without some information that Matt had either taken to his grave or had hidden in a place no one knew about. Temperature settings for the heating elements, pressure settings for the pressurized vessels, and the wavelength settings for the light-based catalysts were all unknown. The department's consulting chemist calculated the combinations of pressure, wavelength, and heat could run into the hundreds of millions, and that it might take decades to reproduce the originals.

Nothing came to light about how Matt had stumbled on his discovery. And Wallace hadn't felt the least compunction about lying to everyone when they asked her about the item Don must have taken from Matt. The remnants of the strapping tape Matt used to secure it to the small of his back clearly indicated that something had been there and been cut away. Wallace pleaded ignorance.

She recounted the part of the conversation between her and Don in which he had arrived at the conclusion that Wallace had found and was still in possession of the little pouch. She insisted that it was an erroneous conclusion—one she had manipulated him into and had allowed him to labor under all the way to the end. She had needed Don to believe she had something to trade for Colley and Stella, so she would have time to free them. No one disputed that if Don had ever come to believe the whereabouts of the pouch were unknown or beyond Wallace's reach, he would have immediately killed his hostages and fled.

Now, Gable's discovery was beyond everyone's reach. At her first opportunity, Wallace had ferreted out the online hiding places that Don had so scrupulously written down in the back of the little notebook and she deleted all of the files. Once she was confident no trace of the files remained, she fed the notebook itself through her shredder and then burned the shreds. After she erased the flash drives, she pulverized them with a hammer.

Eight days after he was shot, Mason was moved to a regular room. Wallace slipped in, wearing sandals and a thigh-length sundress.

"Hey, cowboy. How are you feeling?" She gently brushed the hair back from his forehead.

"Everything hurts. A lot."

"I know. But your prognosis is pretty good."

"Nice outfit," he said, looking her over. "I've never seen you in anything besides work stuff."

"I seem to remember showing you my birthday suit, not so long ago. Am I so forgettable?" A low-voltage thrill scampered up her spine as Mason's cheeks tinted bright red. There was something irresistible about a man who embarrassed so easily. "You really like my dress?" She crossed the room and yanked open the curtains, letting a blaze of sunshine flood into the room. Backlit by the intense light coming through the window, her dress became translucent.

"Now you're just being cruel," he said, unable to take his eyes off the outline of her body clearly silhouetted beneath her clothes.

"Am I that transparent?" she asked, laughing at her own joke.

Mason started to laugh too, but the pain from his injuries turned it into a tournament of groans and spasms. When he looked at her again, something changed. A weight came down behind his eyes. She knew what was coming.

"What happened?"

"Maybe this isn't the best time," she demurred.

"Just tell me."

Carefully, Wallace climbed onto the bed and curled up next to him. She laid her head on the pillow next to his uninjured shoulder and took his hand in both of hers. "What's the last thing you remember?" she asked, staring toward the foot of the bed.

"Walking in through the back door of Carla's house."

Mason was visibly relieved when she told him about Carla's escape. After cutting herself free, Carla had found her way to a nearby highway, where she was picked up by a sheriff's deputy who had been cruising the area looking for Don. The news about Matt had, at first, devastated her. But, after she learned that Matt's criminal activities were the cause of her miseries at the hands of Don Brindl, her sorrow had quickly turned to anger and resentment. She had called a few days ago to tell Wallace she was sorry for all the nasty things she'd said during the investigation, and to say that she was moving back home to try and make a new beginning.

Mason's physical recovery would be long and difficult, but at least he wouldn't have to contend with guilt over Carla's death. She remembered how mortified he had been in the car the day they went to Bayou Sara to look for Carla. The day he was so worried his conversation with Don had put her in jeopardy. The day the world had come apart at the seams. Even though he had been terrified at the prospect of what he had done, he had had the courage to let his fear show. Any reservations she had about him started fading that day in the car. Then, after she found the envelope, she saw him in an entirely new light.

"Thank you," he whispered, his voice husky with emotion.

"For what?"

"For saving my life."

"Thank *you*," she whispered back, her eyes starting to glisten.

"For what?" he asked.

She thought about the mementos in the envelope. The fact that Mason had begun saving things, almost from the moment they met, told Wallace that something had sparked very quickly for him. The fact that he had continued to save things told her he had seen her more clearly than she had realized. She pulled the envelope from one of the deep patch pockets on the front of her dress and held it where he could see it.

"For bringing me back from the dead."

Ten days after Medicated Mike Harrison had his unfortunate encounter with Arthur Staples and nine days after Wallace had rescued the Greenbergs and put an end to Don Brindl, she was still on restricted duty, pending the outcome of the Internal Affairs investigation. Restricted duty meant she reported to work and shuffled papers but she didn't meet the public and she didn't carry a weapon. It was like being at work and being under house arrest at the same time. The worst part about it was being in such close proximity to her boss virtually all day, every day. Things were still uncomfortably chilly between her and Chief Burley—a state of affairs she was unwilling to live with.

She expected him to rebuff any attempt to resolve the issues that had arisen between them, but Burley surprised her. When she had taken the bull by the horns and invited him for a clear-the-air meeting at one of the little outdoor restaurants down by the river in Catfish Town, a few blocks from headquarters, she felt sure he would turn her down. But he had accepted. That was a good sign. At three o'clock on a Monday afternoon, the place was practically deserted.

"Have you seen Mike Harrison in the last few days?" Burley asked.

"Yesterday. He was wide awake, but he didn't seem to be processing at full speed. His wife was there. I'd never met her before. She seems . . . I don't know, not what I expected."

"I knew her before she married Mike. I told her not to do it, but she evidently saw something. I don't know." He smiled and shook his head, then he gave her a watcha-gonna-do shrug.

"Do you think he'll return to active duty?"

"If he asks me, I'll advise against it. It was ruining his life. He deals with the pressure in too many unhealthy ways. The things everybody thought were character flaws were just bad coping mechanisms."

Wallace started finger-tracing random figures on the tablecloth. Her eyes followed her fingertip as it moved across the fabric. "I feel really bad for him."

"You should. We all should," he said, staring at the tabletop. "He had a bright future at one time. He made some bad decisions and he had absolutely no idea how to get back on track. He had people in his corner, but he couldn't figure out who to trust. That's a very lonely, scary place to be—where there's a cloud of suspicion around everybody in your life."

Burley had never before been so free with his thinking about the men and women who worked under him. It was throwing Wallace off balance.

The waiter brought their food, but she pushed hers aside, no longer hungry. "I've been advised to file a grievance against you," she said.

"I know, and I'm not telling you not to. I'm not allowed to tell you not to."

"I don't want to." She looked past him at the decommissioned naval vessel moored along the pier. "I think you were wrong about how I handled Mike and I think you were wrong to take me off the case. I'll probably always think that and you'll probably always think exactly the opposite."

Burley pushed his lower lip out and tilted his head. "What you think or I think may be less important to your career than what the official record says."

Wallace gave him an irritated, dismissive wave. "I want things between us to be the way they were. If I drag in pressure from the outside, that'll never happen." She hunched over the table, leaning on her elbows.

"That's probably true. So, what pathway do you suggest we take to get back to the way things were before?"

Wallace sat up straight, and a tentative smile flirted with her expression. Burley wasn't saying it directly, but it seemed he was admitting that turning the clock back was important to him as well. She knew there was a price for everything, but he was inviting her to open the bidding.

"Was the reassignment of the case ever made official?"

"Afraid so. And there's no way to reel it back in. In the old days, when everything was paper, files with inconvenient information could be lost. Not so easy now, and besides, that leaves tracks that are like blood in the water to the sharks in Internal Affairs."

"But the contents of the file could be modified or added to, to reflect a more convenient truth."

"That would be a little easier and certainly attract less attention." He gave her a wary, amused look, like her cards weren't as good as she thought they were.

"Perhaps the file should reflect that the new detectives were not displacing me. It's possible, given the complexity and gravity of the case, that they were actually being added to my team?"

"That wouldn't stop Internal Affairs from investigating your role in the demise of Don Brindl."

"I'm not worried about that. Honestly, I almost don't care what they say. Besides, that's not an issue between you and me. Unless you have to testify against me in the hearing."

"Why would they be interested in hearing me go on about why I was assigning additional personnel to your case?"

"So we have a deal?"

Burley laughed. "A deal implies both parties get something. What's in it for me?"

"What do you want?"

Burley looked at her, as if he were surprised by her question. "Don't quit me."

"Excuse me?" Wallace nearly choked on her coffee.

"Just don't quit." He leaned forward and looked her square in the eye. "I know what it looks like when an officer feels like they've had it up to here, like they're not making a difference anymore. I've lost too many good people because they lost hope. And now, this fatalistic attitude you've got about the upcoming investigation, it's like you've already decided that if you don't like what you see coming, you'll just pack up your little kit bag and move on. Don't."

"Come on. Surely you want more than that." She leaned back in her chair. "This is just too easy. You know what I think?"

"Tell me." The amused look was back.

"I think I see Colley's blackmailing little fingerprints all over this."

"Busted." He threw his hands up in mock exasperation, but his expression was completely unreadable.

"I can always ask Colley. He tells me everything."

Burley roared with laughter, then slid his phone across the table to her. "You want me to dial his number for you?" His expression became serious again. "The force needs you to stay. I need you to stay."

Wallace could feel her eyes starting to sting. "That night, outside the interrogation room, where you had Arthur Staples? The way you railed at me before throwing me off the case—it felt personal." This was the real quid pro quo for her, and she could see that Burley understood. The business with the file wouldn't mean anything unless he was willing to cross this last bit of distance between them. Fear rose in her as Burley let the silent seconds tick by. "I won't quit, but it won't work with that still hanging in the air." She leaned forward, feeling as if she couldn't breathe.

"You're right. Things were out of control and I lashed out at you because you were there. It was wrong." He looked directly at her. "I'm sorry. It won't happen again."

She inhaled deeply. "All square?" she asked.

"All square."